SHE IS THE LAW

SHE IS THE LAW

TERRA KRIS™ BOOK ONE

MICHAEL ANDERLE

LMBPN Publishing
PMB 196, 2540 South Maryland Pkwy
Las Vegas, NV 89109

First US Edition, July 2021
Version 1.01, July 2021
ebook ISBN: 978-1-64971-911-9
Print ISBN: 978-1-64971-912-6

DEDICATION

*To Family, Friends and
Those Who Love
to Read.
May We All Enjoy Grace
to Live the Life We Are
Called.*

— Michael

CHAPTER ONE

The air smelled of smoke and rain. Lamplights reflected yellow in the puddles on the cobbled street.

All was quiet. At the corner of the street, a group of tourists stood, gathered around their *Guide to Atlantica.* It wasn't an unusual sight. For years the outer world had been obsessed with the treasures that Atlantica had to offer. It also wasn't uncommon for the call to come through to HQ.

"Shots fired down Cartwright Avenue," Corporal Leonie Black informed Atlantica Officer for Justice, Terra Kris. "Upper East Side."

Terra heeded the call, accompanied by her partner, Tommy Vincenzo. Three years her junior, Tommy exhibited several traits that rubbed her the wrong way. He always smelled of peppermint, for one. Another was the derogatory tone that accompanied every word that left his lips and aimed toward her.

"Nothing to be done," Tommy remarked. His almond eyes peered through heavy lids at the apartment across from them. A milky light leaked into the streets, silhouettes dancing behind the glass. Another gunshot fired, and all they could do was twitch.

Terra shook her head, her jaw clenching. She scratched the

place where the arm of her smart glasses hooked over her ear, her HUD currently inactive. "We can wait. Let's see how this plays out."

Tommy squared up to Terra, eyes locking onto hers behind his glasses—a new addition to the AJS forces across the island. He was an inch smaller, which removed some of his bluster. Terra had seen many guys like Tommy in her old precinct, back when she was sitting in the higher ranks of officer justice. Men like Tommy were a dime a dozen, and her cold stare met his as the silence spoke between them.

Tommy smirked. "Need me to report back to Black? Give her the full report that you disobeyed a direct order from your superior officer?"

"Superior?" Terra chuckled. "I thought we were partners."

Tommy let out a derisive snort. "I outrank you, Kris."

"Only on paper," Kris spat back. She nodded at the apartment where a third shot had fired. Someone inside screamed. "You're telling me that we'd do better off to leave the chaos inside and trundle back to the station empty-handed?"

Tommy straightened his spine. "This is exactly the kind of bullshit that had you kicked down to the realm of the commoners. Anyone would think you weren't Atlantican through and through." He holstered his Glock 99—standard Atlantica Justice System issue—and turned his back on her. "Come on. Get in the goddamn car. Now."

Terra gritted her teeth, eyes lingering on the conflict inside the building. It was true that she was born and bred on this island, a scrap of land that was discovered back in the latter half of the twentieth century, floating about a thousand miles east of New York City and permanently shrouded in a layer of protective fog. Still, even in the year 2027, she couldn't believe that this was what the law had come to.

The wealthy flooded Atlantica the moment the treaty was established between nations. The rules were simple, printed in black and white, and abused by mob bosses, drug lords, cartel runners, and billionaires the world over: what happens on private property stays on private property. The AJS carried no jurisdiction in any area that wasn't public. For a justice-loving officer like Terra Kris, this was a real problem. Too many times had she watched offenses carried out from afar, unable to do anything to stop them while the perpetrators smiled from the sidelines.

This resistance had previously landed her in trouble.

"Kris," Tommy barked. "Now."

He stood by the car, fifty feet from where she stood. The tourists shuffled away, disappearing around the side of the corner building, a skyscraper so high that Terra couldn't see the rooftop through the fog. Rain chilled the skin on her face as she shook her head and reluctantly made her way toward the black sedan.

What's the point in responding if all you can do is watch from the outside?

Terra drew level with the window. She tapped a metal touch pad by her ear. The street lit up in a string of neons and digital script as she looked inside the apartment, the experimental artificial intelligence program attempting to decode what was happening before her. While it couldn't see through curtains or walls, a message on her display did read:

74 Cartwright Avenue, Upper East Downtown, Atlantica, 753-TTY-2.

Property owner, Sandy Tomlinson.

Age 37.

Criminal background: two cases of illegal narcotic vending, five DUI offenses, two cases of grievous bodily

harm. Four years served in jail. Last convicted offense 22 November 2026.

Tommy's voice patched through the radio. "Officer Vincenzo to AJS Command Four, call off dispatch units to Cartwright Avenue. Dispute remains internal and out of our jurisdiction."

Terra deflated. Her eyes lowered to the cobbles, spotting the large puddle before her. She sidestepped, lip curling as the internal shouting grew louder.

"Kris!" Tommy called. "Last warning. Ass here. Now."

Terra curled a fist behind her back, then stuck out a middle finger. She smirked, wishing that Tommy could see it, but knowing that it wasn't the best idea to aggravate your partner, especially when under probation.

Just ride out the probationary period, Terra. You'll be back up in the big leagues before you know—

Voices exploded inside the building. A shrill, female voice cried, "You dick! You absolute dick! You thought you'd get away with this? You thought I wouldn't see through your bullshit?"

Terra dove to the ground as a series of bullets sprayed the glass. They *thunked* against its thick layers, forming several spiderweb cracks around the puncture hole. The window shook in its frame.

"You idiot!" a male voice called, aged or affected by cigarettes, Terra assumed. "Are you trying to get us in the shit? You know what happens if the AJS—"

More exclamations rang as shots fired again. Four more bullets *thunked* against the glass, the pane shaking dangerously in its moorings.

Come on, Terra silently urged, her eyes fixed on the window. Distantly, she heard the black sedan's engine rumble into life.

A window rolled down. *"Terra!"*

"Eat lead, fuckers!" the female voice crowed. A final spray of bullets rained against the glass. Crimson droplets splattered against the pane. The curtains shredded as the bullets tore through.

The glass shuddered. The cracks grew larger

The window disintegrated, bursting forth in an explosion of tiny glass fragments. Terra pushed herself to a crouch, then took a knee. Behind her, the bullets *thunked* against the brickwork of the opposite building.

Terra's face broke out into a satisfied grin. *Houston, we have lift-off.*

She could now make out the shadows of figures inside from her position down low. She counted five of them, frantically running around as they were granted a short reprieve from gunfire.

Terra glanced at Tommy. Tommy shook his head, eyes wide, realizing what was about to happen.

Terra sprinted toward the apartment, remaining low. She pressed her back to the brickwork and drew her Glock.

A man's voice called, "You fucking moron. Now you've done it. Count the seconds until the AJS comes knocking on your door—"

The woman's voice returned. "Shut your dirty mouth, asshole. How about the next time I invite you over, you fucking pay for the *good* ink, instead of giving us this shit-heap, you cheap-assed second-class dealer. If I wanted blood poisoning, I'd stain my arms with Biro."

"It's top-grade, we swear!" another woman retorted. "Archimedes only deals in the best."

A warning shot hit the ceiling.

Terra drew her weapon and spoke softly into her HUD. "Officer Kris to AJS Command Four, amendment to my partner's previous callout. The situation has progressed. Gunfire has entered the streets. About to perform a B E and AA on the scum."

Terra popped out the pistol's magazine and checked her

rounds. Satisfied that they were plentiful, she reseated it and thumbed off the safety.

A reply came over the radio, the response firing straight along the arms of her HUD and buzzing quietly into her ears.

"AJS Command Four to Officer Kris, can you confirm your terminology?"

"B E and AA," Terra repeated, steeling herself. "Break, Enter, and Attitude Adjustments." She muted her radio responses, eyes darting to Tommy who drew up beside her.

"I'll take it from here," he mouthed. "My command."

Terra scoffed.

"I'm not buying your bullshit," the woman continued. "Tell Archimedes that if he wants another sale from us, he best bring his A-game, not this piss-water. I've finished with you bitches. Get the fuck outta here."

Tommy held up three fingers and started counting. Before he could get to two, Terra stood to her full height, pistol aimed through the broken window. "Too late, fuckers. Hands where I can see them. This is official AJS business now."

CHAPTER TWO

For a moment, all was still. Terra had the chance to count the five thugs inside the filthy kitchen. A warm stink of marijuana, sour milk, and body odor hit her nostrils as she used her peripheral vision to scan the room and search out all possible entrances and exits.

The woman who had been making all the fuss froze with her AR-32 pointed at the floor. The shock of Terra standing there, her body shimmering in her metallic blue one-piece uniform was enough to buy Terra a few seconds to assess.

She was older than she sounded. The woman was at least fifty years old, her head sunken into her body with little sign of a neck. She wore a stained tank top, which revealed long, thin arms decorated in red sores. Her veins stuck out from her pale skin, dark grey instead of their typical blue.

Ink-heads, Terra thought. The reports had been going crazy for the latest in the narcotics sensation. Most of her meetings for the last few years had revolved around cases of ink being shipped, sold, and abused in the dark hollows of Atlantica. There was big money in prime product although from the state of this woman's apartment, you wouldn't think she knew it.

"Drop your weapons," Terra warned, eyes flicking between the group. "Down on your knees. Hands behind your head."

Tommy grumbled something beside her, then appeared in the window, pistol pointing at the thugs.

The woman smirked. She looked between the two officers, a pregnant tension hanging in the air. "You shouldn't have come."

"You shouldn't have invited us." Terra firmly fixed her stare. "Bad move breaking that window. Now you've moved into outlaw country, and the sheriffs are here to take you in."

Someone moved in another room, footsteps on carpet.

"Drop. Your. Weapons," Tommy repeated firmly. "Don't make us shoot."

"Of course." The woman nodded at a man standing near one of the doors. A goatee decorated his chin above a black turtleneck. He crouched slowly, then placed his pistol on the floor.

Tommy pointed his Glock at the other three gathered near the corners of the counter. "You, too. Now."

The three exchanged a glance, then slowly worked their way into a crouch.

Terra's eyes bore into the woman's. "Are you deaf or just stupid?"

The woman's grin remained. Her hand twitched, the mouth of the rifle looking as though it was about to lift and point at Terra. Instead, it dropped lower to the floor.

"There we go," Terra soothed.

The woman crouched, the mouth of the rifle touching the dusty tiles. Something knocked in another room. Terra glanced at Tommy. He paid no attention.

The rest of the group had their hands behind their heads. On the table was a black briefcase with foam padding, a series of vials, syringes, and something in a metallic case.

"Read them their rights," Tommy instructed.

Terra straightened, emboldened at their cooperation. "You have the right to remain silent—"

"Now!" the woman shouted. The word exploded like thunder in the room. A man crashed through a door at the back of the kitchen, rifle in one hand, bullets spraying in all directions as the silence broke. Terra ducked below the window. Tommy spun, his back against the side.

All hell broke loose. The woman laughed manically, reminding Terra of the witches she had seen on children's TV shows. Her shots added to the din. Someone yelled in pain as droplets of blood flew through the window.

Tommy's face soured. He shook his head with a disapproving glare at Terra. Terra's face hardened, staring at the building opposite as she listened to the noise within, trying to glean the best route forward. She spotted herself in the reflection of a nearby window and noted for the first time that she could now see the thugs inside the apartment.

"Bitch didn't let me finish," Terra muttered, the smile returning to her lips as she tracked the thugs in the makeshift mirror. A moment later, a bullet found the glass and shattered the reflection.

Terra had only seconds to make her shot count. She rose from her crouch, high enough for only the top of her head to be seen. She fired her Glock, her bullet sailing expertly through the kitchen and embedding itself in the thigh of the man who had burst into the room.

There was half a moment of breathing room in which Terra pivoted her aim and shot at the woman. The bullet screamed toward her. Bloody fireworks exploded from her shoulder as her body was knocked off-kilter.

Terra returned to her crouch. Tommy leaned in, pistol pointing toward the group of three. Before he could fire, he drew back. A string of bullets cracked the plaster of the window frame, dust and brick exploding in all directions.

"Fuck," he grunted, the word coming clearly to Terra through the HUD.

Terra chuckled. "Can't stand the heat, Vincenzo?"

Tommy glared at her.

"This is a warm-up in the inner city," Terra continued. "I order an arrest like this with my Starbucks in the morning. Goes down well with an almond croissant."

Tommy frowned. He shot blindly through the window, aiming at the ceiling. Shouts of alarm sounded in the bullet's wake. "Wait until Black hears about this."

"I'm sure she's already plugged into our HUDs. Not that she'll be watching live."

"Get out here, you sons-of-bitches!" the woman exclaimed.

Terra shrugged. "That's our cue. Now, where was I?" She peeked over the lip of the windowsill, careful not to cut her hand on the fragments of jagged glass remaining like broken teeth. The woman writhed on the floor. The large thug was unconscious beside her, a pool of blood gathering beneath his leg. Turtleneck and the other three were nowhere to be seen, though a door stood ajar to the side.

Terra stood to her full height. "You have the right to remain silent. Anything you say can and will be used against you in a court of law. You have the right to speak to an attorney and to have an attorney present during any questioning. If you cannot afford a lawyer, one will be provided for you at government expense."

The woman reached for the rifle. Her hands were bloody, and the gun slipped from her grasp. Terra brushed aside the remaining teeth of glass with the side of her firearm, then vaulted through the window.

Her ass slid across a countertop. Her feet touched the floor. The woman yelled for backup. Terra placed her hand under the kitchen table and flipped it onto its side before crouching behind it and using it as a makeshift shield.

The woman cried out again. "Now, you assholes! Get her! Get her!"

Terra peeked out from behind the table as a face appeared in the gap in the door. She shot, the shadowed man collapsing instantly to the floor.

"Get out of there, now," Tommy growled. The words came through her ear canal via her HUD as clearly as if he was standing beside her. "Kris. I'm not fucking around anymore."

"Neither am I," Terra retorted. "Get on board, or go home. Justice can be my partner tonight." She thumbed the HUD and the information faded. The visuals powered down. Terra could hear Tommy talking outside, but his words remained there, unable to contact her through the glasses.

She peeked around the doorway again. The woman had the rifle in one slick hand. Her clenched jaw and bared teeth added to her manic look. Terra ducked out of the open as bullets crashed into the table's surface. Wood splintered in all directions. The noise was deafening. Terra clapped her hands to her ears, accidentally triggering the HUD.

"—for fuck's sake, Terra," Tommy continued his tirade of profanity unbroken from the dead line.

Sorry, buddy, Terra thought as she tapped the button again. *I'm afraid I'm working above your pay grade.*

A large section of the table broke away. Terra shrank behind its protection, feeling the vibrations of the bullets against the hard surface. When it seemed that she was running out of options, the rifle jammed.

"Damn it," the woman complained. She whacked the gun against the floor. "Tyson!"

Terra peeked out from cover. Another face appeared in the doorway. This time, Terra aimed at his feet, the shot catching the man's toes.

Terra broke cover and ran over to the woman. She kicked the rifle out of her weak grasp, sending it sailing across the room. It clattered against the wall.

She twisted away, ducking behind the refrigerator as more

activity caught her attention, coming from the room with the open door. A hurried frenzy of voices reached her. "Come on, come on, come on."

Terra looked around the fridge, able to see into the room. The three dealers stood by a large sash window and were fighting with the catch to get the damn thing open. They shoulder-barged each other, frantically looking over their shoulder in case she stormed in.

Terra placed a finger to her ear. "This is Sylvester to Tweety Bird. Get your ass in here and cover my six."

Tommy started calling something back, but Terra switched off the HUD once more. She stalked out from the fridge, then dashed to the opposing wall. She pressed her back to the plaster, her body inches from the open door.

The sash window slid open.

Terra broke cover, appearing in the doorway, gun aimed at the three. One of the men was half-out, straddling the frame. He gave a brief yell of surprise before throwing himself out and onto the hard ground.

The others turned to follow suit.

Terra leaped over a large double bed, the covers yellowing with streaks of black. She fired a warning shot at the wall, which caused the other two to freeze in place. "Freeze. Hands where I can see them."

The woman obeyed and raised her hands. The man, however, turned with an enraged look. His lip curled as he advanced on Terra, his hands balled into fists.

Terra smirked. "I hoped you'd play it my way."

Someone landed in the kitchen. Tommy's voice addressed the woman.

The man swung at Terra. Terra holstered her pistol and swept an arm in front of herself, her forearm blocking the punch and deflecting it out of the way.

The man's shoulder lurched left. Terra delivered a hook to his ribs. The man switched momentum and brought his fist back, almost catching Terra in the chin. She leaned back, grabbing his wrist on the swing. With a firm twist, he doubled over. She raised her elbow and struck the back of his neck. The man grunted and fell face-first to the floor.

Someone appeared beside her and shoved Terra off-balance. The woman had broken her cooperation and slammed into her side. The pair crossed the room, not stopping until the wall hit Terra's back. She expelled a mouthful of air, then fended off a rapid flurry of blows from the woman.

The woman was fast, but with adrenaline and likely some other substances running through her, the blows were weak. Terra hooked a foot behind the woman's ankle and shoved. The woman fell backward, the bed catching her and softening her fall.

Terra wasted no time advancing on her, one hand reaching behind to draw out a pair of handcuffs. She slapped one ring on the woman's wrist.

The suspect flailed, kicking and wriggling on the bed. Terra's jaw clenched from the effort as she straddled the woman, grabbed the other wrist, and secured the cuffs. "Funny. In another time and place, this would be considered sexy," Terra mused.

With the final *click* of the handcuffs, the woman deflated. She stopped fighting, instead choosing to lay on the bed. Terra climbed off her, eyes locked in case she moved again. "We good?"

The woman spat in her direction. Terra shook her head disapprovingly. "You want to be careful, ma'am. Jail in Atlantica isn't as safe as it is in the rest of the world. A lot of bad types in there. Particularly for…" She tapped her HUD. Immediately Tommy's voice filled her head, but Terra ignored it. Instead, she focused on the information appearing on the screen of glass. "Particularly for a woman who is wanted for three counts of assault, one of solicitation of a political figure—Markus Rubin…interesting—

and breaking and entering into a public documentation office. Huh…"

"What?" the woman growled.

"Nothing on here about drugs." Terra tapped the information away. "Must be a new line of work for you. I'd recommend going into something more morally upstanding."

The woman grumbled but chose not to reply. Terra crossed to the window, stepping over the unconscious man, and clicked the latch back into place. She crouched and cuffed his hands behind his back before standing and giving a satisfied nod. "Much better."

She crossed to the door, casting a furtive glance over her shoulder. "Be a good girl for a moment, won't you?"

"Fuck you," the woman shot back.

Terra chuckled. "No thanks."

A pistol cocked. Terra sighed. She faced the hallway, unsurprised to find a man standing a foot back from the doorway opposite. Inside, the room was dark. Light from the doorway revealed only part of his silhouette, but Terra had accounted for the one man missing from their number. The turtleneck was a dead giveaway.

The man sneered, eyes flashing as they caught the light when he shifted. Not twenty feet away, Tommy was putting the woman in handcuffs as she protested on the floor.

Turtleneck raised a finger to his lips, teeth shockingly white in his mouth.

Terra's shoulders softened.

The man signaled that she should lift her hands.

Terra didn't move.

The man's smile faded.

Terra's grew.

Her hand whipped to her pistol.

The man pulled the trigger.

Terra ducked. Behind her, sheetrock cracked.

Terra fired.

The man buckled over, looking shocked as he wheezed his exhale. He dropped his pistol and fell to his knees.

Tommy's ears pricked up. He ran toward them, then stopped to take in the scene of Terra crouched with her gun out in front of her and yet another dying man in the apartment.

A moment of quiet passed between them. Tommy's nostrils flared.

Terra raised her eyebrows. "Did I do something wrong?"

CHAPTER THREE

Terra crossed her legs, her ass going numb from the cool, hard steel of the cheaply built chair beneath her. AJS officers strolled along the corridors, eyes fixed to their tablet displays, occasionally almost bumping into each other as they each hurried to their next assignment.

Across the hallway, large glass dividers separated the bullpen from the private offices of the senior officers.

The "bullpen..." Terra felt a pulse of irritation well within her as she scanned the dozens of open desks with their standard computer systems on top. Screen displays showed photos of family and friends—and even a few pets. There were ficuses and cacti and mugs that read "World's Best Dad" on the messy desks. The bullpen was a term that she hadn't heard in the inner city HQs, but the precincts she used to look down upon from high used it. She hated it. It was bad enough that the term "pig" still followed officers of the law into Atlantica, but to adopt the term and embrace it, implying that the officers were considered "bullish" and in as much need of restraint as the prisoners...Where was the respect? Where was the authority, pride, command...

"She'll be with you in a moment."

Gina Williams stood in the nearby doorway. She'd pulled her hair back into a tight bun, and glasses perched on the end of her nose. She was young, with bright red lips that drew the attention of the male officers—it was either that or her pencil skirts that stopped just above the knee. She flashed a bright smile, then ducked back inside the office.

Terra sighed. She didn't see the problem. She had brought in four criminals, quelled what could have been an explosive gunfight, and helped the AJS glean information on Archimedes. Sure, two perps had lost their lives in the process, but it had been them or Terra, and that was a battle Terra was never going to take lightly.

"Corporal Black will see you now." Gina offered a warm smile, then held the door open for Terra.

Terra entered the reception area. A small walnut desk sat in the corner, the smell of vanilla and perfume lingering in the air. There were metallic filing cabinets, security cameras fitted to the corners of the room, and a door with frosted glass and large golden lettering reading "Corporal Leonie Black."

Unconventional, but what does Atlantica care about convention?

Terra glanced at a clock on the wall. It was wood carved into the shape of an owl. The pendulum swung back and forth, the rhythmic ticking enough to make Terra sleepy and a little dizzy.

Gina moved in front of Terra and knocked on the door. A voice called, "Come in."

Gina opened the door for Terra. Terra stepped inside.

Corporal Black's office was double the size, yet also twice as empty. The only light source was the yellow bulb inside the desk lamp, and the temperature dropped several notches upon entry. A ribbon of smoke ascended from a glass ashtray on the corner of a metallic desk.

"Take a seat." Corporal Black motioned to yet another metal chair across from her desk, then folded her arms. Terra obliged, wishing that she was back in the inner city, where the chairs were cushioned and did something beneficial for lumbar support.

"Thank you," Terra offered.

Corporal Black was quiet and kept her eyes fixed on the wall across from her. She was tall, at least six feet at a guess when standing. Her shimmering blue uniform complemented her dark skin. Hexagonal patterns ran across the body piece in large sections.

Each hexagon was the very latest in Kevlar protection, nanoparticles that hardened under sudden stress and protected the officers from the worst of gunshot attacks. They weren't foolproof—each could only withstand a handful of shots before the technology disintegrated— but they were the latest and greatest in personal protection. Terra was surprised that the AJS budget in the outer districts stretched that far, but Lord, was she thankful.

Corporal Black's emerald eyes narrowed. Her arms remained folded. There were two golden stripes on her left breast. Her left cheek was sunken slightly, the puckered ridge of a scar running almost the whole way from her ear to her lip. She drew a long breath and shook her head. "We have a problem."

Terra followed her gaze to the wall. Projected onto the entirety of the large square was first-person camera footage of a place that Terra recognized. She heard snippets of her voice. She saw flashes of her hands as she raised the gun and vaulted into the kitchen. In the background, Tommy was mumbling and muttering as Terra plowed forward with her mission.

They watched the full feed together in silence. Terra relived the experience, feeling the adrenaline, the excitement, the fear once more. Corporal Black paused the footage as Terra and Tommy stood outside the sedan. The senior officer was pissed off, and rain fell hard from the sky. In the background were flashes of AJS lights from their backup.

Corporal Black let the silence hang. She uncrossed her legs

and arms and leaned forward onto the desk. "You have a problem with authority."

Terra met her gaze, silent in the absence of a question. Corporal Black's stare was intense, but there was something else behind it. Forgiveness that Terra didn't often see in the faces of her former bosses.

"Do you have any words to defend yourself?" Black asked.

"Defend myself from what?" Terra asked.

"Disobedience," Black replied.

"The situation escalated," Terra returned. "Tommy was out of the—"

"Officer Vincenzo," Black interjected.

Terra closed her eyes to regain her composure. "Officer Vincenzo was out of the line of fire. You saw the video. The window shattered, bullets entered public space. I needed to react, to respond—quickly. We train to de-escalate situations to protect the public. Protect and serve—that's our creed, right?"

Black's nostrils flared, though it was brief. Her expression remained calm. "I don't need reminding of our creed and morals, Officer Kris. In case you had forgotten, you're addressing a senior officer of the law. I know what I saw and what I saw was a direct disregard for commands from another senior officer."

"Tommy is *not* a senior officer—"

"Officer Vincenzo," Black corrected.

"Officer *Vincenzo*," Terra shot back, temperature rising. "He is not a senior officer."

"He is *your* superior," Black reminded. "You are on probation, Officer Kris, in case you had forgotten. It's because of situations like this that you're in my ranks and on a probationary period where you will be watched, monitored, and babysat by my officers until you're in a position in which we once again deem you fit to serve the Atlantica Justice System with full credibility."

Terra stood sharply. "I brought you a link closer to Archimedes. I handled a situation that Vincenzo—with all of his infinite superiority—was reluctant to get a grasp on. I applied the training and code of the Atlantica Justice System to bring criminals to justice. If that's not what we're here for, then I don't know what we're doing anymore."

Her chest rose and fell with each breath. Her gaze bored into Corporal Black's, who appeared unfazed. She gazed back with the lazy curiosity of a woman watching the elephants stroll at the city zoo. Terra could understand why they assigned her to Black's unit. Most of the other officers would have let their egos get in the way, their heat matching that of Terra's until the whole situation descended in a flurry of fire and fury.

At least, that's what she remembered from Garcia's office. Her former captain might have had the illusion of being a nice guy—a desk smattered in photos of his wife and two children, each one depicting a perfect suburban family—but she still saw the hatred in his eyes, the glee on his grin.

None of that reflected in Black.

The door opened. Gina poked her head inside, glancing between the pair. "Everything okay?"

Black gave a warm smile and nodded. "Just venting some emotion," she explained. "We all need it from time to time. Thank you, Gina."

Gina closed the door, leaving them both in quiet.

"Sit down," Black instructed, gentle but firm.

Terra slowly lowered herself back to her seat.

Black sat back in her chair and laced her arms behind her head. There was a harsh light from the computer monitor that caught the contours of her face. "You're passionate. I can see that. I don't blame you for being pissed off at the position in which you find yourself. A fall from grace is never easy to take."

Terra ground her teeth, knowing better than to say what she wanted to say. That it shouldn't have been a fall from grace. It should have been an ascendance to greatness. She and her partner had uncovered the holy grail of internal corruption.

They had followed the White Rabbit down Alice's rabbit hole and exposed the whole sting.

The only thing they couldn't do was prove it.

"Tell me," Black offered, narrowing her eyes on Terra. "What are your retirement plans?"

Terra froze, a cold wash running through her. "Retirement plans? I'm twenty-eight years old. I haven't even thought about retirement."

Black held her gaze.

"No." Terra's face hardened. "You can't make me. This is everything to me, Corporal. I live to serve."

"Calm down," Black placated with a lazy wave. "I'm not here to force you into early retirement, though I do need you to think. Your behavior among your colleagues has been noted, from the inner city and now here. You're lucky to have been cast down into my little pond. Another precinct would have had you out on your ass so quickly that the scrapes on the asphalt would set you on fire."

She studied Terra for a moment.

"Thank you," Terra offered weakly.

"Don't thank me with words. Thank me with action. I said that you're lucky to have me, not that I can save you forever. You're a great officer, Kris. Anyone can see that. If you could only learn to get along and work with your partners here, it would make my job a hell of a lot easier. I might be able to see my family when I'm home instead of drowning under a thousand pages of paperwork."

Terra glanced down at the table. Silence stretched between them.

Black sighed. She opened her top drawer and removed a pristine cardboard box. That, in itself, caught Terra's attention. Nothing in this shit-heap precinct was ever brand new. Everything was a hand-me-down from the top wolves. She slid it toward Terra. "I think I have a solution for your problems."

Terra raised an eyebrow. She stared at the package. "What is it?"

Corporal Black didn't reply.

Terra reached for the box. It was lighter than it looked. She pulled open the tab and slid out a white box with an image of a pair of smart glasses on the front.

"APRIL?" Terra read, examining the large bold letters on the front.

"Brand-new, sent from HQ," Black continued as Terra took the glasses from the box and rotated them in her hands. They were sleek, midnight black with tinted lenses. A faint pulsing blue light in the intersection where the arms met the lenses made Terra think of the AJS cruisers and their flashing cherries. "Experimental and the first of their kind. The latest in emergency service AI."

Terra snorted. She composed herself when she saw the tired expression on Black's face. "Forgive me, but what are HQ doing sending you guys the latest and greatest in Atlantican technology? Last I checked you guys were still using printers the company stopped manufacturing in 2001."

For the first time, Black smiled in amusement. "Remember, Kris. You're one of us now. There is no 'you guys.' You're as much a part of this precinct as Maria's ficus is. That coffee stain on the kitchen cupboards in the shape of Italy? That's you, now. Get your head down from the clouds and accept where you are, and you can do amazing things here. Who knows, with a little encouragement, maybe you'll finally end up back with your old pal in the inner city. But, for now…" She nodded at the glasses.

"What am I supposed to do with these?" Terra asked.

Black grinned. "Put them on."

Terra turned them over once more in her hand before placing them on her face. The bridge was a little rough in design, and it was irritating her nose. She reached for the button she had seen on the side of the arm and tapped it. The lenses exploded with light, a message scrawling into the space between her and Corporal Black.

Advanced Police Relationship Intelligence Liaison.

Powered by Tynamo Inc.

Terra nodded, impressed by the clarity and the smoothness of the display. The words danced in front of her. Some of them faded until all that remained were the letters **APRIL**.

"Pretty sweet graphics…" was all that Terra managed before a voice spoke in her ear.

Hello, Officer Terra Kris. How are you today?

Terra looked to her side, almost certain that someone was standing beside her. She turned over her shoulder but only found the frozen image from the projector cast onto the wall. "Hello?"

Yes, "Hello." It's a typical greeting that most humans provide each other upon their first interaction with one another. It offers a pleasantry and increases the likelihood of positive interaction. If I didn't know any better, I'd say that you were perhaps the artificial one. Should we check your programming?

There was a smirk in that voice, sarcasm leaking off the final sentence. Terra raised her eyebrows, turning to find Black with an earpiece in and grinning. "Quirky, isn't she?"

Terra let out a soft chuckle. "AI has certainly come a long way—"

New officer detected. Scanning now.

The office turned semi-transparent as a series of neon blue grid lights scanned and mapped the environment. Terra could see enough of it to identify features, threats, or movements, but her primary focus became a high-definition image of Corporal Leonie Black. She went from sitting to standing, floating in the air. The projection turned the corporal in a three-sixty view as statistics appeared around her.

Corporal Leonie Christina Black.

Age: Thirty-nine.

Height: Five feet, seven inches.
Weight: One hundred thirty-four pounds.
Married to Dwight Harvey Black.
Children: None.
Occupation: Senior Atlantica Officer for Justice.
Time served on the force: 6,205 days.
Criminal record: Clean.

The list went on, detailing a bird's eye view of Black's house, her registered vehicles, her medical history, all of it scrolling before Terra in a blur of words and lights.

The speed of the information was rapid, and Terra grew breathless while trying to keep up with it all. When the words **Last location** appeared, Terra followed as the lenses zoomed in on the real world, passing through a series of interconnected camera feeds, slowly working toward the precinct. Terra saw streets, stores, restaurants, and pubs until finally, the station came into view. The camera zoomed in, hopping between feeds until eventually the unit in the corner of Black's office started to blink.

Terra looked at the image of Black and herself in the office from behind. From here she could see the corporal's computer monitor, a replica of what she saw on display.

"Pretty sophisticated technology, isn't it?" Black asked.

Terra nodded, a little light-headed as small lights blossomed in the corner of her vision. She tried to reply, but her throat was dry. The attack of lights was dying, but still, the residual images remained.

Terra raised her hand to the glasses to take them off. She managed to only get them a centimeter from her face when a blinding pain surged through her head.

Terra toppled off her chair, grunting in agony. Her hands rose to her head. The hard floor met the back of her skull. She blinked away the worst of the pain, but her head began to thump. "What the hell?"

She opened her eyes to find Corporal Black standing over her. "The glasses are designed only to be removed by a superior officer when you are off-duty. They are fitted with a command sequence that can only be accessed by your ranking officer, meaning that when you clock in at the station, you place APRIL on your face. When you finish your shift, I enable you to remove her."

Terra grunted, accepting the hand that Black offered her. She wobbled slightly on her feet. "Why? What's all this for?"

Black half-shrugged. "Since I've run out of prospective officers who are willing to pair with you on a day-to-day basis, this is what it's come down to, Kris."

"What do you mean?" Terra knew the answer.

"Officer Kris, meet your new partner."

CHAPTER FOUR

Terra popped two aspirin from the metallic sleeve and watched the bubbles form inside the cool glass of water.

She stirred the drink with her finger, encouraging the pills to dissolve faster. The headache wasn't too bad, but the dull pain irritated her. Terra was always at her best. She slept the recommended amount of hours, ate the recommended diet according to the latest offerings of the food wheel, and drank the recommended daily dose of fluids.

By all accounts, she considered herself a model human. A headache wouldn't do anything to help that.

She brought the glass to her lips. A sharp *yap* made her flinch. The glass slipped an inch in her grasp, some of the water almost spilling on the floor.

Terra cocked an eyebrow at the fluffy white creature standing by her feet. Skooch's tail wagged enthusiastically, a long flag of fluff and fur. Her large, bat-like ears pointed at Terra, and it looked as though she was smiling.

The AJS officer hadn't ever seen herself with a toy dog. She had always wanted something big and sturdy, a mastiff or a Doberman. Still, with the demands of her job and the limited time she had to exercise a larger dog regularly, she had settled for the little Papillon.

She had been a gift from an ex-lover. Now four years old, the Papillon had become one of the highlights of her day. Skooch hadn't complained when Terra moved to the outer city. She had merely licked the officer's face and curled up to her in the evening for cuddles. That was all Terra needed, and Skooch was happy to provide.

"You scared the shit out of me," Terra softly stated as she set the glass of water down. She picked Skooch up and cradled her in her arm. "You need to be careful of alerting Mummy. You know I'm a trained killer? I'm licensed and armed at all times."

She smiled at Skooch as the dog strained her neck to lick Terra's nose. Terra brought her closer and closed her eyes as wet kisses warmed her face. "How's *your* day been?"

She placed Skooch down on the floor, then downed her drink. Skooch ran excitedly in circles around her feet, following Terra as she strode to the cupboards to pour her dinner—dog kibble and jellied meats.

Satisfied, Skooch tucked into her bowl. Terra rubbed her temples, then turned her attention to her dinner. Her head still throbbed, and occasionally her mind flashed with the lights of the APRIL system. Corporal Black had typed a command into her computer to release them from Terra's head, but the pain very much still followed her.

She flopped onto the couch with a tray laden with a roast chicken ready-meal. A cup of steaming black coffee rested on the side. She flicked on the TV and consumed the latest in the onslaught of miserable media that painted the head-lines. Another murder in downtown, drug busts, corruption chains, the latest revelation in a wealth and power struggle from the millionaire moguls scrapping it out in the inner city.

When a face came on the screen that caught her attention, her ears pricked up. She thumbed the volume up and narrowed her eyes at the red-haired bearded wonder shown

"Today marks a historic day in the story of Atlantica justice," a perky blonde journalist stated into an oversized microphone. "Tobias Archer, head of the Aphrodite Cosmetics Corporation and director of the Atlantica Beauty Pageant has finally been found guilty and convicted for more than two hundred sexual offenses. As you can see here, Christian, the streets are packed with angry Atlanticans, including many of Tobias' victims who have been seeking and demanding justice from this Atlantican giant for more than two decades."

The cameras swept along the city street, with towering buildings in bright lights all around. Hundreds of civilians marveled in wonder, throwing "Boos" and hisses as Atlantica Officers for Justice marched Tobias into their cruisers. His expression was surly, and his dark eyes caught the camera.

Terra spotted several of her former colleagues on the case. When the footage showed an athletic woman holding up a hand and keeping back a screaming woman trying to break the barriers, Terra turned the TV off.

"I guess Imani's going to be late for our date, then," Terra muttered to Skooch, who had returned from her food and now waited by Terra's feet. "The life of an inner-city officer, eh?" She pushed the tray aside, then picked up the dog and ran her fingers through her soft fur.

"That was supposed to be my sting," Terra complained. "Three years I spent gathering evidence on that one." She looked at the TV. "I wonder who got the final catch in the end."

Terra sighed but forced a smile. Skooch placed her front paws on Terra's chest and stared into her eyes. "You really are a smart girl, aren't you?" Skooch flooded her face with kisses.

Terra placed her gently beside her on the couch. She turned the TV back on, this time flicking the channel to cover the news in the United Kingdom. The reporters sat side by side with large, cheesy grins on their faces and a picture of Prince Charles behind them.

"Not long to go now," Terra muttered as the reporters detailed the upcoming coronation of the new king of England. "Can you imagine a stranger world than that with a king?" The smile was back along with a look of fascination in her eyes. "The outside world is a marvelous thing, don't you think?"

She turned her head to a glass display cabinet at the far side of the room, filled with trinkets and souvenirs that friends had brought her back from their travels. From here she could make out the Leaning Tower of Pisa next to a replica of the Eiffel Tower. There were china plates with "I Heart London" written around their circumference. There were flags and glasses and trolls and bears, each with the stamp of a different culture on them.

Terra sighed and rested her head back on the couch. "One day," she whispered to Skooch. "One day…"

Night fell, and the city came alive.

Terra straddled her Ducati XDiavel Dark, the city blurring past her in a flurry of speed.

The engine rumbled beneath her, filling her body with vibrations and adrenaline. She stayed low, leaning forward as she slalomed around the steady stream of evening traffic.

Heads turned as the bike ripped past. Terra had customized it herself, painted the body in a sleek array of midnight black and neon blue. She sourced the parts for maximum efficiency and made what had been state-of-the-art for its model year even better. The seat was comfortable, the machine responded to her every move, and every second spent speeding on that seat had Terra smiling.

She parked by the curb outside Bougey's Bar. Glass panels

decorated the front of the bar, with an array of neon lettering scattered across its front to spell its name. It was quirky, modern, and if Terra lived a normal life, she could consider spending much more time here.

The place was jumping. The air warmed the minute she stepped through the door, the music louder than it needed to be. She sidled through the crowd and joined the mass around the bar. Ten minutes later, she stood at the front counter.

Although two barkeeps wandered up and down the wall-length counter, they rarely addressed the customers. Instead, a series of screens decorated the countertops with a menu of cocktails, lagers, ales, ciders, and spirits. Terra swiped through the menu until she found the hot drinks and ordered a coffee. She found the Appletinis and ordered one of those as well.

She confirmed payment with a wave of her phone. The device buzzed in her hand. Two round receptacles opened beside the monitor, the mechanisms whirring away out of sight beneath the counter. A moment later, two perfectly poured drinks ascended.

Terra nodded at one of the bartenders—a tall man with a broad chest and a v-neck that showed off a mat of curly blond hair. He flashed a grin back. One of the girls beside Terra swooned, which sent her into a fit of giggles.

Terra rolled her eyes and squeezed through the crowd, barely managing not to spill a drop.

She found a recently vacated table in the center of the room. The tabletop was still sticky, and Terra waited as a small string of jets squirted from the table's rim into the center. A wiper blade swept across the table in a perfect circle, dragging the liquid residue into a plug in the center.

A buzzing indicated the automatic function had initiated the heater. By the time Terra sat, the table was spotless.

She sipped her coffee and observed the crowd. The music did nothing to help her headache. Young men and women packed the bar, most in outfits that seemed far too revealing for public consumption. Plastic smiles covered faces, men stalked the borders of the bar, and by the time Imani Thomas arrived, Terra had rejected four eager men who seemed unwilling to take no for an answer until Terra flashed her AJS badge.

"Sorry I'm late," Imani offered, reaching down to hug Terra.

Terra squeezed her back. A strong cloud of sweet perfume enveloped them both. "Don't mention it. I've sorted you out."

Imani sat across from Terra and shrugged off her coat. She was beautiful. Tall and athletic with a frame that lent itself perfectly to police work. Her muscles strained beneath her cream blouse, and her long legs stretched on for years. She flashed a bright smile, then took a long draught of her Appletini.

"Busy day?" Terra flashed a knowing grin.

"You saw the news?"

"I did." Terra looked down at the table. "Quite the capture. I doubt you'd have gotten that far without all the foundational groundwork laid for you. You really are stepping on the shoulders of giants." She looked up and grinned.

Imani tilted her head with a hint of pity in her eyes. "We couldn't have done it without you. You know that, right?"

"I needed to hear you say it."

They sat a moment in quiet. A man around twenty years old strutted toward them, then turned when Imani pointed. She returned her attention to Terra. "How is life in the projects?"

"It's good." Terra sipped her coffee. "Pretty basic. But, it's good. None of the glory of what you and the guys are claiming."

Imani reached across the table and took Terra's hand. "It won't be forever. Play ball for a little while, and you'll be right back where you belong. They'd be stupid not to recognize your talent, and once we have Garcia pinned with evidence, they'll be begging to have you back."

Terra's blood boiled at the mention of his name. Captain Parker Garcia was the worst of the worst among the AJS ranks. A crooked cop bulked up with power. It had been an accident, at first. Terra had been working late one night, typing away at her computer until the early hours of the morning. She had fallen asleep at her keyboard. When she awoke, dazed and confused, the office was empty, all except Parker Garcia.

The conversation was in whispers, but it was loud enough for Terra to glean the information as Garcia spat down the phone, demanding that the ink sales move faster. He scolded whoever was on the other end of the line for not transferring money, threatening to end the sting and send them to jail.

Terra remained motionless, waiting until the office was empty before heading home.

There began Terra's downfall. She informed Imani, her AJS partner, of what she had heard. At first, Imani had been dismissive, but after further digging, the breadcrumbs started to appear. Imani and Terra had worked in secret, following the trail and attempting to accrue evidence to bring down the asshole in charge of their troop.

However, they slipped up. Parker became wise. Soon the river ran dry, and before Terra and Imani could do anything further, Terra got her marching orders. She protested and tried to call Garcia out, but it was too late. In her final scrabbling attempts at saving face, she absorbed the blame for them both. Freed Imani of any cooperation with their operation, and so the weight fell on Terra Kris.

"As long as he's there, I won't be," Terra replied. "You know that as well as I do." She drew a long breath. "Are you still…"

"Following up?" Imani finished. "You bet your ass I am." Her smile faded. "It's slow, though. Garcia has his back up. He talks to me like everything's normal, but I can see the suspicion in his eyes. You may have taken the blame, but he's not stupid. He knows that I'm a threat."

"*We're* a threat. Just because I'm a few miles out from you guys doesn't mean that has faded. I can still help."

"*No.*" Imani looked over her shoulder. "No. You need to sit tidy, Terra. It's the only way anything's going to change. The moment he finds you sniffing around again, we're screwed. I'll be out on my ass, too, and I need to be there, close to the fucker so I can bring him to justice."

"*We.*" Terra locked her gaze with Imani.

Imani raised an eyebrow.

"You said 'I.' We're a team." Terra's lips thinned.

Imani nodded, offering an apologetic smile. "Yes. Yes, we are." She took her lipstick from her bag and applied a fresh layer. "How are things down in the little leagues?"

"Going steady."

Imani gave her a knowing look.

"Fine, they're…rough." Terra informed Imani of her struggles in being surrounded by cops with less ambition and less skill while still being under the microscope from the seniors.

"Sounds tough," Imani agreed. "I mean, I get it, too. They're going to be jealous. Everyone wants to outdo the disgraced inner city cop. But the fact that you can still show them up and hold your flame, that's got to get their egos bruised."

"There's no one left to partner with me," Terra continued. "They've had to bring in technology to help." She laughed. "Ridiculous, huh?"

Imani cocked her head.

Terra took out her cell phone and tapped the screen. She brought up an article about the APRIL glasses. "Have you seen these before?"

Imani brought the phone to her face and shook her head. "Can't say I have. What are they?"

Terra raised an eyebrow.

"What?" Imani asked.

"I'd have thought they'd have at least passed the inner city test first. That's the way of the force. All good things filter from the top."

Imani narrowed her eyes, then shook her head again. "Nope. Nothing. Never seen them before in my life. What are they?"

Terra nodded at the phone.

Imani read the screen. "Advanced Police Relationship Intelligence Liaison." She laughed. "A babysitter in a pair of glasses?"

Terra nodded. "Can you believe it?"

"So they've run out of real-life humans and decided to fit you with a robot," Imani continued. "Man, you really are rocking it down in the slums, aren't you?"

Terra snatched her phone back with a playful smile. "Watch out. Terra plus robot equals mega justice droid. They won't need to assign me back to the HQ. I'll be a one-woman fighting force. I'll be the law."

Imani laughed. "You wish."

Terra smirked. "When I'm ruling Atlantica on a throne of justice, I'll be sure to bring you along with me for the ride."

"Pinky swear." Imani offered her pinky finger.

Terra took it. "Done."

They sat a moment in quiet, each woman scanning the room and taking in the sights as the grins faded from their faces. A dance floor flashed its lights over the far side of the bar, filled to the brim with writhing and dancing drunks. Terra chuckled.

"You laugh now, but we're going over there." Imani grinned.

"No, you need booze for that. I'm not in the zone."

Imani waved that off. "Girl, come on. You work too hard. Why don't you play a little, too?"

"No, I can't." Terra shook away Imani's hand.

Imani gave Terra a stern look. "Here." She handed Terra her Appletini. Terra took a reluctant sip. "There. Much better. Let's go."

Imani wasn't taking no for an answer. She brought Terra to her feet and walked her toward the dance floor. Before they reached the crowd, she glanced over her shoulder with a quizzical look.

"What?" Terra asked.

"I don't get it. Why would they give you advanced tech that up top hasn't seen?"

"Maybe it has?" Terra offered. "Maybe they've hidden it from dirty cops like you."

Imani gave Terra a playful shove. "You're awful."

"I know." Terra turned to head back to the table.

"Nice try." Imani laughed. "Come on, let that hair down for five minutes."

CHAPTER FIVE

Scanning perimeter.

Terra stood by the chain-link fence in the darkness, a small pocket of shadow between where the cones of light from two sodium floodlights shone. The glasses rubbed the bridge of her nose. She felt the skin getting raw, no doubt leaving a bright red mark that would annoy her the moment Black released her from their grasp.

Across the vacated parking lot, the building stood in darkness. Terra, however, could see a lot more than she knew she should.

The darkness of the world faded as the glasses scanned. The building mapped out before her, showing a 3D image of each floor and the layout of the apartments. She could see the stairwell, bathrooms, bedrooms, kitchens, every room. Infrared scanners displayed people's bodies moving around inside, their shapes appearing in shades of orange, red, and yellow.

"Impressive," she approved.

Thank you. Your admiration further fuels my motivation to succeed and achieve.

Terra cocked an eyebrow, almost hearing the hint of a motivational speaker in her head. "You're a chirpy system, aren't you?"

My design encourages and motivates my partner. Your approval sends a positive message to my database of a job well done. Shall we proceed with the arrest?

Terra put her hands in her pockets. "Not yet, APRIL. I want to find out what else you can do. Show me security footage from inside the building."

Terra let out a surprised grunt as her world lurched beneath her feet. Everything that was in front of her faded in a blur of color. The next thing she knew, she was looking down at the top of the stairwell from the security feed in the corner of the room. Terra looked side to side, feeling as though she had morphed into the camera. She tapped her foot and reassured herself that she was still in the parking lot when she felt the asphalt beneath her toe.

"You have to warn me before you do something like that," Terra stated. "You really send a girl's head in a spin."

Noted. Warnings initiated for future data jumps. Updating system with gender information on cognitive stability.

Terra raised an eyebrow. The bridge cut into her nose. "Wait, what?"

You stated that data jumps trigger light-headedness in female humans. I have updated my database to reflect observation. Male humans are yet untested with data jumps. Flag raised on system database.

Terra shook her head, trying to clear the encroaching dizziness. "Whatever, APRIL. Just...take the note for me, okay? Slow down a bit. I'm not used to this amount of virtual reality in one go. Plus, I can't lose situational awareness without risk of harm."

Of course. Also, I monitor our surroundings continuously and would warn you of threats.

Terra looked around the stairwell, noting the numbers on the doors. Beyond that was the shining red outline of a man perched on the edge of the couch. He was leaning low over the table, his nose close to something she couldn't make out but could assume what it was. "Are you unable to enter into the perp's apartment?"

Due to Atlantican regulations on public versus private property, official authority systems cannot breach the data walls of private residences.

Terra chewed her lip. The apartment building's shared spaces were public, but the residences were out of her jurisdiction. "Then we're going to have to find a way to get in there."

Terra took a step forward when a blinding pain flashed behind her eyes. She grabbed both sides of her head and grunted. "What the shit, APRIL?"

It is forbidden for an officer of the law to break the regulatory guidelines set out by the Atlantica Justice System headquarters. Any notable action taken to break the rules will result in negative reinforcement on the acting officer.

"So, you're basically a human shock collar?" Terra growled. "What is this? Pavlovian training?"

I can find you a treat if you like?

Terra gasped as a sudden calmness washed over her. The arms of the glasses vibrated rapidly, soothing her temples and momentarily erasing her headache. After a few seconds, the vibrations stopped. Terra opened her eyes and saw the parking lot before her. "What was that?"

Temporal nerve stimulation. By sending small electrical frequencies to your temporal lobe and other quadrants of the brain, one can trigger the sequences associated with increased levels of adrenaline and serotonin.

"You're altering my biology?" Terra scolded. "What the hell?"

Not altering. Manipulating. There's a significant difference.

"Semantically," Terra spat back.

Not in semantics, in definition. Here, let me explain. According to the Merriam-Webster Dictionary—

"APRIL, shut up," Terra stated. "I don't need to hear a goddamn definition to know that whatever the fuck this is, it isn't natural. I want you out of my head—*argh!*"

She pulled the glasses away, initiating another sudden shock to her temples. Terra placed the glasses back on, falling to her knees in pain. Nearby, a light switched on in an apartment.

Caution, APRIL stated. Civilian suspicion is increasing. The element of surprise is fading.

"Stop shocking me, then."

My basic programming prevents my partner from altering my mother code. To initiate changes to foundational coding, please speak to your ranking officer.

"Fuck..." Terra grumbled. She glanced up at the window where Ollie Verdana sat on his couch and snorted blow. "How am I expected to arrest him if we can't get in there?"

Terra expected silence to answer, being used to having to deal with these thoughts by herself. Instead, APRIL answered. **You would have to lure him out.**

Terra raised her eyebrows. A grin appeared on her lips. "I didn't know you had it in you, APRIL."

I do not understand these colloquialisms, Officer Kris. In me, I have circuitry, wires, and a great deal of advanced computer coding.

"You suggested luring the perp out of his apartment. That's something that not many officers are keen to try and do. Too much paperwork, you see."

You asked a question. I merely supplied a logical response.

Terra cocked her head, her neck cracking. *I may warm up to you yet, robot.*

She played around with APRIL's settings, exploring the information provided on the display screen. Outside of the apartment, there was little they could glean without getting a physical view of the man, but a revelation came when Terra muttered a question to herself. "What's a good way to lure someone out of their home?"

Incentives, prizes, and rewards are all great motivators. Many civilians are also partial to phone calls, takeaway foods, and shopping trips for alcohol and other such narcotics.

Terra gave an approving nod. "Not bad, not bad…"

Footsteps sounded nearby. Terra shrank farther back into the shadows as two more red shapes appeared on her display. She could see the pair arriving around the corner before they appeared out in the open.

Terra crouched low.

Civilians approaching, APRIL declared. Terra hoped the voice was only inside her head.

The two figures appeared under the streetlights, skinny and withered. They had their hoods raised around their faces, but long gangly arms poked out the sleeves of their sweatshirts. Judging by their gait, she was looking at one man and one woman. They crossed to the apartment block, then buzzed the panel.

A tinny voice replied, barely audible. "I can't hear them," Terra whispered.

Amplifying audio, APRIL announced. A moment later, the words were clear inside her head.

"Ollie, it's us. Open up." A woman's voice.

The red shape of Ollie moved from the couch to a wall. He tapped a button. "You're late."

"Fashionably so," the woman replied.

Data jumping, APRIL announced, only giving Terra a second before the world lurched and she was looking down at the pair by the door.

"Yeah, I'm going to need more of a warning than that," she declared.

Noted.

The pair looked up at the security camera, and for a heart-stopping moment, Terra feared they could see her. The anti-tres-pass light shone down on them, illuminating pale faces and gaunt cheeks. A tangle of beard hid the man's chin. The woman's eyes were slitted, her eyelids looking almost bruised.

"Come on, Ollie. It's cold out here," the woman complained.

Terra turned her head, surprisingly closer to Ollie's red shape now. She heard him sigh down the transmitter before a buzzing announced that he'd unlocked the door.

Data jumping in three...two...one...

The world lurched. Terra returned to her position in the camera on top of the stairs. Her stomach flipped over. She put a fist to her mouth to prevent her heaving. "Maybe it's not the warning I need. That did nothing to help."

Searching for alternative methods for travel sickness...

"Not now," Terra declared. "Focus on the job at hand."

The camera tracked the pair as they stalked up the stairs. Terra frowned as she saw the pair's hands dig into their pockets. There was a large shape inside that looked familiar.

"Shit," Terra muttered. "They have guns. They're going to kill him. Zoom in, APRIL."

APRIL obliged, and Terra made out the flash of metal on the barrels of the guns they drew as they approached the door. Ollie crossed his apartment, one hand rubbing his nose as he moved to the door. He stretched, taking his sweet time as the pair knocked on the door and waited.

"APRIL, pull up the phone records of Ollie Verdana," Terra instructed.

Pulling up phone records.

The pair knocked again.

Three records found.

"Dial them all. Call the numbers," Terra urged.

I can only call one line at a time. Calling first line.

A phone started ringing in Terra's head. She took a step

toward the building, one hand automatically resting on the butt of her gun.

The line went dead.

Calling second line.

Terra drew her weapon. She could see the red figures with their weapons drawn out of sight of the apartment's peephole.

Ollie reached for the door handle.

Data jumping in three...two...one...

The world lurched.

Terra looked down on the pair exchanging a glance, hardened expressions on their faces. A red mass was on the other side of the door.

The phone rang.

Ollie stopped and glanced over his shoulder. He held up a finger. "Two secs."

The pair did not like this. The woman brought her gun up. The man placed a hand to lower it.

Ollie waited for the phone to go to voicemail. A message played in Terra's ear. "The person you have dialed is currently unavailable. Please leave a message after the beep."

A long *beep* played, then cut to silence.

Terra paused a moment, then whispered, "Ollie. Get out of there. Run."

Ollie looked around the apartment as if someone was in there with him and giving him instructions. He cast an uncertain eye to the door, then strode to the blinds. Two fingers poked between the wooden slats, then pinched them open as two eyes appeared in the window.

Exiting data jump in three...two...one...

Terra stood in the parking lot, staring up at the window. A soft glow of light leaked out from the apartment, but that wasn't the main focus of her attention.

Scanning target, APRIL announced, as a series of illustrative images and reams of text appeared around Ollie Verdana.

Target confirmed: Ollie Verdana.

Strings of text displaying Ollie's age, height, weight, eye color, date of birth, family history, criminal history, even his temperature, and blood type appeared in Terra's vision. A meter appeared on the right-hand side labeled, **Suspicion**, with a gauge that read **fifty-nine percent.**

The bar slowly increased as Ollie glanced around the parking lot. When he closed the blinds, the information stayed on him, as though APRIL had tagged him and could now track the target since he was still in their field of vision.

"APRIL, you did it," Terra muttered.

Ollie turned to the answering machine.

Shit. Terra cleared her throat. "Ollie, if you can hear me, get out of there, now. You have two attackers outside your front door. They're carrying…"

Nighthawk Custom T3 Luger, 9mm, four-inch semi-automatic, eight rounds.

"…Nighthawk T3s," Terra continued. "They're coming for you. Get out of there."

Ollie cast a furtive glance at the door.

Data jumping in three…two…one…

Terra closed her eyes before the jump, hoping that might remove some of the nausea that came with the leap. It took the edge off, though she was still discombobulated. The pair at the door was growing irritated. They knocked again.

"Ollie, sometime today?" The man growled.

Ollie took a few steps back. "Hold up. I've just got to…" He looked around. "I've got to check something."

The woman lowered her hood. She'd shaved half of her head, and even on a low volume, Terra could hear her teeth grinding. "This is bullshit," she muttered.

Ollie walked into a room at the back of the apartment. Terra couldn't make out what he was doing, with only the shape of his red silhouette to guide them. In her vision, she spotted the words,

Elevated heart rate, and **Adrenaline levels above typical measures**.

Yeah, no shit, she thought.

Ollie scrambled around in the back room.

"Ollie!" the woman shouted.

The man knocked again.

Ollie didn't answer.

"Fuck this," the woman declared, raising the handgun and pointing it at the handle.

"APRIL, take me back," Terra ordered, feeling her body running toward the building, even though her mind wasn't with her. It was a strange sensation, like traveling on an escalator while wearing a VR headset.

Exiting data jump in three...

"Now!" Terra called.

That was a mistake. The world spun around her. She hadn't prepared for the mental jump while running. Her ankle rolled as she misstepped and she fell to the ground. Rough asphalt scraped her cheek. She grunted, fighting to get up.

A gunshot fired from above. Terra sprinted toward the door. The two red silhouettes at the door barged inside the apartment. Terra reached the doorway and scanned her AJS badge. A green light allowed her entry—one of the perks for cops living in a digitally advanced city.

She heard their voices above her, talking to each other and calling for Ollie as she climbed the stairs. A readout in her vision fed her information about how many decibels she was making with each step.

Careful, APRIL warned as a picture-in-picture image appeared of the top of the stairs. Terra could make out the shape of herself climbing the stairwell. It was like walking with a rearview mirror attached in your eyesight, except the mirror showed whatever camera feed lay ahead.

She slowed down. Ollie's red silhouette was stationary in

another room. One of the pair was at the table, rubbing a finger along the place where Terra assumed a trail of white powder would be. The other was slowly creeping around the apartment, exploring in the doorways.

Terra tiptoed to the top of the stairs. The landing creaked beneath her feet. If the pair heard her, they didn't show it.

Terra placed her back against the wall beside the door. It was still ajar, and she could see the shadow of the man stretched along the floor.

"Any advice?" Terra whispered to APRIL, steeling herself for entry.

Public versus private protocol breached. Take them down, officer.

Terra smirked. "Oh, I don't mind if I do."

C H A P T E R   S I X

"Ollie…" the woman crooned, her voice carrying across the apartment as the man took a deep inhalation through one nostril on the table. "Come out, come out, wherever you are."

"Freeze!" Terra shouted, emerging in the doorway and training her Glock at the woman on the far side of the room. "Drop your weapons and put your hands in the air."

The man was kneeling by the table, cheek pressed to the wood, a streak of white powder across his face. His eyes were rolled back in ecstasy as he sluggishly turned to face Terra.

Troy Rampton, APRIL declared. **Threat level: forty-three percent.**

The woman spun, her eyes wild, her hair a tangled nest.

Veronica Rampton. Threat level: eighty-seven percent.

"Drop your weapon!" Terra repeated. "Don't make me shoot."

Terra ducked behind the door as Veronica opened fire. Wood splintered as the bullets struck the door. Plaster exploded as her aim followed Terra and more projectiles found the wall. Terra ducked low, avoiding the one or two bullets that ripped straight through the cheap plasterboards.

Two bullets remaining.

Terra grinned. *I could get used to this.*

"Give it up, Rampton," Terra declared. "Come quietly, and we'll make this easier for you."

"Bullshit!" Veronica retorted. "I know what you pigs are like. Spewing bullshit like you gobbled shit-flavored ice cream. Stay the fuck out of our business and go back to your pigpen."

Another shot fired. Terra threw her hands over her head.

One bullet remaining.

"What about the other guy?" Terra asked quietly.

APRIL showed Terra a scan of Troy, who was now lying on the floor and gently writhing.

"Beautiful." Terra peeked around the door. The moment her head appeared, another shot came. She narrowly avoided its trajectory.

She beamed. "APRIL?"

Out of ammo, the AI confirmed.

Terra rose to her feet and emerged into the room. She pointed the gun at Veronica, who was pulling the trigger but only eliciting empty clicks. She growled, then slapped the side of the gun. Scrambling to do *something*, she fished in her pocket and drew out a fresh magazine. Her hands shook as Terra advanced, closing the distance between them.

"Give it up, Veronica," Terra announced.

"How do you..." Veronica began.

"Know your name?" Terra grinned. "Doesn't matter. What matters is you're under arrest for attempted murder." She read Veronica her rights as she grabbed the gun barrel and wrestled it from Veronica's grip. "Do you have anything to say for yourself?"

Veronica desperately searched around. "Troy! Get off your ass and do something."

Terra twisted her wrist sharply, forcing Veronica to twist. She placed her in cuffs, then turned to Troy.

Troy was struggling to get himself to his feet. His eyes were glassy, his movements labored.

Warning. Threat level rising, APRIL informed her.

Terra pointed her weapon at him. Troy paid no notice. He grasped his gun in sweaty palms.

"Stop," Terra announced. "Final warning."

Troy ignored her, the gun swinging in a slow arc toward her.

"Fine." Terra pulled the trigger. Her bullet found the top of his thumb. A large groove followed its wake, and a small spray of blood came from his hand. He yelled and dropped the weapon.

Terra rushed him before he could make another move. She crouched, able to easily move him onto his front as she brought his hands together and slapped the cuffs on his wrists. The wound was minor. It would heal. His pride wouldn't.

Terra stood above him and gave a satisfied nod. "Looks like we've had our first successful mission," Terra stated.

Warning, APRIL announced in Terra's ear. **Imminent threat. Watch your six.**

Terra raised an eyebrow as she turned. A door near Veronica flew open. A panicked, drug-addled Ollie stumbled through with the barrel of a sawed-off shotgun leading as he frantically searched for his invaders.

His eyes locked onto Veronica's. Malice and anger painted his face. Without warning, he pulled the trigger. All that had been Veronica was no more as her mid-section disintegrated. Red droplets rained down in the apartment. Segments of Veronica's stomach and organs splattered the walls.

The only part of Veronica that was unaffected was her mouth, fixed into a perfect circle as she folded to her knees and her body thudded to the floor.

Find cover, now. APRIL's voice was stern.

Terra threw herself down behind the couch.

Ollie swept his aim around the apartment again, this time finding the non-lucid form of Troy still trying to writhe on the floor. Terra cried out to stop him, but the report exploded, drowning out any words that might have reached Ollie's ears.

Troy's hips and thighs were the most affected, blood spraying near Terra, some arcing to the ceiling and painting the cream color an awful shade of crimson.

You have a window of three seconds to respond, APRIL stated.

Terra wasted no time rising to her feet and finding Ollie in her sights. Already she was beginning to trust the AI, though the idea of it seemed absurd to her. None of it made any sense, but that was something to worry about later.

She trained her weapon on Ollie and fired. She shot his kneecap, causing him to buckle to one side. He cried out as he went down, slamming to the hardwood floor. His shotgun flew from his hands.

Terra kept her pistol trained on him as she stalked across the apartment. She blocked out the puddles of blood leaking from Veronica and Troy, eventually finding her place standing over Ollie. "Oh, boy. You are in trouble, aren't you?"

Ollie grimaced, eyes narrowing. "Fuck you, pig."

Terra shook her head and tutted. With her spare hand, she reached for a set of cuffs looped around the back of her belt. "Careful, my friend. I saved your life. This isn't how you speak to your heroes."

"Heroes?" He spat on the floor, the saliva thick and white. "You're as much a piece of scum as they are."

Terra wasn't delicate as she rested her knee on the back of his thigh. She twisted his body and placed him in the cuffs as she read him his rights. When she finished, she sat back on her ass and gathered her breath. "Such a shame that you pieces of shit don't embrace the generous nature of us AJS officers. I could have let you die here." She raised an eyebrow. "I still could."

Negative, APRIL countered in her head. **Homicide is a sackable offense, followed by a minimum possible jail sentence of fifteen years.**

Ollie grunted in pain, trying to reach for his leg, the lower half bent at an awkward angle.

Terra rolled her eyes. *I didn't mean literally.*

Terra rose to her feet. "APRIL, put in a request for medical assistance at this residency. We'll get Ollie some medical attention for that knee."

Ollie gave Terra a strange glance as he looked around the apartment. "Who are you speaking to?"

Placing call. Request filed. Medical unit on their way. Updated progress report sent to Corporal Leonie Black.

"Wait, no." Terra cast her eyes downward. "We're not done yet."

Offender to be brought in and questioned following medical attention. Officer Terra Kris to stay put until medical services arrive, then remove herself from the case.

"Huh?" Terra frowned and paced the room. "No, wait, APRIL. This is my case. I caught the guy. I get to follow up and ask my questions."

Your ranking officer has verified instructions.

"No," Terra growled back. Her lips thinned. "You can't throw me off a case when I'm in the middle of it." Ambulance sirens blared outside. Flashes of light illuminated the vacant parking lot. Terra looked out the window.

Your heart rate has elevated.

"No shit, Sherlock," Terra retorted. She ran across the room and crouched beside Ollie. "Who's your dealer? Tell me where I can find him."

Ollie grinned, a goofy gesture as his eyes grew glassy.

Terra shook him. "Tell me where I can find your boss."

She pulled Ollie's head up. His eyelids fluttered. A drunken grin spread across his face. "Oh, man..." His words were slow, soft. "I remember you." He chuckled. "You're in trooouble now..."

Terra's brow creased as confusion overcame her. "You remember me? Remember me from where?"

The man's chuckle faded as his eyes rolled back in his head. He was still breathing, but that was all she was getting from him. She shook him again, throwing a glance over her shoulder as the ambulance doors opened and closed.

She tapped the arm of her glasses. "APRIL, inform Black that I'll stay on this case.

Heartrate elevated above typical levels.

"APRIL," Terra urged. "Send the message, now."

Initiating temporal nerve stimulation.

Terra opened her mouth to argue, but all that came out was a sigh. All the frustration and tension left her in a heartbeat as her body softened and a feeling of bliss washed over her. She sat back, resting against the side of the couch as her smile grew.

Heartrate decreasing.

"Fuck you," Terra replied, laughing as she did so. She closed her eyes, her breathing coming slower and deeper.

The ambulance staff arrived in a flurry of neon yellow and white. Terra pointed at Ollie and slurred information about his condition. It didn't take a rocket scientist to spot that the other two were beyond help.

Then Terra was being assessed. She didn't remember much of what came next. All that she knew, twelve hours later, was that she was back in her apartment, her sheets were soft and warm, and she had awoken from the best night's sleep she'd had in some time.

CHAPTER SEVEN

The wind licked Terra's face as she strolled through Kingston Park.

She hadn't felt this refreshed in years, yet there was still a bubble of irritation in her stomach. The sun shone its milky light through the Atlantica haze as dog owners, parents, and joggers made their way around the several acres of artificial woodland placed amid the mass of concrete and steel skyscrapers.

Kingston Park was to be an homage to New York's Central Park. It was only after the first year of the park's existence that Kelly Kingston realized the mistake she'd made. While New York's ode to nature consisted of a variety of elms, each flourishing and reaching for the sky, blossoming and fading throughout the year across a spectrum of pinks, greens, and oranges, the elms didn't do well in Atlantica's humid sub-climate.

Over the years, Kingston experimented with the choice of trees. In the end, she settled for a combination of oak and birch, with the occasional palm tree stuck in there for variety. All in all, the homage to one of the world's most famous manufactured nature parks had turned out to be a Frankenstein creation of colors, plants, and design.

Not that it was unusual. That was one of the few things Terra loved about Atlantica. You couldn't look up without spotting an influence from another culture or country. Every building in Atlantica was custom, every street a mismatch of design. There wasn't so much a Chinatown in Atlantica, rather a sprinkling of Chinese culture among the offices, restaurants, bars, statues, and corner stores. She didn't need to leave Atlantica to see what the outside world had to offer.

Although she planned to one day, to see if it stood up to her expectations.

Terra glanced down at Skooch, her fluffy white feet padding excitedly ahead of her, straining on her lead. Terra had one hand in her pocket as she processed what had happened last night and did her best not to lose that feeling of calm while her insides attempted to boil over.

They had manipulated her. Corporal Black had used the APRIL AI to control her. Terra had performed her duty and brought the bad guy to justice—albeit in a terrific display of gunfire and blood—but she hadn't been able to follow through and enjoy the fruits of her labor. The glasses were amazing at helping Terra perform her duties, but what was the point when she couldn't see things through to the end?

Worse than that, there had been no explanation. Terra had awoken in her bed, the glasses nowhere in sight.

Where is he now? Terra thought back to Ollie Verdana and wondered what Black had done with him. He could still be in the hospital. Or, depending on how they'd patched him up, he could have been carted to the station and was now sitting in the interrogation booth, his leg in a cast as they tried to draw out the information that Terra should have rightfully earned.

Terra shook her head and tried to focus on the park. The brickwork path snaked ahead before her, leading her and Skooch toward a water feature where children were running back and forth through sprays of water that burst out of the ground at seemingly random intervals. An older woman with a beautiful snow-white husky strolled past, nose in the air as though she was trying to sniff out trouble. Near a series of picnic benches and a large sandpit, a jogger bounced past on the tips of her toes, wearing bright pink wireless earphones on either side of her head.

Terra's eyes went to a man sitting on the bench. He sat alone, a bottle of Coke in front of him. He wore a thin cotton hoodie with the hood pulled up over his head, his eyes tracking Terra as she walked past. Perhaps it could have been the aqua blue yoga pants Terra wore and the sleeveless jacket that hugged her athletic frame—it wouldn't be the first time creeps had spied on her as she strolled through the park. Still, something about it felt off. The man was sitting with no one, and as Terra moved out of sight, she felt his gaze following her somehow.

She stopped near the fountains, letting Skooch strain at the lead as her tongue lapped the wet holes in the ground. She looked back, unable to see the picnic benches past the thick trunks of the trees. She closed her eyes and locked the mental picture of the guy in her mind, her years of training acting on autopilot.

A burst of water sprang from the ground.

Skooch shot back toward Terra, standing by her feet. She barked, flashing her teeth at the attacking spray.

Terra crouched to pick Skooch up, softly laughing as she ran her fingers through her fur. "Easy, girl," Terra soothed. Nearby, a middle-aged woman laughed. Terra waved. "Skittish little thing."

"She's adorable," the woman replied.

"And light," Terra returned. "If she had been standing over that jet, I'd have to get her down from the trees by now."

The woman laughed again. Terra placed Skooch down. "Come on, girl."

They followed the path around the trees, Terra's eyes straining to catch a glimpse of the guy at the table. She caught brief flashes through the trees, but when she finally got a decent glance, the man was gone.

Terra looked around, eyes peeled for any further sighting.

She found none.

The rest of Terra's day wasn't worthy of note. She called her parents, cleaned her apartment, and tried to return to the nutrition plan she had followed back in the inner city. It turned out that demotion had given her a craving for Twinkies and Milky Way candy bars.

When night fell, she arrived at the AJS station and halted outside its red brick façade for a moment.

She stared up at the less-than-impressive building and chewed her lip. She had worked her ass off to find her way into the AJS' premium police force and still remembered that first day, standing in front of the ivory pillars, a gleaming gold crest hanging above the supporting arch. Cops looked flawless in their uniforms, muscles bulging, hardened expressions on their faces as they went about their business to serve and protect.

This, though...

The building was dilapidated. The windows wore a sheen of grime that blurred the officers moving around inside. Clusters of weeds grew through the cracks in the stone path that led to the front door, where the words "Atlantica Justice System" were printed and hung above it. One "c" was at a crooked angle and looked as though it were about to fall off.

Terra sighed. *It's not forever. You can do this.*

She entered the building and signed in at the front desk. A cherry-cheeked recruit sat behind the counter, shielded by bullet-proof glass—or so they said. Terra didn't believe that glass would stop a fly from smashing through.

Custer was young and had joined the precinct around the

same time that Terra had. He beamed at Terra now, offering a, "Right on time, Officer Kris."

"Please, just call me Terra. And you don't have to say that every day. I've told you." She returned the smile, his innocent face reminding her somehow of Skooch, before pressing her thumb against the scanner and registering her arrival at work.

"Sure thing." Custer gave her a theatrical salute. "Oh, the corporal was looking for you, by the way. Asked me to tell you she'll be in her office."

"I'm surprised she ever leaves," Terra returned.

Custer chuckled. "Right on."

Terra passed through a large rectangular body scanner, aware that Custer had his eyes glued to the computer screen. The scanners were smart, able to detect any equipment, drugs, or weapons that hadn't been registered safe with the AJS system. Terra had only seen these scanners trigger their alarms once, and within seconds the officer was pinned to the floor by half a dozen colleagues before being brought in for questioning.

It hadn't been anything serious, only the residual powder of a late-night binge. They were soon stripped of their privileges and taken down to the lower ranks.

How's that different to you? Terra shook her head, rounding the corner to the farmyard.

Terra skirted the edges of the main area, a thin hallway that bordered the bullpen with large panels of thin glass. There was even a couple of steps that descended into the main activity area, just adding to the effect of pigs trapped in a pen. Terra observed at least half a dozen officers sitting at their computers, with four of those leaning back in their chairs and drinking their coffees. The smell of greasy fast food hung in the air. In the space nearest to Terra, a large woman with dark braids—"Slim," to her friends —scrawled a series of lines and circles on a whiteboard, her face a mask of concentration.

"There she is!" a voice crowed.

Terra drew a calming breath and turned to see two men in uniform blocking her way. Officer Alex Dunston beamed at her. A thinning patch of hair circled his crown, and deep laughter lines bracketed his eyes. He had a stomach that bulged out from the rest of his body, reminding Terra of the alien from the Stephen Spielberg movie, and a stale scent of coffee followed wherever he went.

"Fancy bumping into you down here," Dunston exclaimed. "Always great for the gods to come down from Olympus and grace us mortals with their presence."

Terra bit her tongue. Dunston had been the first officer she'd partnered with upon her arrival. Things had taken a turn when staking out a known pedophile's house. Dunston had refused to follow the perp, and Terra chose to climb out of the car and pursue on foot. She had brought the asshole to justice, though as she brought him to the cop car, Dunston decided that would be the time to play the hero.

Even now, the faint outline of a black eye shone on his face.

"Ah, leave her alone," the other man replied, the words "Officer Hewlett" scrawled on his badge. He eyed Terra up and down, eyes lingering on her breasts. Hewlett had been assigned to Dunston only a few days ago. Terra had seen them stalking around the station from afar but had done her best to avoid them both.

She knew Dunston's reputation, having studied his files. He had ascended from an accelerated training program, the leading officers deciding that it was fine to overlook his several mentions of sexual harassment throughout the years. "Can't be easy for an angel to fall from Heaven, can it? Did it hurt, sweetheart?"

Dunston laughed, bringing the remains of a sticky powdered donut to his mouth. He took a large bite and spoke through the food. "Angel? A rule breaker like this bitch?" Bits of donut sprayed in the air. "Nah. She's too much of a renegade to be an angel, ain'tcha Kris? No wonder the boss partnered you with a goddamn robot. No one else would take you." He laughed. A wet mass of dough hit Terra's cheek.

Her nostrils flared. She wiped the dough away with her finger.

"Cut her some slack," Hewston offered, placing a hand on her shoulder. "I get it, darling. It's tough in a place like this. Friends don't come easy. If you need someone to talk to about…" He drew a long breath, eyes straying again to her chest. "…anything, you let me know, okay? We're the same, you and I—"

Terra swept an arm across Hewlett's, knocking his grasp away. He twisted to the side but quickly regained his balance. Anger flashed behind his eyes, though he diffused it with a laugh. "You have some fight in you. I like that."

Terra rolled her eyes. "Whatever it is that you assholes think you know about my situation, you don't."

Dunston nodded thoughtfully. "I know that the boss doesn't trust you. That's why you now have a collar on your eyes."

Hewlett laughed. "That's what all good bitches need—"

Terra's knee met Hewlett's crotch. Hewlett exhaled sharply, a soft "Ooft," expelling from his lips. His face went red. A couple of the heads in the bullpen turned.

Dunston frowned. Slim gave him a stern look from the other side of the glass. She exchanged a glance with Terra, then carried on her work.

Terra strode between the pair, shoving her way past them. "Stay the fuck out of my way," she instructed before finding her way to the corporal's office.

***

"You have a right to be angry," Corporal Black soothed, that same sober tone of voice that Terra had become accustomed to. Perhaps that was the reason that Black had risen to her seniority, the ability to remain calm in any situation. Or maybe it was because she had accepted that the peak of her career was going to be this rank forever, and there was no point in rocking the boat.

Terra wasn't sure which one yet.

"Angry?" Terra barked. "I'm furious. You stole my arrest. You knocked me out and shipped me back to my apartment without my consent. What the hell was that?"

The glasses rested on top of the table. The lid was off the box, the words APRIL printed along the side. A blinking light caught Terra's attention.

"We are experimenting with new modes and methods of serving justice," Black replied. "The big guns want to see if this technology can be useful for an officer in our division. If we can fit each officer with a virtual partner, we can double our protection, reduce the rates of crimes, capture twice as many criminals. This is about expansion, Kris. Moving with the times and embracing technology as a fundamental part of the force. The world is moving on."

"Bullshit," Terra hissed. "Why me? Why do I get the choker collar? Why would I even wear those again? At the tap of a button, you can knock me out? What is that? You're altering my brain chemistry for the sake of justice?"

Black tilted her head. "They warned that there could be some teething problems."

"Teething problems?" Terra scoffed. "I lost twelve hours of my life."

Black nodded. There was no apology, only deeper thought. She tapped her keyboard, and the wall lit up with video footage of Terra's previous night's encounter with Ollie. Terra spun in her chair, taking in the visual information that APRIL offered, catching snippets of their conversation, seeing the thermal imaging of their targets.

"But look what you gained," Black offered.

They watched the footage in quiet. Terra had to admit that something was exciting about the amount of information that

APRIL provided. No other officer could have given her a view from the CCTV cameras or showed where the targets were through the sheetrock walls. The glasses offered a chance for independence as an officer, an operative working at an increased capacity, giving the force the benefit of technology, intel, and insight that their targets wouldn't have access to.

Then the footage showed Terra's point-of-view, as APRIL soothed her temporal nerves and shut down her consciousness. The screen continued to project the apartment and the medical staff, APRIL's feed unaffected as Terra was lifted and carried to the ambulance.

Terra shook her head and turned back to Black. "No."

Black raised her eyebrow. She tapped her keyboard and the video feed cut. "No?"

"I'd rather go out there solo than have to deal with…that," Terra declared.

Black sighed. "I'm afraid that's not an option you have, Terra." She tapped the screen of an idle tablet and slid it toward Terra. An official-looking contract with the AJS crest in the top right corner was on display. "This is your final warning. Since your descent into our ranks, you have shown a lack of respect for authority and an unwillingness to comply with your fellow staff. This contract outlines that you can continue your service on the force, only under the condition that you embrace the APRIL technology and wear it at all times while you are on the clock."

"Corporal, I…" Terra started.

"The moment you clock in, you are to come to my office," Black continued as if Terra hadn't said a word. "You will put on the glasses, and you will listen to instructions. Any more displays of unwillingness to cooperate with your superiors will lead to your immediate suspension and possible permanent expulsion from the Atlantica Justice System."

Terra frowned. Her eyes bore into Black's. Her corporal

appeared indifferent. It was impossible to tell how she felt about it, other than this was serious, and there would be no arguing.

Terra glanced from the agreement to the glasses.

Black leaned forward, a warmness crossing through the cold office. "Terra, I know this is hard for you. It's difficult for anyone to fall from a height as you did. But, let me assure you, I'm on your side."

"Doesn't seem like anyone is on my side right now," Terra admitted, the words slipping from her lips.

Black showed the shadow of a smile. "You are a rare breed, Kris. There's a reason we selected you for this program and not any of your colleagues."

Terra narrowed her eyes. "What are you saying?"

The corner of Black's mouth eased up. "I'm saying that you should sign the agreement."

Terra drew a deep breath.

Black continued, "It's that, or you're out."

CHAPTER EIGHT

Terra stared at herself in the floor-to-ceiling mirror in the locker room.

Lockers were all around, each one with a name scrawled on the front in Sharpie. Pin-code locks secured them. Terra had a flashback to the locker room in the inner city, the names written in digital LED displays—easier to change and clean with the endless influx and clock-outs of new and old officers.

Long wooden benches occupied the spaces between them. Showers were on the right from the entrance, with a faded unisex sign painted on the wall. Long gone were the days of gender separation in utilities.

Terra leaned close enough to the mirror that her breath fogged the glass. The glasses were rubbing her nose again, and a red streak spread out from the bridge between the lenses. Terra lifted them tentatively, enough to afford her a moment of comfort, her body tensed, waiting for the glasses to emit a shock for the mere audacity of moving them two centimeters from her face.

You appear nervous, APRIL remarked.

No shit, Terra thought, concerned that speaking out loud

would only draw the attention of the few officers in the changing room.

"Nice eyewear," Slim commented, appearing in the locker room behind Terra.

"The latest trend." Terra forced a smile. "They're all the rage over at Bon Vivant Valley."

Bon Vivant Valley was a large quadrant of the inner city dedicated to the latest and greatest in fashion, sporting influences from across the globe, and creating a home for the greatest designers the world had ever seen.

"So, expensive?" Slim sat on a bench and tapped the screen of her tablet.

"The priciest." Terra shifted over to her locker and entered her code. "Thousands. Could even be more."

"You don't know the price?" Slim laid a hand on her chest.

Terra smirked. "Too many suitors, that's my problem. Men in this place throw their money around. Who can keep track of who sent what and what costs how much?" She laughed. "Are they that bad?"

Slim locked her tablet, then strode over to Terra. She stood a clear foot taller than her, and the minute she entered Terra's immediate field of vision, her public information appeared, floating in digital displays around her body.

Threat level: three percent APRIL declared.

"APRIL, power down," Terra replied automatically.

You don't have permission to grant that request.

Terra grimaced as Slim raised her eyebrow. "Sorry, talking to the glasses."

"Oh, really?" Slim looked impressed. "Do they talk back?"

"Unfortunately, yes." Terra tapped her ear. "Only to me, though. Straight into the noggin."

The statistical information hovered, with another graph showing Slim's heart rate, as well as her oxygen intake levels. Terra tried again, "APRIL, clear statistical information."

Do you wish to launch "Civilian Mode?"

Terra told APRIL she did.

"APRIL?" Slim asked.

"Advanced Police Relationship...something or other," Terra replied as the data information faded from her vision and she could see Slim properly.

Slim raised her hands. "May I take a look?"

Terra flinched. Slim's guard raised.

"I was only asking," Slim stated.

Terra sighed. She glanced down. "I know. It's not you. It's these...they..."

"They really do have you on a leash, don't they?" Slim asked.

Terra turned to her locker and pulled out her one-piece under armor. She proceeded to shrug out of her tank top and pants. "What are you working on at the minute? Any big operations for you?"

Slim took a step back, losing herself again in her tablet. Out of everyone at the station, Slim was the most likely to gain rank in Terra's books. She had her eye on the prize. She had the right attitude and the moral compass to keep her on the right track. "Nothing huge. A couple of domestic disturbances and reports of a possible dog-fighting sting out on the Verge. Should be enough to keep me busy for one night."

Terra stepped into her under armor. The metallic blue cloth hugged her frame tightly. She pulled the sleeves up her arms, struggling a little to close the zip over her breasts. Slim chuckled, knowing the struggle well. Terra inhaled, managed to secure the zip, then exhaled. "Never gets any easier."

"That it doesn't." A *beeping* sounded from Slim's wrist. "That's Carla. She's out front and waiting. You have a good night out there." She turned to leave, then looked over her shoulder. "You, too, APRIL."

Terra wondered how Slim knew the glass's name, then

remembered the print on the securing arm and her earlier commands.

Pleasant operations to you, Officer Jenna Newman.

Terra chuckled. "Please. We just call her 'Slim.'"

Updating database. Jenna Newman's alias update confirmed. "Officer Slim."

Terra pinched her brow, then set about attaching her utility belt around her waist. She holstered her Glock before pulling on her jacket and boots.

When she finished, she stood and automatically looked for her tablet. Realizing her error, she addressed APRIL. "Pull up my agenda for this evening."

APRIL obliged. An array of articles and scrolling documents flashed before one settled at the forefront of her vision, floating before her as though suspended in the middle of the locker room.

Terra gave a stern nod, a slight hesitation in her step as she remembered her blackout from the evening before.

Terra sped through the streets, her motorbike silent as she rounded corners and closed the distance between her and her target.

The bike was police issue and one of the most advanced parts of the precinct she had come across. A rhythmic blue pulse came from the Atlanticore module installed inside the bike's central chamber. Terra couldn't understand how the AJS had secured enough of Atlantica's exclusive power source to propel their vehicles but couldn't confirm a contract with the tech companies to update their outdated computer systems.

The Atlanticore power was clean and sustainable. It provided energy to the bike without the need for internal combustion or rechargeable batteries. These bikes could go for years on a single cell of Atlanticore, which might have been the reason why they were so often the focus of attempted thefts and attacks. Luckily, in all of Atlantica's history, only a handful of AJS vehicles had ever been successfully hijacked and their Atlanticore extracted. Most thieves attempted to flee the island, but for whatever reason, the moment the Atlanticore passed a five-mile radius of the island, they became unstable, exploding in an impressive array of fireworks and destruction. Even the island's top researchers had failed to determine why.

Justice quickly found those who stayed on the island. The AJS was smart enough to install trackers that were notoriously difficult to extract and recovered the Atlanticores within a twelve-hour window. Only one was not.

That officer now rested in the city cemetery, decorated and never forgotten.

Still, she missed the rumble of her Ducati. While the custom AJS-issue bikes were practical, they lacked a little something in their character.

Terra pulled to a stop next to a row of bicycles. The smell of freshly baked goods filled the air, even though the last of the bakes must have finished hours ago. She dismounted and headed down a narrow one-way street. Apartment buildings occupied either side of the road. A six-step stoop on the front of each led to their front doors.

"Bring up the thermals," Terra announced.

Initiating thermal scan.

Terra's breath caught as dozens upon dozens of bodies appeared around her. In the bedrooms and lounge spaces of the apartments she could make out figures of people sitting, sleeping, standing, and even a few lost in the throes of passion. The crowd of thermal figures spread into the distance, reaching at least thirty feet ahead.

"Which one's our target?" Terra asked.

Scanning images.

Terra glanced around while APRIL performed the scan. She

could make out the forms of a man beating a woman, her eyes narrowing as she took in the scene. In the apartment above them, two figures sat side-by-side, presumably watching TV. In the apartment below, a crowd of men spun something on a table. "APRIL, zoom in."

APRIL obliged. There were seven men at the table, one of them the target of their focus. The man raised something to his head, and there was no doubt what it was in Terra's mind. Anyone could identify the motion of someone raising a gun to their temple, even if the gun wasn't in the picture. They pulled the trigger, then the men cheered.

*Russian roulette...*Terra frowned. *They're within the bounds of private residence...*

Unable to confirm target, APRIL announced at last.

"What do you mean?" Terra asked.

Target is not in vicinity.

A series of images flashed into Terra's field of view. One showed the man that they were after—a forty-year-old with a bad mullet and a gold tooth named Charles Strahovski—followed by a close-up image of his registered vehicle. The image switched to CCTV footage of Charles' custom Bentley driving through the city before settling outside a liquor store ten blocks away.

The next feed showed Charles walking into the store with a bulge in his jacket pocket.

Licensed gun owner. NAA mini-revolver. 2023 model. .22 caliber. Registered 13 May 2026.

"Thanks, APRIL," Terra muttered. "Civilian mode, please."

Civilian mode activated.

The information dissolved as Terra hopped on her bike. Three minutes later she arrived outside Tony's Seven Eleven. The lights were bright, an array of commercial posters displaying half-naked women and branded beer bottles. Terra approached the store, pausing when she heard raised voices.

Terra waited around the corner. Across the street a couple

walked hand in hand, dressed to the nines as they made their way toward a bar on the corner. A couple of people strolled the sidewalks nearby, one with a large mastiff dog.

Terra thought of Skooch.

"Get the fuck outta my store," the voice called, laced with an Italian twang. "You ain't got no business in here, Chuck. Get the fuck out. Now."

Terra was about to turn her head when something caught her eye across the street. A Lamborghini with tinted windows had parked near a meter. A blinking light on the dashboard alerted possible thieves of its alarm system. Terra was almost certain she could make out the shadow of someone inside.

"APRIL. Thermal scan." Terra narrowed her eyes.

The people walking lit up in shades of fire. The scan confirmed Terra's suspicion as it revealed a man sitting in the driver's seat, head turned toward her. She met his gaze for a moment, unsure whether he knew she was looking at him.

"Last chance," a deep, baritone voice growled. "Don't make this harder than it needs to be."

"You haven't got the balls to—" the Italian started, cutting short as glass shattered and someone cried out.

Terra turned toward the store. Inside were four civilians and the store clerk.

"APRIL, show me inside," Terra called.

Data jumping in three...

"Now," Terra instructed.

Altering protocol...

"Now!" Terra's world lurched as she found herself inside the camera feed, looking down on the store to where Charles Strahovski was leaning over the counter to grab the necks of as many bottles as he could manage within his reach. A thick-necked Italian with a dark beard crouched out of the way of his shattered protection. Several of the bottles now spilled their contents on the floor.

Charles made a run for it.

The store clerk stood with a Magnum in his grip. He shot at Charles, who ducked out of the way, slamming into a nearby wall. A number of the bottles tumbled to the floor. He bounced back and headed for the door.

Exiting data jump in three...

"Forget my three-second warning," Terra exclaimed. She could hear Charles next to her, but her vision was still in the camera. She reached out, hoping to grab him, but only felt the leather of his jacket slip through her fingers as he sprinted away.

She ran for him, blindly following the direction he started. When APRIL gave her vision back, her head filled with statistics. They showed Charles' heart rate, his threat level, the current speed of his run. They showed the contents of the bottles in his arms, the decibel levels of his shoes, surrounding traffic levels, car registrations. Arrows pointed in all directions, and numbers scrolled all around him.

"APRIL, civilian mode." Terra felt sick.

It is unwise to initiate civilian mode during apprehension of a criminal—

"Now!" Terra declared. "Please."

The world spun. She pumped her arms, gaining on the man. Somewhere behind her, an engine rumbled into life. The vehicle accelerated, the roaring growing louder.

The stats slowly faded, though they left a residue in her vision. She rubbed her eyes, but her hand only met glass. The bridge of her nose flared with pain, and Terra wondered if she would develop some kind of blister.

Charles made a sharp left down an adjacent street. Terra just about managed to keep up. He clutched his goods in one arm, then drew his mini-revolver with the other, blindly firing at Terra as she found her footing and started to gain traction.

"Son of a bitch," Terra exclaimed, zigzagging and putting phone boxes, street lights, and cars in her path to avoid the bullets. She drew her gun but was hesitant to use it. "Freeze. Atlantica Justice System."

The man paid no heed. He shot again, nearly clipping Terra's hip. She darted out into the road. A car engine revved. Terra turned in time to see the black Lamborghini speeding toward her.

Terra dived out of the way, feeling the wind rush past her as the car sped on.

Charles turned down another street.

Terra pushed herself off her stomach, eyes fixed on Charles. The Lamborghini, however, had other ideas. The driver drifted the vehicle at the end of the street, then returned toward her.

Terra aimed the gun at the car, feeling naked and alone in the center of the road. "APRIL? Where are you?"

You activated civilian mode. My programming awaits instruction.

"Useful," Terra muttered, taking a shot at the Lamborghini. "Black, I hope you can see that this is justified."

She blew out the tire. The car jerked to the right, skidding back and forth until it slammed into a parked Rover. Glass shattered. Lights flicked on in the windows of the surrounding buildings. Terra exhaled, gun trained on the driver.

From this angle, she couldn't quite see him. Steam poured in billows from the radiator. She advanced slowly, all thoughts of Charles gone from her head.

Initiating thermal imaging. APRIL displayed the figure behind the wheel, slumped over. The vibrant red was cooling to a low yellow tinged with icy blue. **Threat level: undetermined.**

"You can't tell the threat level?" Terra asked.

Unable to gain a clear reading through vehicle heat expulsion and smoke particles.

Terra strafed to her right, eyes fixed on the car. She drew closer as smoke now mixed with the steam. Soon she was standing beside the crumpled hood of the Lamborghini, the tinted window of the driver's side cracked but not entirely smashed.

A crop of dark hair was visible through the small gaps in the glass.

"Is he…" Terra asked.

I don't understand the question.

"Is he dead?" Terra finished. The yellow coloring was cooling to an almost total blue.

Civilian is in a critical condition. Heart rate below typical levels. Medical attention required.

Terra opened the door, vaguely aware of the gathering crowd behind her. She kept the gun aimed at the man's head. When she had room to move closer, she grabbed his shoulder and forced him back.

He was gasping for air, his face covered in lacerations and blood. His eyes fluttered as a faint grin appeared.

"Who is he?" Terra asked APRIL.

As statistics and information started to appear in Terra's vision, the man uttered one soft, airy sentence that would alter the course of Terra's world forever.

"Your worst nightmare," he stated.

Threat level: ninety-seven percent APRIL announced as the man raised his hand and thumbed the device's trigger in his hands.

Terra screamed, knowing only white-hot heat, blinding light, and the pain of a thousand daggers of shrapnel as she was blown backward from the car.

CHAPTER NINE

Terra ran, though she didn't know what from.

The world was dark, pitch-black on either side. The floor was hard and smooth. Her bare feet drummed their beat as she sprinted. Her arms pumped on either side, her gaze unfaltering. Air came and went in sharp bursts in her lungs, and all she knew was that she needed to keep going.

She needed to run.

The world slipped away beneath her. The road showed no end. Ahead of her was a flare of light the size of a dime. Her gaze pinned on the light, eyes unblinking. The rhythm was hers and hers alone, her body making music in the otherwise silent world.

She didn't think. She didn't need to, not now. Determination was her guide, and her faith was unwavering. The answers were ahead. All she had to do was keep doing what she was doing. She needed to trust the process. She needed to keep fighting.

Terra was always a fighter.

From the moment she was six years old and received her first bicycle from her parents, she knew she would change the world. While other girls in the suburbs rode their bright pink tricycles with rainbow tassels and white wicker baskets, Terra sped by on two wheels, her frame metallic blue, with flashing blue and red lights on the front. While other girls in her neighborhood sold lemonade and cookies on their front lawn, Terra pursued rule-breakers. She monitored dog owners who walked away from their pooch's steaming piles of poop and brought them to justice. She waved her hands at the speeding cars that roared down her street. She stepped between bullies and their prey—even if that meant Terra took a beating sometimes—to ensure that justice prevailed and she was leaving the world a better place than she had found it.

It wasn't difficult, not in Atlantica. This city was a breeding ground of corruption, and any intervention was enough to leave a mark. Terra was one of the few officers who truly believed in an Atlantica where one day, the rich and corrupt wouldn't be the only ones sitting at the top of their towers. She believed that she could help alter the course of the legislation that prevented officers from being able to bring assholes to justice within the confines of their own home—what kind of backward shit was that?

Logic enforced by the corrupted founders who forged the rules of this goddamn island. A conglomerate of nationalities, billionaires, and trillionaires, all looking for a safe place to hide from the world and perform their wicked deeds. While the rest of the world strived to improve their moral compass, Atlantica sank deeper and deeper into the dirt.

One foot in front of the other. Terra was laser-focused although she didn't know why. Run, run, run. That was all she needed to do. To fight, to run, to fight some more.

I haven't finished my work yet.

A beeping sounded. Rhythmic and regular. Voices mumbled, amplified in the darkness around her but indistinct, their tone reaching an almighty panic.

The beeping turned to a long whine, a high-pitched note running without end.

The note ran, but Terra stopped. She wanted to continue, but her body wouldn't let her.

Her chest rose and fell. The light grew brighter, or maybe it finally came closer.

Terra fell to her knees in the darkness and waited.

She waited.

Corporal Leonie Black was in the gallery. A large glass window allowed her to look down into the operating theater.

A dozen surgeons and medical staff coordinated their efforts, loitering over Terra's body. The white paper bib was stained with blood as they prodded and poked with their steel instruments. Leonie sat upright, posture clean and perfect, the way she had learned as a little girl and continued to this day.

"This is a mess," a voice declared, the tinny sound coming through the overhead speaker, Leonie's direct link into the surgery. Her expression was calm, but her heart was beating fast. Her gaze was hot and intense, trained on the pale face of the AJS officer.

A door opened, then closed.

Scattered around the gallery were a handful of junior staff members. Their heads were low over their tablets as they took notes and studied the procedure.

Somebody moved across the gallery to Leonie and sat beside her.

They were quiet for a moment, the large woman filling the room with her presence as well as her bulk. Her gut spilled over Leonie's armrest. Leonie adjusted her arm and crossed her legs.

"Is she going to make it?" the woman asked.

Leonie drew a long breath. "I don't know. It doesn't look positive."

The woman nodded. Leonie saw it in her peripheral vision. "She needs to."

"I know," Leonie replied.

The woman didn't need to say it. A lot was riding on this program. They had made that abundantly clear from the start.

The EKG spiked as a fountain of blood squirted from Terra's chest. The beeping rose dramatically as the surgeons scurried around, increasing their activity. Then came the flatline.

Leonie stood. She pressed her hands to the glass, breath fogging up the space in front of her. A couple of juniors turned their heads.

"She's fading," a surgeon reported although it was pointless. They could all see it.

Leonie's eyes shimmered. "No."

"Calm down," the woman stated calmly, as though they were simply watching a movie. "There's always another path."

Leonie looked back at the woman, her head low as she tapped the screen of her cell phone with stubby fingers. Each stab left a greasy mark on the surface. The phone *beeped* with each keystroke. The juniors looked her way with distaste.

"There," the woman announced.

Leonie turned back to the operating theater as someone arrived through the door. The lead surgeon busied himself with the defibrillator, charging the pads to jolt Terra back into the world, while the new arrival wheeled in a metal trolley with strange-looking components resting on top.

A handful of the surgeons watched with interest.

"Clear," the lead surgeon called. Terra's body jolted.

"Tell them," the large woman stated, her eyes dark as beetle shells.

Leonie moved to the corner of the room and pressed the round silver button on the receiver. "It's time, Dr. Sanchez."

Dr. Sanchez turned up to the gallery and met Leonie's eyes. He scanned the seats and found the large woman. A heavy sigh weighed down his chest. He saw the tray for the first time, the assortment of components resting on top, then gave an affirmative nod.

The newest arrival handed the surgeon a silver package the size of a Zippo lighter. Leonie couldn't see it from above, but she'd seen the items in the lobby not too long ago. Steel-blue letters read "APRIL" along the side.

Dr. Sanchez placed the package inside Terra. He carefully located its position. Satisfied, he picked up the paddles once more. "Charging… Clear."

Terra's body jolted.

The long, high-pitched whine became a slow, rhythmic pulse.

Leonie turned back to the woman, but she was gone.

CHAPTER TEN

Terra's throat was dry.

She swallowed—or tried to, at least. The walls of her throat constricted and rubbed together, feeling as though they were sandpaper. She grimaced and tried to move, then realized she couldn't.

She became aware of a rhythmic beeping, and it threw her mind back to the strangest dream she had. Something to do with…running? A light at the end of the tunnel.

She coughed.

Pain flared across her body.

"Easy," a voice soothed.

Terra peeled her eyes open and stared down at the woman standing at the end of her bed. The linens were a perfect white. The woman's features were blurred, but Terra could tell that the woman was kind.

Terra tried to speak, but all she managed was, "What…" Her voice raspy and without substance.

The woman finished tapping on the screen of her tablet. She placed it in a cradle and tilted her head. "You're okay, Terra. Take it easy. You're in Atlantica Central Hospital. You had an accident."

Terra frowned. More pain flared. She softened her expression and tried to swallow again.

Ouch.

"Here." The woman skirted the bed and held a glass of water with a straw for her. "Take a sip and try to keep calm. You're okay. Your vitals are stable, though…"

Terra sipped from the straw. The water was like liquid happiness, trickling easily down her throat. It cooled her insides as it traveled down.

"What happened?" Terra managed.

Conflict shadowed the nurse's face. "I should let the doctor know that you're awake."

Terra tried to sit up, but her arms didn't have the strength to raise her. The woman hurried from the room.

Terra closed her eyes, sleep coming over her almost instantly, but not before she noticed the shape of a large woman watching her through the glass window at the end of her room.

"You've been in an accident," the doctor informed Terra. He sat at the end of her bed. A pair of glasses perched on his nose. He had thick blond hair neatly combed back and eyes that seemed to see straight through her. His badge read, "Sanchez."

Terra frowned. This time the pain was less. Her recent hit of morphine had seen to that. "I don't remember."

"That's perfectly natural," Dr. Sanchez soothed. "You've been through a traumatic experience. It's not uncommon for patients to experience slight bouts of amnesia. It's the body's way of coping with devastation by compartmentalizing and often hiding the information for you to cope.

"I imagine that your memory will return with due time. All we need you to do is to take it easy for a few days, okay? I want to ensure that your vitals remain stable following the procedure."

Something flickered in his eyes.

"What procedure?" Terra asked.

Dr. Sanchez drew a long breath. "There were complications with your surgery. You flatlined in the middle of the operation, and we had to find…methods to get your heart beating again."

Terra glanced down at her chest. The scar ran along the center of her ribs, a leak of dry blood running along the incision. "You mean like a pacemaker?"

The doctor considered his words. "Kind of." He rose to his feet. "Get some rest, Terra. I'll inform your visitors that you'll be able to see them soon, okay? I'd like to see that heart rate come down a little more before the excitement of a reunion takes place." Dr. Sanchez adjusted his glasses and crossed to the door. He paused. "I want you to be aware that you'll need another minor procedure before you're able to be discharged."

Terra raised an eyebrow. "What kind of procedure?"

"Maintenance," the doctor replied. "We need to check that all of the cogs and gears have been aligned and lubricated correctly."

He left the room.

Terra snorted in derision as she adjusted herself and tried to get comfortable. She was thankful for the morphine.

She lay there for some time considering the doctor's words. It was a strange choice of phrase, and she wondered if every doctor saw their patients as pieces of machinery, with themselves as the mechanics.

Slim placed the stack of books on the side table then sat.

"I didn't know what kind of thing you liked." She flicked through the various volumes. "I brought crosswords, sudokus, a mix of word puzzles, dot-to-dots, color by numbers, the whole works."

Terra smiled. "Thanks. It's good to see you."

"I brought fruit as well." Slim handed a paper bag to Terra. "I don't know what they're feeding you here, but you need to keep up your strength. I need a rival to compete against when you get back on your feet."

Terra chuckled. "Who knows when that'll be."

Slim stared intensely at her. "What happened out there, Kris?"

"I don't know." It was the truth. Almost twenty-four hours had passed since she had awoken, and she had gleaned nothing from the medical staff. They tiptoed around her questions as though the very act of giving her the truth would set off a bomb inside her mind.

"You were in an accident." Corporal Black's voice was soft but commanding. She stood in the doorway, a steaming paper cup in each hand.

Slim adjusted in her chair then dragged a second beside her. "Corporal. I didn't know you were here."

Black sat beside her and handed Slim the second coffee. "I knew *you* were." She offered a reassuring smile. Terra thought back to the last conversation, how tense it had felt and how cornered she had been into accepting the agreement presented to her.

"I guess those glasses weren't so great after all," she joked. "They couldn't stop whatever happened to me, could they?"

She expected Black's face to reflect the same humor in Slim's, but instead only got a thoughtful expression. "Have they not told you yet?"

Terra shook her head. "Told me what?"

"You were in an accident," Black replied.

Terra rolled her eyes. "I know that much."

"It was a car accident," Black replied.

Terra searched her mind, but all she could see was white light. "I crashed?"

Black nodded. "You were driving too fast, apprehending a suspect. Your bike skidded out of control and smashed into the side of a parked car. The engine caught on fire and...well, you can guess the rest."

"My bike?" Terra asked.

"We salvaged it. The mechanics say they can fix her up as good as new."

Terra moved a delicate hand to her head. There were lacerations on her arm that would take some time to heal. Her thumb felt strange, numb beneath a thick white bandage. "I remember none of this."

"The doctors say that you won't," Black confirmed. "I've seen it all on the camera footage." She sighed. "Mistakes happen, Terra. All we can do is learn from them. Pick ourselves up and carry on."

"Two weeks is what the doctors are telling me," Terra added. "I mean, from the final surgery. Then it's all a healing and waiting game. I hope I can get back to peak performance."

Black offered her trademark warm smile. She touched Terra's hand and a tiny jolt of static pinched Terra's skin. Black didn't seem to notice. "You'll be fine. Your spot will be waiting for you when you've fully recovered."

Slim chuckled. "Come on, Corporal. Terra's better than half of the squad you have in the bullpen, even as she is now." She winked at Terra. "You'll be back in no time, Kris."

Terra returned the smile, but something niggled the back of her mind. She just couldn't put a finger on what it was yet. She glanced at her thumb, then the scar on her chest and a strange feeling washed over her.

They gave Terra her date for the final surgery. Two days after her initial wake-up, they wheeled her into the operating theater once more.

The wheels squeaked with each rotation. The bed jolted over

the lip of the elevator. When they passed through a plastic-strip partition and settled under the spotlight, pain flared in the back of Terra's head. The light was bright, but that wasn't what pained her. Something glinted in the corner of her eye as though a piece of shrapnel was still lodged somewhere in her cornea.

The anesthesiologist hovered over her with a plastic mask in his hands. "You won't feel a thing. I promise you that."

Terra steeled herself, unable to shake away the cold ache inside of her. It was the same ache that came every time the morphine started to wear off, a feeling of something having invaded her body—a feeling of something *not right*.

She gave a small nod. The mask lowered over her face. She breathed the chill gas that funneled down the tube.

As the edges of her vision darkened, something entered the room. A soft, blue, glowing pulse that flashed like the lights atop the AJS cruisers.

Terra slipped into a dream of car chases, handcuffs, and APRIL.

Good morning, Terra.

"Hmmm?" The words sounded muffled, as though Terra was listening to them underwater.

Actually, good morning is factually inaccurate. It is, in fact, afternoon. However, colloquial discourse often incurs some inaccuracies in communication. Allow me to begin again. Good afternoon, Terra.

Terra shuffled in her cocoon of drowsiness. She brought a hand toward her eyes, feeling for the glasses so she could remove them. She caught the bridge of her nose and felt the place where the skin had hardened beneath the irritation from the metal frames. She felt cotton across her eyes.

"Huh?" Terra swam to the surface of consciousness. She was

lying in bed, *that* she could feel. But all was dark. If the voice was correct, it shouldn't be dark in the middle of the afternoon.

She opened her eyes and met a burning pain. Her hands fumbled for her face and traced the bandage that wrapped around her head. Much of the other pain from before appeared to have eased. She wondered how much morphine they had pumped her with.

"What's going on?" Terra asked.

The medical staff have completed their initiation of the APRIL protocol, and startup has executed. Your body is currently battling in the stages of acceptance and rejection, although my programming will soothe the transition. Please allow approximately thirteen hours and twenty-six minutes for the sequence to complete.

Terra's heart jumped. "Sequence? Is this some kind of a joke?"

Terra dug her fingers beneath the cotton that covered her eyes. It hurt to blink, and as she eased a small gap to see by, light flooded her vision. She cried out, hands slipping from the bandage as a throbbing erupted in her head. As if of its own accord, her hand fell neatly by her side and stayed there.

Footsteps sounded from down the hall as a voice called a doctor. Terra was aware of someone in her room, then weight shifted at the bottom of her bed, and she knew he was there.

"You have to remain calm, Terra," Dr. Sanchez instructed. "You have nothing to be concerned about. This is all part of the procedure."

Terra gritted her teeth. "You best tell me what the hell is going on, Doc, unless you want to be the headline of tomorrow morning's paper."

Dr. Sanchez let out a long breath. "Your accident was severe. You were alive when the ambulances got to you, but the shrapnel that exploded from the vehicle badly injured you. While your major functions remained intact, a large section of your spine was damaged. There was also major trauma to your motor cortex and brain stem. One of your optical nerves sustained a laceration, and unfortunately, you lost your thumb, too."

Terra's jaw clenched.

"We had to employ new methods of repair," Dr. Sanchez stated. "Cutting-edge technologies designed to give you the greatest chance of recovery we could provide."

"What did you do?" Terra felt like she knew the answer.

Dr. Sanchez was quiet for a moment. "We installed the latest in prosthetics and electronics to repair your critically damaged pieces. Your lower spine is now titanium. We installed biotech in the parts of your brain that were beyond repair, as well as replacing your optical nerve."

She heard the smile in his voice. "It really is impressive stuff. With any luck, you should be one hundred percent back to normal within only a few weeks. We'll obviously monitor you and ensure that you stay healthy, but after those bandages come off your face, you'll be free to go."

Terra stewed as she processed all of this information.

Heart rate above typical levels.

Terra's heart dropped. "Doctor?"

"Yes?"

"What did you install to ensure that the biotech systems worked?" Terra licked her dry lips. "I've read into this stuff before. Experimental. You need an operating system, don't you?"

Dr. Sanchez stood, his weight leaving the bed. "You get your rest, Terra. We'll talk more once you've had some time to process all of this."

His footsteps faded before Terra could reply. She sank back into her pillow and drew a few steadying breaths.

"Hello, APRIL," Terra whispered.

Hello, Terra, came the reply.

CHAPTER ELEVEN

Marie and Michael Kris lived in a suburban residency on the east side of the island of Atlantica.

Picturesque houses lined wide roads bordered with white picket fences. Red brick walls rose and fell in waves, and automatic golden gates detected the arrival of the owner's vehicles and parted automatically to allow entry. The sidewalks were clean and neat, with an array of trees blossoming in neat rows.

The Kris household wouldn't have looked out of place in the rolling hills of the French countryside. The rooms were quaintly decorated, with posters and paintings of grapes and French landmarks, and family portraits and photos from bygone vacations littered every surface.

On this morning, only one week since Terra had awoken from the surgery to be greeted by APRIL, she sat upright in the four-poster bed with a steaming mug of black coffee in her hands. It felt strange to be back in her childhood bedroom, but she had to admit that it was nice to see her parents again.

Although they lived busy lives, with Michael offering his services as a forensic scientist for the nearby AJS precinct, and Marie working with the French diplomatic service of Atlantica,

Terra had seen more of her mother over these last seven days than she had in a long while. Her father couldn't book the time off, but her mother had accrued quite the vacation stack, having worked hours beyond overtime over the last few years.

"Morning, sweetheart," Marie offered as she entered the room.

Terra smiled. Her mother had crept into the room to bring her drink while she slept. Terra had pretended not to notice, although APRIL had made a show of announcing the intruder into the room.

Threat level: four percent.

A bit high, surely?

As Terra kept her eyes closed, she felt the mechanisms within her getting to work. In the fuzzy red of her closed eyelids, information appeared, hovering in the space with temperature read-outs and decibel levels of footsteps.

Terra assumed the technology didn't work unless she opened her eyelids. That was something, at least.

"How are you doing?" Marie sat on the bottom of Terra's bed.

"Much the same as yesterday," Terra replied. Light streamed in through the window, glinting against the metal of her prosthetic thumb. Her mother's gaze followed, too. Terra gave a thumbs-up.

"Healing takes time," Marie soothed. "You should know that better than anyone. How long did the doctors say before you're back on your feet again?"

"A few weeks." Terra sat back and exhaled, eyes finding the canopy above the four-poster. "Hoping it goes quicker."

"I'm sure it will," Marie replied. "You're a Kris. Nothing keeps us down for long."

Terra offered another smile. A *yap* came from downstairs. Marie rolled her eyes and turned to Terra.

"She's fine. Send her up."

"Are you sure?" Marie asked. Skooch had been in Marie's care since Terra's transport to the hospital. They had managed to keep her away from Terra for a few days while she began her healing, but Terra had to admit that she missed the eager warmth of the Papillon's tongue on her cheek.

Marie disappeared down the stairs, and Terra made out her voice softly talking to Skooch. She spoke as if addressing a child. A moment later, excited feet scurried up the wooden stairs. Skooch sped into the room and bounded up to the side of the bed, where she placed her paws on the sheets and stared up at Terra.

"Come on," Terra instructed, patting the linens.

Skooch obeyed, jumping higher than should have been possible. She pawed her way up Terra, sniffing and kissing her shoulders, neck, then cheek. Statistics appeared around the dog, including her breed, her age, her blood pressure, and more.

Threat level: one percent.

Terra rolled her eyes. Skooch froze, head tilting to the side. Her eyes scanned Terra's face.

"What is it, girl?" Terra asked.

Skooch recoiled a fraction and barked.

Threat level: sixteen percent.

Skooch let out a handful more *yaps*. Terra raised her eyebrows. "Can you hear her?"

She sat forward. Skooch took a few uneasy steps back, flashing her teeth.

Threat level: thirty-eight percent.

"Shut up," Terra instructed.

Marie froze in the doorway. Another wave of statistics appeared around her, a cloud of digital words hovering in the air. "I didn't say anything."

"Not you, Mom," Terra clarified.

Skooch barked.

"Not you, either, Skooch," Terra stated. She waved one hand, then put the other to her temple as a dull throb appeared. "Jesus, this headache."

Initiation temporal nerve—

"No!" Terra exclaimed.

Marie, who had crossed the room to collect the empty coffee cup on a tray, jumped. The cup fell to the floor and broke into large pieces. Skooch barked.

"Engage civilian mode," Terra commanded.

Engaging civilian mode, APRIL replied, the stats and information fading from her view.

Marie shook her head, eyeing Terra curiously. "What is going on with you?"

Terra pinched her eyes and shook her head. "Nothing, Mom. Sorry, it's…just this surgery."

Marie kept her gaze for a moment longer. "Dr. Sanchez warned me about this. He said it would take some adjusting. Something about the body's rejection of foreign components. Here." She handed Terra a couple of large white pills. "These should help."

Terra took them. "Thanks. I think I just need to get some fresh air."

Marie raised an eyebrow as Skooch sniffed around Terra's stomach and started to regain her confidence in her owner. "Are you sure that's a good idea?"

"One way to find out." Terra offered her a reassuring smile.

Marie nodded. "I'll come with you."

"No," Terra replied a little too quickly. "I mean…No, thanks. I want to do this myself. I need to do this myself."

Marie thought for a moment. "Hon, you've just had spinal surgery. They've fixed your brain. You need supervision."

"I'll have supervision," Terra commented. "Skooch can come with me. If anything happens, I'll tie a note to her collar and send her home."

Marie looked doubtful.

"I'll be okay," Terra stated, slowly swinging her legs to the edge of the bed. She took the crutches that leaned against the wall and placed her hands through the loops. She pushed herself to her feet, surprised at her strength.

Her mother was right. A patient recovering from severe spinal trauma shouldn't have been able to stand and walk. However, Terra had been testing the limits of her movement while her mother and father were sound asleep. She'd surprised herself with how stable she was and how confidently she could walk just over a week out of her surgeries.

Whatever the doctors had installed inside her, it was working miracles. For the first time in a long time, she was thankful to be living in Atlantica, on the cutting edge of the world's medical influence.

She was also thankful that her parents had covered her medical bills.

She took a few tentative steps for her mother, putting on a small show to demonstrate that she'd be capable of a short walk around the block. "See?"

Marie's lips thinned. She crossed her arms and looked out from under her brow in the same way she had when Terra first told Marie she'd be following her father's footsteps and joining the AJS recruitment academy. "If one thing goes wrong…"

"I'll be bed-bound until the next blood moon. Honestly, I'll be fine."

"Fine," Marie stated at last.

Terra beamed. "Come on Skooch, help Mummy get dressed, and I'll let you sniff the fox shit around the base of the cedar on the corner."

Marie rolled her eyes.

It felt good to be outside again. Terra kept most of the weight on her crutches as she ambled toward the end of her parent's gravel drive.

The first few steps were alien, but she soon got into a rhythm. Skooch forewent her usual eagerness, seeming to sense Terra's caution, and slowly padded ahead, her lead looped around the handle of the crutch. The gates buzzed open, and Terra offered a small wave of her fingers at Marie, who watched her from the front porch.

She took her time, breathing lungfuls of fresh air as she grew more confident with her steps. By the time she'd made it to the street corner, her weight had shifted more to her feet than her crutches. She waved as she passed Mrs. Thompson and her son on the other side of the street. Mrs. Thompson seemed ready to stop and chat, but Terra turned the corner and left her behind.

The sun was out but muted behind the Atlantica fog. Somewhere in the distance, Terra could just make out the Atlantica jungle, a great mass of green that bordered one side of the suburbs. Several miles to her right was the coastline, and a faint smell of salt hung in the air as great albatrosses swooped overhead.

Terra walked another block to a large open green set in the center of the suburbs. There was a kids' playground in the corner, and a sports field painted onto the grass in the other. Terra worked her way over to a bench and sat.

Skooch hopped up beside her. She lay next to her legs and panted, eyes tracking a greyhound racing across the common between a man and a woman.

Terra was a little breathless, too. She rested the crutches beside her. "Beautiful day to be outside again, isn't it?"

Skooch paid no attention. At the park's far side, where the green met the road, an AJS cruiser slowly passed. Terra's smile faded. "I want to get back there, Skooch."

Skooch's ears pricked up, but her eyes never left the greyhound.

Terra's brow creased. "I wonder what all this will mean." She thought of the digital displays that APRIL cast in her vision. "It can't be right. It still makes no sense. Why would they fit me with *this*? At least with the glasses, I could remove the damned thing, but…to have it installed inside me? There's no escape."

Skooch turned her face to Terra's, eyes wide and intelligent.

"I know it saved my life," Terra replied with a soft smile. "But there could have been another way. Surely there must have been another way?"

The AJS cruiser parked. Two officers exited the vehicle, dark shades over their eyes which seemed unnecessary given that the sun had a filter in the fog. She watched them with strange envy at how normal and human they looked. Terra glanced at her thumb, the steel bright and jarring against her skin. She flexed the thumb, and Skooch's lips peeled back into a snarl.

"You'll get used to it," Terra soothed. "I'll have to take my advice too, I guess."

The officers crossed to the playground. A man was sitting on a bench and watching the children. His arms stretched out on either side of the back of the bench. He looked warm and friendly, as though one of the girls playing on the frame would soon shout, "Daddy, watch me!" before whizzing down the slide.

The cops approached from behind. She wondered if she recognized them, but they were too far away. She thought for a moment, then stated, "APRIL, activate scan."

Initiating scan.

The plethora of digital information appeared once more, with small nuggets of data showing on everyone within sight. Terra couldn't help but notice her vision was considerably more crowded than it had been when she only wore the glasses.

"Focus on the AJS officers, APRIL," Terra commanded.

It doesn't hurt to say "please," APRIL replied before the litany of information faded and only the officers' details came into view.

"Zoom in," Terra continued. There was a moment's pause. "Please."

It was disconcerting. The sight in her left eye zoomed in, while the right remained where it was. She closed her right eye and could now see the two officers in clear profile. An AJS ID image popped up beside the male officer, Officer Rico Frisk. It wasn't a face she recognized.

The second officer, a blonde-haired woman with a dark unibrow, was identified as Jessica Gotham. Their statistics were impressive, each with clean records and a fair amount of time dedicated to their precinct. A red stream of information at the bottom of the screen displayed a message.

Current objective: Locate and identify local child molester, primary suspect Thomas Parker. Last known location, 35 Evergreen Drive.

Terra tilted her head as they closed in on the man on the bench. He was in his mid-thirties, and wore a broad smile as he tracked one of the girls playing on the frame.

Terra leaned forward. "APRIL, zoom please."

APRIL zoomed in on the man's face. There was something slightly off in the way that he smiled at the girl. His green eyes barely blinked, and he uncomfortably shifted as he crossed his legs. Terra could see each hair on his chin, the clarity of the imaging impressive. APRIL slowly pulled up bio information about the man, identifying him as *the* Thomas Parker. He had an elevated heart rate, and his cortisol levels were fifty-six percent above typical levels.

"What does cortisol relate to?" Terra asked softly.

Cortisol: a steroid hormone associated with the "flight or fight" response. Increased cortisol levels are indicative of fear, excitement, and arousal.

"Fuck." Terra turned back to the officers. They were within feet of the man. One of them said something Terra couldn't hear.

Enhancing audio, APRIL offered, without Terra needing to say anything.

"…can we talk to you for a moment?" Jessica asked. They were pleasant enough, with little cause of raising alarm in the man.

He turned, jumping as if they had shouted, "Boo."

"You frightened me." He offered a warm smile. "How can I help you, officers?"

"We have reason to believe that you are Mr. Thomas Parker?" Rico replied. "Can you confirm this?"

Heart rate and cortisol levels high.

Thomas' eyes shifted. "I get this a lot. Apparently, there's a doppelgänger that looks like me in the neighborhood. Not yet crossed paths, but Benny at my local hangout says the resemblance is uncanny."

Rico and Jessica exchanged a glance. "Can we see your ID please?"

Thomas patted his pockets. The little girl slid down the slide letting out a squeal. His eyes flickered her way. "I'm sorry, I've left it at home."

The officers' shoulders softened. "We're going to have to ask that you come with us—"

Thomas rose swiftly, launching a fist at Rico. The attack caught him off-guard. Rico twisted, knocking into Jessica.

Thomas ran.

He sprinted across the lawn, putting distance between himself and the officers. Terra stood without thinking. She tracked his trajectory, got a readout of his speed, saw a visual display of arrows on the ground showing where he would end up if he kept running. A second arrow appeared from her feet into the cross-section, showing the shortest distance to run for her to intersect his path.

She ran.

She didn't give any thought to her surgery. There was no pain with each step. Adrenaline flooded her body as she pumped her arms and ran faster than she ever had in her life. Grass tore up beneath her feet. Thomas noticed her making a break toward him. He tried to alter his direction, and the visual display adjusted in real-time, intercepting his every move.

Threat level: eighty-nine percent. Warning. Weapon: switchblade.

Her vision focused on the lump in his pocket, which Thomas reached for. Her scan showed the knife before he drew it. She didn't back down, coming straight at him as he stabbed the knife toward her stomach.

She dodged the blow, bending so that the knife found air. Her arm moved almost of its own accord, and her senses sharpened as she tracked his movements and caught his wrist.

Thomas dropped the knife. He brought his other hand to catch it as it fell away from Terra's grasp. Before he snatched it, Terra swept a leg in front of her and kicked the blade away.

Thomas' eyes bulged. He sneered as he threw blows with his fist. Terra dodged them all. Thomas punched Terra's arm, then recoiled. The sound of a rubber mallet hitting metal sounded. Terra raised an eyebrow, then kicked his stomach.

Thomas shot back a couple of meters. His ass skidded across the dirt. He rolled over his shoulder, then got back to his feet. He looked pissed, but instead of fighting, he hunted for his escape route. Jessica and Rico closed the gap from the park.

He broke to his right, arms pumping as he made his way toward the edge of the green. Terra chased him, gaining ground with every step. Her breath was measured, not a bead of sweat on her. She got within reaching distance and jumped.

Her arms wrapped around his neck. Her weight bore him down. He crashed to the ground, eating several chunks of dirt as his face mashed into the grass.

Terra took his arm and twisted it behind his back. There was little resistance. She took the second, then sat and waited for the other officers to catch up.

Rico and Jessica called for Terra's attention. "Put your hands up. Please dismount the civilian."

Terra obeyed, knowing the protocol through and through. "It's okay." She turned slowly. "I'm Officer Terra Kris. I'm an officer of the Atlantica Justice System. I'm on your side."

Jessica lowered her weapon after Terra eased a hand into her pocket and pulled out her badge. She scanned the badge with her phone. "Officer Kris, says here that you're not currently on duty. You're on medical leave."

"That's correct." Terra looked back at her crutches resting against the bench. For the first time since she'd started running, she looked down at her legs.

It seemed that Jessica was having the same thoughts as she scrolled down her cell phone. Rico busied himself with securing Thomas in handcuffs.

"You've recently had spinal surgery, correct?" Jessica asked.

"Yes." Terra nodded. "Yes, I have."

Jessica's expression was priceless. Rico turned his head, his disbelief evident. "Spinal surgery? Her?"

Jessica raised an eyebrow. "That's what it says." She showed Rico the phone. He gave an approving nod, then dragged Thomas to his feet. Thomas struggled but couldn't escape.

"Impressive," Rico replied. "They must have you on one of those accelerated programs. Ain't standard procedure for us city officers. How'd you get approval through the big boys?"

Thomas wriggled. Jessica punched him in the ribs. "Down, boy. Yeah, how did you manage that?"

Terra shrugged. "I don't know what to tell you."

Rico smiled, offering a friendly hand. "Well, we appreciate you, Kris. Take care now. Rest easy."

"Don't think she needs it," Jessica added as they carted Thomas toward their cruiser.

Terra watched them leave, her disbelief visible as she tested each of her legs in turn, feeling for any sudden pain or soreness. There was only a dull ache.

"Not bad," she muttered.

She started back to her crutches when she noticed that one of them was lying on the ground. With sudden sharp clarity, she looked around, hunting for the little Papillon, forgotten as she pursued the asshole.

"Where is she?" Terra asked.

Papillon, Skooch, identified. In pursuit of enemy.

Terra's vision filled with a series of arrows pointing to her left. She followed them, then saw a flash of white cross her vision. The digital signatures followed the dog. Eventually, Terra caught up to find the Papillon chasing eagerly after the greyhound, both pooches in their chase element.

If only the greyhound's owner wasn't so disgruntled.

Terra considered grabbing her crutches but instead decided to leave them. She started forward, picking up into a jog as she attempted to herd her stubborn little dog.

CHAPTER TWELVE

A block from her house, Terra adopted the crutches and slowed her approach.

Her mother was waiting for her downstairs. The moment Terra opened the door, she appeared, fussing and helping her into the kitchen where she sat Terra at the counter and offered her a grilled cheese sandwich.

Terra ate it eagerly, fielding questions about how long she had been out and why there were grass stains all over her. Terra put it down to a small tumble, and Marie clicked her tongue. It was a good half an hour before Terra could escape back into her bedroom and find solace in quiet once more.

She placed the crutches by her bed, then slipped beneath the covers. Skooch followed her, finding a nesting place on the sheets beside her. She was soon snoring.

Terra sat in bed, head full of thoughts. APRIL was still active, and Terra could almost feel her gears whirring inside her head. She tentatively touched the skin around her eye, feeling its tenderness beneath her touch.

As she shrugged out of her jacket, she pinched her skin, feeling for the places where it was sore. In her sprint after Parker, she was almost certain that someone had replaced her limbs and extremities with pistons. She examined her thumb, scrutinizing the neat stitching around its base.

"APRIL, answer me some questions," Terra stated quietly.

Of course, Terra. What would you like to know?

Terra considered this. She settled with the biggest question of them all. "What did they do to me?"

You'll have to be more specific.

Terra smirked. *Of course, I will. Now she wants specifics.*

"What surgery did Dr. Sanchez perform on me?" She examined her hand again. "What is all of this?"

APRIL repeated the same information that Dr. Sanchez had told her, detailing the damage done to her spine, optical nerves, and brain. She informed Terra of the software that APRIL ran on —an advancement from Tynamo Inc. and a future evolution of the AI lenses.

"You're saying I'm a guinea pig?"

No. A guinea pig, Cavia porcellis, is a species of rodent belonging to the genus Cavia in the family Caviidae. Despite their common name, guinea pigs are not native to Guinea...

"Okay, I get it, APRIL," Terra interrupted. "Enough." She rubbed a hand down her face. "What I meant to say, am I just some test subject for Dr. Sanchez and his team?"

I am not able to determine a sufficient answer. Insufficient data to make a statement.

Terra nodded. "Of course. Of course, there is. Why would anything be clear or useful in all of this? You said that you're an evolution of the APRIL lenses. What does that mean?"

I have advanced coding. APRIL biotech can offer a wider radius of scanning abilities with an improved knowledge base and to-the-minute synchronization with the Atlantica Justice System servers. Some models allow an override of biomechanical movements, with enhanced speed, strength, and—

"Wait a minute," Terra instructed.

Timer set for sixty seconds.

"No," Terra grumbled. "Cancel timer."

Canceling timer.

"You said enhanced speed and strength?"

Experimental models allow synaptic overriding of major nerves and muscle groups. When synchronized with partnering prosthetics, the APRIL software is capable of pulling a host from a dangerous situation and providing increased biochemical assistance to aid in escape and capture.

Terra thought back to the green, how she could run and jump and move so much faster than she believed that she should. "Is that what you did to me?" She patted her body. "APRIL, how much of me is altered biotech? How much of my body did they actually replace?"

A 3D image floated in the air before her, a perfect match of her body shape. It spun in a slow three-sixty as labels and arrows appeared, and particular body parts lit up in time with APRIL's analysis. A mistrusting voice in the back of her mind told her to expect a full skeletal reconstruction, organs that were mesh instead of flesh. Instead, true to the doctor's words, her thumb, spine, eye, and a couple of sections of her brain illuminated.

Scan complete. Hardware confirmed. No foreign objects or intellectual alterations detected.

"Well, that's something." It still didn't make sense. How was Terra able to heal and perform so well on the green? "APRIL, you mentioned biochemical alterations. Can you clarify what that means?"

The APRIL program can stimulate the nerve centers and hormone distributors associated with particular types of bodily stress. APRIL can keep you calm under pressure, flood the system with adrenaline, and balance out your hormones to prevent the inevitable crashes that humans have following periods of intense adrenal activity.

"Like medication? Beta-blockers and pills designed to stop depressive episodes?"

Negative. APRIL provides you with only what you need to perform your duty, using a sophisticated algorithm and continually scanning your bodily data. This program will keep you at your best instead of preventing you from reaching your worst.

"Interesting…" Terra grinned. "And the healing?"

With APRIL's bio scanning and manipulation program attached, your central nervous systems, platelets, white blood cells, and red blood cells are better controlled and distributed around the body. Epidermal stimulation can also increase skin recovery time by forty-eight percent.

"Holy shit…" Terra breathed. She was superhuman. Marginally so, but still, the possibilities of this technology could be amazing. If she could apprehend every criminal as she had in the park, she'd be an unstoppable one-woman justice force. "What are the limitations?"

You'll have to be more specific.

Terra considered her questions. "Who has current access to the system? I'm assuming that someone will be able to access your server, similar to the glasses we shared. You're not in here with me alone."

Information is classified.

Terra's stomach fell. "Do you have a camera feed?"

APRIL's program provides a constant data stream of visual information.

Terra rubbed her chin. She closed her eyes, conscious that somebody else might be seeing through them. An idea occurred to her. "APRIL, can you show me the night of the accident?"

For a moment, nothing happened. Then, Terra's world lurched. She opened her eyes and found herself looking down at a busy evening street from a CCTV camera fixed above the entrance to an apartment block.

The footage was dark, but with a few enhancements, she could make out the shape of people walking along the sidewalk. Cars drove steadily up the street. The sound of merriment and music thumping came from a bar that was out of sight.

Terra recognized the street. She could see it flashing in her mind as she apprehended a man on foot, and then it was gone.

An engine roared, growing louder. A car sped into view, headlights bright. They reached the intersection and drifted around the corner, narrowly missing a transit van that had stopped at a red light.

Terra's bike sped into view, her AJS' engine silent as she sped along the road. She attempted the drift, but the transit van jumped forward. She adjusted her angle, but it was too late. The bike fell beyond her control. She skidded into a parked car. Her body crashed against the trunk.

White light exploded. It was so sudden that it didn't seem real. Terra could make out the shape of something thrown backward, but it was hard to tell if it was her body or a chunk of the car. White filled the screen. There were screams.

The light cleared. Terra was nowhere in sight. A crowd gathered.

"Cut the feed," Terra stated.

Her body lurched. She was back in her bedroom, staring at the far wall. Sweat peppered her forehead.

Initiating temporal nerve stimulation.

Terra didn't bother to argue. Her heart rate slowed as a sudden calm washed over her. She didn't fall asleep, but she did close her eyes. For a long while, she sat there and thought about her accident. For a long time, she tried to make sense of it all.

CHAPTER THIRTEEN

Imani was waiting for Terra when she arrived at the quaint cafe on 35th Street.

She waved her over with a pitying smile. It was how everyone who hadn't seen her since the accident greeted her. It was the same way people greeted a cancer patient after being first diagnosed with the news, a pitying expression as if anything too rough or enthusiastic might break them and shatter them into a thousand pieces.

A black coffee waited on the table on a white saucer. The saucer perched upon a paper doily. Scones, jam, and cream occupied the center of the table. "It's supposed to be Cornish," Imani informed Terra. "Apparently, there's a whole debate across England over what to call them."

Terra read the label. "Scones? Like, sc-own-s, right?"

Imani laughed. "Some people say it like 'gone.' Sc-on."

Terra waved a hand. "You're stupid."

Imani showed Terra a clip of the debate on her cell phone. A riled-up man with a strange accent engaged in a heated discussion with a woman who spoke as if she was parroting the king. "See?"

"Ridiculous." She spread a thick layer of jam and cream on her scone. Imani watched her. Terra grew self-conscious and put her hand under the table to hide her thumb.

Imani tilted her head. "Show me."

Terra brought her hand back up and laid it on the center of the table. Imani reached out her hand, then turned Terra's over to examine. "Impressive work."

"I give it a thumbs-up." Terra smirked.

Imani laughed. She looked closely at it. "Could they not have issued you a skin-colored one? Or one that had faux flesh on it?"

"I don't know. Never thought to ask."

"What can it do?"

Terra raised a finger. "I'll show you. This is pretty awesome." She picked up her scone and took a big bite. Jam stained her lips. "It's really good at picking things up."

"You know what I mean," Imani retorted with a head shake. "You said there was more."

Terra leaned across the table conspiratorially. "APRIL, engage civilian mode."

Civilian mode engaged. The date that floated around Terra's vision faded to nothing, though she was still cautious with her words. "You remember those glasses that Black partnered me with the last time we met up?"

"Sure," Imani replied. "The robot sidekick."

Terra nodded. She tapped her temple. "Guess who's riding shotgun."

Imani's brow creased. As the realization dawned over her, her mouth fell open. "Shut up."

Terra nodded.

"You mean…they've fitted you with an AI? They've implanted technology into your body?"

"Yeah. The same as the glasses. The APRIL system. A more advanced version, according to the woman in my head."

Imani frowned. "How can they be more advanced? Weren't

those glasses the latest in partner in crime advancement? If they're the latest, how can you have something more advanced living in your head?"

Terra shrugged. She hadn't considered that.

"What can you do with it?"

Terra showed her. They pointed out people in the cafe, and Terra listed their details. She told Imani their name, height, weight, age, marital situation, everything down to their specific listed medications as well as the number of incarcerations. Ninety percent of Atlanticans had *some* form of a criminal record to their name.

"That's impressive." A hint of jealousy entered Imani's voice. "You're a one-woman show."

"I can also tap into security feeds, as long as they're networked to AJS-secure servers. I can access information on everyone—*everyone*," she emphasized, nodding to a camera in the corner of the room. "There's also a feed recording my activity, so I can go back and replay the footage of my captures."

She waited for Imani to pick up on the hint. Imani's face fell. She sat back, becoming reserved. "Terra. They're tracking you?"

"Every move."

"Who? Who is it linked to?"

Terra shook her head. "I don't know. I don't have access to the permissions. I'm speaking to the corporal later today. Hopefully, she can shed some light on the situation—where are you going?"

Imani gathered her things in her pack and stood. She glanced awkwardly down at Terra. "I'm glad we took the time to catch up. I'll talk to you soon, yeah?"

Without a word, she left the cafe.

Terra sat a moment, staring down at her half-eaten scone. She understood every part of Imani's sudden departure. No cop liked the idea of being tracked, particularly given the nature of the subjects they often spoke about.

Terra sighed. She finished her scone, then paid the check.

When she was outside, she straddled her motorbike and sped toward the precinct.

Terra felt as though she was reliving her first day at her new school.

She had been three months into her sixth grade when her parents moved house and into a new area of the suburb. The school transfer had been tough, with most kids having made firm friends by the time Terra graced their classrooms. She remembered walking down the halls, heads turning her way as people muttered about her, not making an effort to mask their words, judging the new girl who roamed their building.

Now it was very much the same.

Custer greeted Terra in much the same way as he always did, his eyes only briefly flickering to the scarring on Terra's eye and the metallic thumb that poked out from her sleeves. He offered his cursory, "You're right on time, Officer Kris," and this time Terra didn't have the patience to quip back. She signed in, then made her way toward the bullpen.

Officers smiled, but they were empty gestures. She could tell they were asking questions about her recovery and what she was doing back so soon. Rumors must have been flying because those who walked toward her soon curved out of her way, giving her space to make haste toward Black's office.

As she passed the bullpen, glass panels on her right, she spotted Hewlett and Dunston looking her way. Dunston broke into his best version of "The Robot" while Hewlett chuckled and chewed a pen between his teeth.

Terra entered Black's office. Gina stood sharply, a hand moving to her chest. "Officer Kris, you startled me."

"I need to talk to Black," Terra commanded.

Gina looked flustered. "Corporal Black is currently in a

meeting and isn't scheduled to finish for forty minutes. After that, she has another meeting that should last an hour. Then it's her lunchtime." She glanced at her computer screen, examining the calendar. "I'm sorry, she won't be available until…"

"The hell she won't," Terra stated. She moved to the corporal's door and shoved it open. The door crashed against the wall, drawing the attention of the corporal and the last man Terra expected to be sitting in this office.

Captain Parker Garcia offered a smile, the gesture alien on his face, like seeing a lighthouse in the desert. His goatee was grey and shaved close to the skin. There were deep trenches beneath his eye, and his ears seemed too large for his head.

"Officer Kris," he cawed, a deep, growling voice rumbling from his throat. His thick neck was red, his body in fine condition for a man of over fifty years. "You're a sight for sore eyes."

For a moment, Terra stood frozen. Hatred roiled inside her as she gazed down at the sneering man. It had been months since she had last seen him, the man who was responsible for having her demoted into the lower ranks.

The last time they had encountered each other, his face had been beet red, the vein in his forehead poking out as he roared at her and gave her marching orders. As far as Parker was concerned, the AJS should kick Terra off the force. After a review, the board gave her a second chance.

Terra looked at Black for answers. "What is he doing here?"

"I'd be careful how you talk about your superiors," Garcia interjected. "That's always been your problem, hasn't it? Black was saying that you've scared off half your partners in this precinct. Down to you and the robot to watch out for each other, aren't you?"

Terra wondered how much Garcia knew. For a vomit-inducing moment, she could feel him inside her head, watching her through the camera fitted inside her eyes. Only when he pulled out the APRIL glasses and waved them in the air did she calm down.

"Officer Kris is getting by," Black stated. "She's cooperative, and she's performing the duties I set out. A few teething issues, but it's nothing we haven't seen through, is it, Terra?"

"No," Terra answered uncertainly. It felt as though something had sucked the air out of her lungs.

Balancing biochemicals, APRIL soothed in her ear.

Then it was over. As though someone had flipped a switch on her back, Terra found herself. She unclenched her fists and regained her decorum. "No. Things have been fine here, Captain. Nothing for you to worry about."

"I'm sure she'll be rising back to your ranks in due course," Black stated.

Captain Garcia chuckled. "Sure. And the bullpen ain't full of pigs." He peeled his gaze from Terra. "Is there a reason your subordinate is interrupting our meeting? Is this something I should inform the Chief about?"

"No." Black smiled. "No, I don't think so. Unless you have something you want to say, Terra?"

Black's expression was inviting, but her eyes warned Terra against any further interruption. Terra shook her head. "It can wait."

Garcia raised his eyebrow, then placed the glasses on the desk.

Black beamed. "If you wait outside, I'll get Gina to let you in when we're finished."

Terra exited the room and sat in the office. For twenty minutes, she waited in the pregnant silence as Gina busied herself with her computer, phone calls, calendar invites, and filing documents in their cabinets. The office was soundproof, and Terra's mind wandered, coming up with topics and scenarios that could be a part of the discussion. It was unusual for an officer of Garcia's rank to visit a lower-ranking officer in the outer city.

Finally, the door opened. Garcia stood in the doorway and thanked Black for her time. As he passed Terra, he looked down on her, his shadow holding weight as a dark glint flashed in his eye. "Nice show, Kris." He tossed the glasses into Terra's lap. "Know that I'll still be watching."

Without another word, he swept out of the room. The moment the door closed, Terra felt the oppressive air lift. Black waited at the door, looking tired and resigned. "You have ten minutes."

Terra thanked her and headed inside the office. The temperature dropped several degrees, which Terra was thankful for. It woke her up and washed off Garcia's presence although a faint cloud of his cloying cologne lingered in the air. "You've got to be straight with me."

Black took her seat and patiently waited for Terra to continue.

"Do you have command over my AI?"

Black was quiet for a long moment. Her gaze was steady and thoughtful. She lowered her head and cracked her neck. "No."

Terra wasn't sure what answer she expected, but it wasn't that. "What do you mean, 'no?'"

Black laced her fingers together. "I mean that I don't have access to the software. I only have permission to command those with the glasses. As it currently stands," she nodded at the glasses Terra hadn't realized she was holding in her hands, "the APRIL technology has been recalled for review."

Terra raised an eyebrow. APRIL displayed information about Corporal Black around her figure. Terra noticed a small green readout that stated, "Telling the truth."

Handy...

"So you deemed this technology unfit for a wider rollout," Terra started, "but decided to fit it inside my body anyway? Untested? Untried? You altered my biology for what? So your superiors could use me as a puppet and see the world through my eyes?"

"It's not like that."

"I've been with my parents since the surgery," Terra continued. "I've released private information from inside my house, unknowingly, so that whoever is watching through my system can see our everyday life. There's ammo there. These are people I care about, and my technology is broadcasting them. I want to know to who."

"No one," Black replied softly. "No one is viewing them." She leaned forward in her chair. "Terra, do you really think the Atlantica Justice System would fit you with a CCTV camera so we can monitor your daily activities? Public versus private still applies. No law in Atlantica would allow anyone to install technology inside you that would give out information without your consent."

"It's not like I gave anyone consent to begin with!" A sudden thought occurred to her. "How did this even happen in the first place?"

"Your mother signed the forms. You listed her as your next of kin on your information, didn't you?"

Terra faltered. Her mum had allowed this to happen? She didn't know what to think.

"Look." Black stood and skirted the desk until she sat in front of Terra. "I understand that this is all new and frightening. I'd feel the same if I were you.

"You have to remember that the AJS is here to protect and serve. The technology inside you is to help you survive. The rest of the database is optional. If you wish to have the AJS servers disconnected from you, I can raise a flag to the top bosses to shut it down.

"Given the discomfort you experienced with the glasses and your lack of willingness to comply with your partners, I suggested it might be an idea to overcome all of that and kill two birds with one stone. I'm sorry if that makes you uncomfortable. It's reversible."

Terra looked at her doubtfully. The idea of being without APRIL made her retreat slightly. "You give me your word that this is one-way technology?"

Black smiled a picture-perfect smile. "I promise."

Terra scrutinized her face. She looked for the little legend hovering around Black's head. "Telling the truth."

Terra drew a deep breath, then relaxed in the chair. "Thank you."

"Good." Black returned to her chair. She slid a tablet across the table. "Your first assignment is back. Think you can handle it?"

CHAPTER FOURTEEN

Terra walked down the stairs with no sign of a limp or injury.

That didn't stop her mother from sticking her nose into her business.

Three place settings lay on the table. Michael Kris sat at the table's head, fingers laced and chin resting on his hands. For a man in his sixties, he was aging gracefully. His hair thinned at the crown, but he still had enough to style at the front, giving the illusion from this angle that he was ten years younger. His face was warm and kind, and a gleaming gold watch decorated his wrist.

"Hey, hon," he remarked as Terra walked in. His brow creased.

"Something wrong?" Terra asked.

"You've picked up quickly," Michael stated. "Weren't you incapacitated in bed when I left you this morning?" He leaned back, angling his words toward the arch leading to the kitchen. "Marie! It's a miracle. Our little girl healed. You have to come see this."

Terra chuckled as she sat to one side of him. Marie emerged from the arch carrying a plate in each hand. She looked angry, as though it was disgusting that Terra dared to heal so quickly.

"Don't get me started," she remarked. "I've been telling her to take it easy all day, and she's barely been home." She finally looked at Terra, scanning around her for something she couldn't see. "No crutches, either?" Her shoulders sagged. "Terra, you have to look after yourself."

"I'm fine."

Marie stared at her.

"Honestly, Mom. I feel fine." She picked up her fork and stabbed a potato. "I'm a big girl. I can take care of myself."

Marie huffed and disappeared into the kitchen.

"She's only looking out for you," Michael commented beneath his breath. "We both are. We almost lost you a few weeks ago, or did you forget that? Is that part of the amnesia?"

"There's no more amnesia," Terra lied. "I feel fine. I remember it all like it was yesterday." She thought of the bike skidding into the car and the subsequent explosion. "I wish I didn't remember it all so vividly."

Michael shook his head. "When they showed me that son of a bitch's body, I was fuming." He shoved a forkful of lettuce into his mouth. "Was barely any part of him left."

Terra nodded, losing herself in the taste of her food. If she didn't know any better, she'd think that APRIL was heightening her senses there, too.

Marie strode back into the room and sat across from Terra.

"Thanks, Mom," Terra commented.

Marie waved but didn't look up.

They ate quietly until their plates were empty. When Terra finished, she looked at her watch. "Oops, time to go."

"Where are you off to now?" Marie asked. "You should be resting. *Tu devrais te reposer.*"

Her French accent was impeccable. Terra rolled her eyes, able to pick up some stray phrases her mother used quite often. She had tried to teach Terra French when she was a teenager, but Terra had other ideas.

"Black's given me an assignment," Terra replied casually.

Marie and Michael exchanged a glance.

"You tell her," Marie exclaimed. "I can't keep going in circles."

Michael placed a hand on Terra's. "Honey, no. You're not ready for this. You're fresh out of surgery. Black shouldn't be asking you to return to work."

"I feel fine." She tried to gain her mother's eye, but she was too busy trying to burn a hole in the table with the intensity of her annoyance. Terra brushed it off.

After all, her mother might have been able to sign the consent forms to undergo the operation, but she wasn't able to keep her at home. She had long flown the maternal coop. "Besides, it's an easy job. Only a routine sweep of Kingston Park. That's all. Clearing out the homeless and making sure no one's up to no good."

Michael looked at his wife. "If she says she can—"

"Michael!" Marie shouted. "You're encouraging this?"

Michael glanced back at Terra, a tired look in his eye. "You can handle this?"

"I can handle this," Terra replied.

For a moment, she was thankful that she'd flipped on civilian mode. She didn't want to know what her mother's current threat level was. She guessed it wouldn't be zero.

It hadn't been a total lie. Terra did drive over to Kingston Park.

She hadn't even needed to go to the station to get her things. Black had handed her a rucksack filled with her uniform and effects, and Terra had snuck out the front door before her mother got a chance to stop her. Skooch followed her every footstep but stopped when Terra told her in a hushed voice to wait at the door.

"Mummy will be home soon." Terra offered a smile and patted the Papillon's head.

By the time she arrived at the park, the sun was on its final legs. The sky was a patchwork of shades of bruise behind the fog, and the park's vintage lamplights gave a warm orange glow. They were painted black and shaped in the fashion of Victorian lamps. Terra stood at the wrought-iron gates and scanned ahead.

"Okay, APRIL, show me what you can do." Terra narrowed her eyes.

I am capable of an array of functions. Please be more specific.

Terra sighed. "Scan the park."

APRIL didn't answer this time. Instead, the world within her view slowly morphed before her very eyes. She closed her right eye to focus on the onslaught of new information.

Individuals lit up, popping into view in their thermal colors. First, there was one, then two, then over two dozen were strolling around the park in different areas. She judged their distance by how small or large they were. A smile appeared. "Impressive."

Information appeared around those closest, and Terra understood that those were the ones that APRIL could physically see from where she stood.

Please turn your head to continue the scan.

Terra obliged, turning first left, then right. More and more thermal people appeared until her count made thirty-two. "Zoom in on that one," Terra requested, unsurprised that she didn't need to specify who. A mass didn't look like a person but like a moving, amorphous rock. Her sight zoomed in, and after a few seconds, Terra realized what she saw as two heads appeared as they gasped for air.

"I guess al fresco lovemaking gets some people's gears going." Terra smirked.

Indecent exposure is an arrestable offense on the island of Atlantica.

Terra nodded. "Yeah." She examined those around the two,

finding no one nearby. "Let's give them a few minutes in the hope they'll finish up. They're not exposing themselves to anybody but each other."

She strolled along the path, examining each digital label as new people came into her sight. Anyone that crossed her path gave her a wide berth as she roamed the edges of the park before working her way inwards. As the night grew darker, Terra found it strange how the park remained so well-lit, with Terra at one point able to track a squirrel running along the grass from a fair distance away.

"Have you enhanced my vision?"

Negative. Dr. Sanchez installed me. I played no part in the enhancement of your vision.

"But I *can* see better."

Your visual ability has increased to a twenty-twenty range. Not only that, but thermal scanners and night-vision views are standard within the APRIL software.

Terra grinned. "I really could get used to this." She thought about her encounter with Imani, and her smile dropped. Black had told her that no one else was watching through her lens, but what would it take to hack into her software and override APRIL? There was so much she didn't understand.

Over the next half hour, Terra managed to disrupt a group of teenagers from loitering by the public bins and attempting to set the contents on fire. She sent the two passionate individuals on their way and gave them a knowing look and a warning wag of the finger. She also managed to move on five vagrants who had fallen asleep at the bases of the park's trees.

"There's a shelter three blocks over," Terra informed a woman in her forties with a filthy face and a knitted cap with several holes. "Book yourself in and get a nice, warm meal. It's either that or the slammer."

The woman grumbled and spat, deeply unappreciative of Terra's aid. According to the woman, the shelter was always full, but APRIL pulled up tonight's numbers, and twenty-seven spaces remained. "Best move quick."

She didn't.

Terra watched her amble away, confident that she would soon find another place to settle in the park. As she shrank into a small thermal image, her information lingered around her, a different name on APRIL's system than the one she had provided Terra. A couple of criminal charges were associated with her name, but they were from over half a decade ago.

Terra turned to the path when she spotted a group of five bodies through the trees. Their images blazed hot. Terra tracked them where she stood, leaving a good distance, wondering what a group of that size was doing in the park at this time. She requested the thermal imaging to fade, and APRIL obeyed.

"Can you leave an outline so I can still see them?" Terra requested.

Negative. However, I can reduce the opacity.

"Let's do that, then," Terra confirmed.

She followed the group, the five appearing in her vision like faded ghosts. She slalomed between trees, cautious of her noise level as she stepped on dry leaves. She managed to gain a clear line of sight a minute later.

APRIL revealed the information around them. Each of the five men had recent criminal convictions, with one red warning appearing above the smallest of their group for an outstanding charge.

"APRIL, load file on Gary Clark," Terra stated.

Pulling up file.

The red writing expanded until it filled Terra's vision, morphing into a series of case notes and images. Gary Clark was a long-time offender of GBH and a peddler of Class B drugs. With over two dozen vacations in the fifteenth district jail, here was a man who was familiar with the Atlantica Justice System.

"How has he managed to get out so many times?" Terra mused

aloud.

APRIL surprised her by shifting the information again. A video clip played of a smug Gary sitting in the interrogation room with a female lawyer who appeared to be lifted straight from a TV crime documentary. Her shirt was unbuttoned enough to show a generous line of cleavage, and her makeup was flawless. Neatly parted long blonde hair completed the image. The cop sitting in the room with her was enamored, too, his eyes drifting to her chest every few seconds.

"Do you understand who my client works for?" the lawyer—identified by APRIL as one Catalina Rubio—barked at an officer that Terra didn't recognize. She leaned across the table, enunciating each word carefully. "Fer-nan-do Cross."

The officer's eyes widened. "That's right, officer. Your boy here is a leading cog of the very company that pays your goddamn salary. You bring him in, and you're kicking a hornet's nest of shit."

The officer sat back, eyes considering.

The woman gave a casual shrug as she closed her briefcase. She glanced at the camera, and for a moment, Terra felt as though Catalina was looking at *her*. "You promised to turn those things off."

The officer glanced her way. "The light just means it has power. Not that it's recording."

Catalina gave him a dubious look. She was right to be cautious. Terra knew the tactic well. She was involved in many cases where they left the CCTV cameras rolling to see what was going on. They couldn't use the evidence as part of the case, but they could glean some information that would lead to future evidence.

"Are we done here?" Catalina asked.

The officer tapped the tablet on his screen. "Miss Rubio, your client was just caught dealing speed to minors on the streets. I'm afraid I can't let him—"

A door opened behind. Terra couldn't see the officer entering, but she could hear his voice. "Harmon, let him go."

Terra's blood boiled at the gleeful expression on Catalina's and Gary's faces. How many crooked cops were working in this city?

The video feed faded. Terra turned her attention back toward the group that had now reached the center of the park. Even as soft outlines she could tell they were up to no good.

Terra approached them, remaining hidden until she was within hearing range. APRIL boosted the audio for her.

"You said two hundred dollars on the phone," one of the men groaned. He was muscular, pale, and bald. "This is bullshit."

"Supply and demand," Gary replied coolly. A cigarette hung from his lips. "You want the good grade? You pay for it." He held out a clear bag filled with white powder. "Or I can take it all back."

Terra noted the upgrade from Gary's Class B drugs to Class A. Cocaine was certainly something he shouldn't be dealing in.

The muscular man, his label reading Curtis Laughlin, grabbed Gary by the throat. Gary appeared unfazed by this sudden attack as one of the other men, a redhead by the name of Phillip West, snatched the bag from his hand. "Who's to say we can't just take it?"

They chuckled. Curtis let Gary go. Gary straightened himself out as Phillip peeled open the bag. He licked his finger, then dipped it in the powder. He sniffed it, then rubbed it on his gums. He closed his eyes and gave an appreciative moan.

"Good shit," Phillip approved.

"The best," Gary sneered. "Now time for you to pay the piper."

Philip and Curtis exchanged a glance. The other three closed in on Gary.

Curtis chuckled. "Who says we need to pay, asshole?"

Terra stepped out of the trees, a hand on the butt of her Glock. "I do."

CHAPTER FIFTEEN

Terra puffed out her chest, her metallic AJS uniform catching what little silver light passed through the fog from the moon. The others turned to her, taking a moment to take in what they were seeing.

"You're under arrest for possession and dealing of Class A narcotics," Terra aimed at Gary. She addressed the others, "The rest of you…well, I'm sure there's a bunch in the pipeline that you need arresting for."

They were stunned for a minute. Curtis glanced over Terra's shoulder as if another handful of AJS officers were about to emerge through the trees. When no one came, he laughed. "Sweet for the AJS to send a lonely cop off by herself." He advanced on her, giving a signal for the others to watch Gary. "You really think you've got what it takes to take us, darling?"

He towered over her, his bulk blocking out the light. Terra met his eyes, unfaltering, hand flexing over her gun. APRIL threw up information about Curtis, with lines pointing to particular parts of his body.

Accessing medical records. Curtis Laughlin: one broken

finger, one fractured femur, three gunshot wounds to the chest, and an allergy to peanuts.

Not sure how useful that can be, Terra thought.

Walks with a limp. Minor, but a weak spot. Approximating force needed to incapacitate.

Terra met Curtis' eyes. "You're only going to make your situation worse by resisting arrest."

"Oh, am I?" He looked around the park. Their group was hidden from the path by a cluster of trees. "If you say so, darling."

He made to shove her shoulder, but she deflected the hit with her forearm. His face morphed from mirth to annoyance, eyes flickering down to her weapon. "You can't shoot unprovoked."

"Who says I'll be unprovoked? You're threatening an AJS officer."

He drew a deep breath, then swung a meaty fist. Terra ducked her head back, moving out of the path of the attack. She raised her boot, then slammed it into Curtis' femur. He groaned as his leg buckled, and he fell to one knee.

The others took a step toward Terra. She drew her weapon and aimed it at them in turn. "Let's keep this peaceful, fellas. I'll make a deal with you all. Come peacefully and help me bring in this asshole to atone for his crimes, and we'll reduce your sentence. Hey, with good behavior, you might be out before Christmas."

They debated this in silence. Phillip clutched the cocaine tightly in his hands. Gary stood at the back of the group. Even speaking softly, she could hear his voice, amplified in her head. "You going to stand there and let a woman take you like this? You're a bigger bunch of pussies than I thought you were."

Threat level: eighty-nine percent, APRIL announced. Terra's vision zoomed in on the hot thermal blob behind the group. It appeared as though Gary was reaching into his pocket for a...

Terra shot. The bullet passed through a small gap between

two of the men. They jumped. The bullet hit grass. "Put your weapon down!" Terra exclaimed.

Gary's arm appeared around the man in front of him. Terra took a sharp sidestep, missing the bullet by only a few inches. "Fuck you. This is our business, asshole."

He shot again. This time he caught Curtis in the shoulder. Curtis rolled back onto the grass, and his eyes screwed shut in pain.

Terra aimed her pistol, training it on Gary's weapon.

Colt 1911 Classic APRIL announced. **Maximum six bullets remaining.**

Terra took the shot. She felt a slight nudge in her hand, merely a twitch. The bullet hit the barrel of the Colt head-on, a strange ringing sound coming from the metal hitting the metal. Gary cried out. The gun fell to the ground.

The others scattered.

They headed in all directions, dividing to conquer. Gary was left alone, shaking his hand as though he had received an electric shock.

Terra kept the gun on him.

"You asshole!" Gary cried. "They're taking off with my product."

"Fuck your product," Terra replied, aware that APRIL was still tracking the others in her peripheral vision. She took a step closer. "Hands where I can see them. You're coming in with me."

Gary growled. Slowly, he raised his hands in the air. His dark eyes glinted. "I'm telling you, you don't want to do this, sweetheart," he warned coolly. "This could lead to a whole load of bad for you."

"I'm a big girl. I can handle it." Terra took a step closer, one hand reaching for her cuffs.

Something moved behind her.

Gary grinned.

Imminent threat. Six o'clock.

Terra whirled as Curtis reached for her ankle. His hands gripped her, but she was one step ahead. She brought the butt of the Glock down onto his head and knocked him out cold.

She turned toward the scurrying footsteps and caught Gary sprinting off clumsily across the grass. The Colt was back in his hand, and he fired three careless shots.

Terra drew a deep breath. "You ready, APRIL?"

Ready. Terra's vision homed in on Gary. **Go.**

Terra tore after him, arms pumping at her sides. A cool wave of something she couldn't describe washed over her as the trees tore past her. She didn't need to think about where they were. Her body just knew. She zig-zagged between them, grinning as Gary, who thought he could lose her in the darkness, grew more alert. APRIL amplified his audio, and she could hear his hurried breaths, his soft declarations of "Oh shit, oh shit, oh shit."

She closed the gap, the pair of them passing the woman Terra had encouraged to go to a shelter. She didn't care about that now. She needed this asshole brought to justice.

He stopped, tucking himself behind a tree. Terra hid behind a trunk as another shot came toward her.

"APRIL, how many shots left?" she asked.

Maximum, two bullets.

Terra called, "Give it up. I have you down to the wire. This is your final warning."

"Fuck you!" Gary yelled. "You think I'll ever come willingly with you shits? All I have to do is outrun you, and you're nothing. *Nothing.*"

Terra watched as he turned his head to the left. They were only a hundred meters from the road that edged the park. She knew what he was thinking. If he could get into one of the private residences, he was free.

He broke for it.

Terra emerged from behind her tree and sprinted after him. Arrows and directions appeared in her vision, showing the quickest paths to intercept. Gary fired one of his remaining bullets, and it nicked the tree beside Terra. A couple of splinters hit her face. Something twinged in her back, but a cool wash of APRIL's biochemicals numbed whatever had happened as she closed in on Gary.

He reached the fence. A gate was to his left.

Terra broke free of the trees. She was so close. He grabbed the gate and swung himself around. Terra gripped the back of his collar. He was strong, but her grip was stronger. She dug in her heels and yanked him back. He swung at her. She ducked, reflexes working instinctively for her. "Got you, asshole."

He toppled onto his back. Terra steadied his fall, aware that she didn't want to crack his head open. As he neared the ground, something caught her peripheral vision.

New threat identified. Nine o'clock—

Terra didn't have time to react as a body slammed into her. She could smell expensive perfume mixed with leather. A strange crimson covered her face. She grunted, rolled along the ground, attempting to shake off this new threat.

Arms grabbed her throat and squeezed. Terra clawed at the arm then pulled. She gained enough distance to writhe out of its grip.

She rolled sideways, then quickly pushed herself to her feet. There was a warmth in her back that she didn't like, but her attention focused on two things: the man running away down the street and the beautiful woman with the crop of red hair who was brushing herself down with an irritated expression.

"You've lost my catch," the woman crooned, her voice as sultry as her scent.

CHAPTER SIXTEEN

Terra aimed her gun at the woman. "Winters?"

The woman was the definition of stunning with a short crop of bright red hair that hugged her sharp features. Her lips matched her hair, and so did her long leather jacket. Beneath it all, she wore a tight corset and pants that hugged her shapely legs. She was a woman who was very easy on the eyes, but that was where men often met their downfall. Terra knew better than a lot of Atlanticans how sharp Valentina was as a weapon.

Valentina Winters rolled her eyes, then placed a hand on the top of the Glock. She lowered its aim to the ground. "Kris?" She glanced around the shadows. "Where are your other guys? Garmin and…Gallows, was it?"

Terra thought back to the last time she had encountered Valentina Winters, Atlantica's most notorious mercenary. "They've been promoted. No longer in the same precinct." There was a hint of jealousy in her voice.

"Wow…" Valentina nodded. "You sound bitter about that. Shame. Sorry about that."

There was a strange tone in Valentina's voice. The last time Kris had crossed her path was when the pair were chasing down a jewelry thief in the cavernous bowels of the Atlantica underground. Valentina had flexed the rules somewhat, and Terra had allowed it to happen. All said, they caught the bad guy, and that was all she cared about.

"Care to explain why you tackled me when I was about to make the arrest?" Terra frowned. "I could take you in for obstruction of justice."

Valentina let out a derisive laugh. "Sure you could, sweetheart." She glanced past Terra and out into the street. "Motherfucker… He's gone. Great. Now I'm going to have to track him all over again." She pointed at Terra. "If I lose this guy you owe me five hundred grand."

Terra snorted.

"Oh, I'm serious," Valentina stated. "Big money needed. I have a lot of ground to cover." She looked around once more. "Seriously, where is your backup? Aren't you AJS guys supposed to always travel in pairs? Don't tell me they're letting you guys roam solo in this city now. You'll lose half your force in the first two weeks."

Terra turned back to the street, choosing to ignore Valentina's question. APRIL offered her a view of the people within the immediate vicinity, the tall faces of the building lighting up like fireworks as hundreds of Atlanticans came into view.

She narrowed her eyes, focusing on the only nearby civilian who still bore a name tag. *APRIL…tell me that's him.*

That's him.

Terra grinned. The shape of Gary was only a block away, the man looking over his shoulder as he scaled a series of stairs inside one of the strangest-shaped buildings Terra had seen.

"Hello?" Valentina cooed. She shook her head. "Fine. Whatever. Have a pleasant evening, Kris."

Terra grabbed her arm before she could run past her. Valentina combatted with a defensive chop. Terra's limbs moved as if of their own accord, matching Valentina's speed and maneuvers. A surprised expression washed over Terra. She released Valentina's wrist and smirked.

Valentina studied her. "You've leveled up," she stated flatly. "Have they upped the minimum training requirements for you lot?"

Terra grinned. "You have no idea." She strode past Valentina. "If you want your guy, you better follow me."

Valentina frowned. A thousand questions lay behind those intelligent eyes.

"How do you know this, Kris?" Valentina asked uncertainly. It was amusing for Terra to have the woman who was usually so certain in all she did against the ropes. They reached the landing, Terra slowly advancing to the nearest door.

Terra placed a finger on her lips. She narrowed her eyes at the shape of Gary standing somewhere inside. He was leaning against something, looking as though he were sipping from a bottle of some kind.

If only I could see inside the apartments.

She pressed her back to the wall, then tilted her head to press her ear flat. She couldn't hear anything from inside. "He's in there," she mouthed to Valentina.

Valentina raised an eyebrow. "You're certain?" she asked with a strong hint of sarcasm.

Terra nodded. "Amplify audio," she breathed almost soundlessly.

Amplifying audio.

A woman's voice met her ears. "…three months since you last came here, and now what? You want help? I should kick you straight outta this goddamn place." Her accent was thick and sounded Bostonian.

"You can't. Not until they're out of here." Gary slurped from his drink. "Just one night. That's all I need."

"Should've thought about that before you left without so much as a goodbye." Something slammed on the table. "You piece of shit. You haven't changed. I thought this was an apology. Instead, all I'm good for is for you to tread on me and use me whenever you goddamn please!"

A glass smashed.

"Sweetie, sweetie…" Gary cooed. "Fine. Fine!"

Another glass smashed.

"Look, I'll be out your hair in an hour, tops." His voice grew more erratic. "Just watch TV or do your hair or some shit, then I'll be gone. No worries!"

Another glass smashed.

"Son of a bitch!" Terra heard the tears in her words. "I thought I'd finished with creeps like you."

"I can make this better." Something wrinkled. Gary reached into his jacket. "Look, I can make this night better for you."

An eerie silence followed. Valentina joined Terra at the wall. "What are you…"

Terra raised a finger.

"Gary…you know I'm clean." The woman's voice was soft.

"You miss it, though, don't you, baby?" Gary cooed. "All those nights. Me and you lost in our wonderland."

"Gary…That was years ago." The temptation overwhelmed her.

Terra's nostrils flared. She drew her Glock, indicating that Valentina should do the same.

She moved in front of the door with her gun trained ahead. She raised a foot and was about to kick when her body twitched. Her foot lowered, and she took a dizzying step back.

"What the…" she started.

An Atlantica Officer for Justice is unable to break into a private residence without permission from the owner.

Valentina cocked her head. "Okay, sweetheart?"

"I can't break the seal," Terra stated, slightly in shock at her body's treachery. "An officer can't enter a private residence uninvited."

"You lot are like vampires." Valentina chuckled. "Good thing I can."

She kicked the door cleanly out of its moorings. It swung open, the handle smacking into the wall. Valentina swept in, gun trained on Gary. Terra approached swiftly behind, her mind a little in shock still. She turned her weapon to the woman. "Freeze. Atlantica Justice System. Gary Clark, you are under arrest for possession and dealing of Class A narcotics, attacking a city Justice Officer, and for avoiding arrest."

They swapped targets, Terra moving toward Gary, Valentina closing in on the woman. She wore a thin pink slip, her blonde hair tightly placed in curlers.

"You have the right to remain silent," Terra started. "Anything you say can and will be used against you in a court of law. You have the right to speak to an attorney and to have an attorney present during any questioning. If you cannot afford a lawyer, one will be provided for you at government expense.

For a moment, Gary looked ready to fight back. His face soured and his lip curled. He growled, arms resting by his side before slowly raising them. Terra barked at him to put his hands behind his head. He obeyed as she moved behind him and kicked the backs of his legs.

He slammed onto the tiled floor on his knees.

Valentina worked on the woman. She spoke softly, darkly, in the trademark way that Valentina did with her victims. Where Terra was a firecracker, Valentina was a Black Widow. The woman bit back words and went to her knees.

Valentina drew a coil of cable and tied it around the woman's hands.

Terra placed the cuffs on Gary's wrists.

They dragged both man and woman onto the couch where they sat side-by-side like some deranged married couple caught in the middle of makeshift bondage. Valentina closed the apartment door. The two women then sat beside each other on the coffee table.

"Who should go first?" Valentina asked. The suggestion that it should be her was clear in her tone.

"I have the law on my side," Terra replied. "Don't worry. We'll each get our turn."

"You can't do shit," Gary exclaimed. He spat at Terra, the phlegm congealing on her sleeve. She glanced down, then back at Gary and punched him. "You wait until my employer hears about this. Your ass is going to hit the curb so fast it'll catch on fire."

Terra smirked. "Employer, huh? Would this be a Fernando Cross?"

Gary's joy died from his face.

"I'll take that as a yes." Terra studied the panel of information displayed around Gary's head. His heart rate had elevated, and his adrenaline levels were spiking. She continued, "What would Fernando have to say about his chief henchman getting caught dealing coke in the middle of Kingston Park?"

Gary didn't reply. He simply grinned.

"Something funny?" Terra asked.

"You pigs are all the same," Gary replied. "All so optimistic and shiny, thinking you can erase the scum that sticks to the bottom of the pan of Atlantica. The problem is, none of you know how high up the ladder this all truly goes, do you? None of you know how infested this place is with the very people you try to capture and bring to justice."

He struggled with his handcuffs, then gave up. "Atlantica Justice System… Ha! It's all a fucking joke."

Terra gave a thoughtful nod as she scanned through the files in her display. "Looks like you've been let off the hook fifteen times in three years. I mean, that would definitely suggest that you're a prime candidate to be busted out and back on the street in a few days. You know what the problem is, though?"

Gary stared at her.

Terra leaned forward. "You haven't met me yet. Now, shit bag, you're coming to the station with me. Your pretty lady can come too if she chooses to kick up a fuss?"

The woman shook her head eagerly.

"Good." Terra stood and grabbed Gary by the crook of the elbow. "I'll call in the units. Let's get you out front."

Calling in AJS units.

Terra's head filled softly with the chatter of radios and police officers talking. A hand grabbed her shoulder. "You haven't forgotten about me, have you, sunshine?"

Valentina's eyes were dark, and she sneered. "My turn with that fucker."

Terra glanced at Gary, then shrugged. "You have eight minutes until backup gets here."

Valentina gave her a strange look, then nodded. "You best clear the room then, people. This shit could get ugly, and if you stay here, you'll have no choice but to take me in, too."

Gary's eyes grew wide.

Terra nodded and belatedly realized, *Dammit, I need to track Valentina.*

Scanning. Placing locator on Valentina Winters.

Terra brought the other woman outside with her. As she bided her time for the officers, she heard Gary call out in pain as Valentina extracted her information. She kept her eyes on the thermal blob that was Valentina, ensuring that the Crimson Countess—how the newspapers and media outlets had come to know Valentina—wouldn't steal her catch.

Sure enough, as red and blue lights appeared flashing outside the windows, Valentina cleared the room. She escaped out of the window, and Terra watched her climb to the rooftop. By the time backup arrived, she was gone.

CHAPTER SEVENTEEN

Terra returned to the station, but only for a short while. Black was still militant about Terra "taking it easy" and was undecided about whether she should be thankful that Terra had brought in Gary Clark or pissed at the situation she had gotten herself into.

After all, police work was no walk in the park.

Terra returned home a short while later. Black had signed her off with a scant thank you and told her not to worry about the interrogation. They'd have one of the others pick up on it. Terra needed rest.

Terra wasn't sure how true that was. She felt wired from adrenaline and a mixture of other chemicals running through her body. Or, at least, that's what she figured until she returned to her parents and her head hit the pillow.

She was almost certain that APRIL had affected her somehow and was equalizing her chemical makeup, but she wasn't sad. That night she had the greatest sleep she'd had for some time.

For a few hours, at least.

Morning was crowing when Terra became aware of movement in her bedroom. A small weight shifted beside her, and as she reached out a hand, she found soft fur to thread her fingers through.

"Morning, Skooch," Terra cooed.

"Good morning, sweetheart," a voice shot back.

Terra sat up straight, eyes slamming open. The room was momentarily blurry until the shape at the end of her bed settled into clarity. Valentina Winters smiled at her.

Terra looked at the open sash window, wondering why she hadn't closed that the night before.

I did. I'm sure of it.

"Breaking and entering a private residence is a criminal offense," Terra stated flatly.

"You didn't seem to have much of a problem with me breaking and entering last night," Valentina replied. "In fact, you encouraged it. I think that buys me a free pass to do it without AJS instruction." She chuckled. "You look like shit."

Terra ran a hand through her hair, attempting to neaten it. Valentina's gaze bore into her, scrutinizing every pore of her body. Terra narrowed her eyes. "Too little sleep will do that to a girl."

"I wouldn't know," Valentina replied. There was no humor in her face.

"What do you want, Valentina?" Terra asked. "You have ten seconds to give me a sufficient answer before I turn you in to the authorities."

Valentina smirked. "I want answers."

Terra waited for her to continue as Valentina mulled over her words.

"Something's different with you," Valentina replied at last. "I want to know what it is."

Terra raised an eyebrow. "What do you mean?"

"Our scuffle in Kingston last night..." Valentina chewed her lip. "It's been a while since I've met anyone who can match my maneuvers."

"Academy training. You said it yourself."

"You found the target from half a mile away," Valentina continued. "You didn't track him, but you knew where he was."

"Lucky guess," Terra stated defensively.

Valentina scoffed. "You called the cops without a cell phone."

That one had Terra stumped.

Valentina picked up on her hesitation. "I figured…" She said it more to herself than to Terra. Skooch sat passively, head on her paws, eyes tracking Valentina.

"Look, I spend a lot of my time keeping up with the latest in AJS training and available technologies to help track my targets. I'm on the 'cutting edge,' if you will." She laughed at her joke, but Terra wasn't sure why.

"You have something that could benefit my work—particularly now. I need to track someone, and your gadgets could be a way for me to bring a man to my form of justice finally." A flicker of sadness crossed Valentina's eyes.

Terra considered her reply. How public should she make this new addition to her biology? "It was a remote receiver," she settled on. "A hand in the pocket. A button pushed. The AJS responds and tracks the GPS."

Valentina nodded although Terra could tell she didn't believe her. She glanced out the window at the reddening sky. Outside, all was calm. It was going to be another humid day in Atlantica. "Fine. Keep your secrets." She rose to her feet. "If you do, however, feel like changing your mind, I'm a dab hand with technology. Make my gadgets, hack into security vaults, track my targets…that kind of thing."

"I know. I've read your case notes."

"There's nothing in my case notes."

April confirmed this unasked. Terra repeated, "I know."

Valentina stopped by a chest of drawers beside the window. She took a card from her pocket, then scribbled something on the back. She placed it on the top. "In case you change your mind."

She studied Terra with a look that penetrated through Terra's lies. Valentina wasn't stupid, but neither was Terra. To hand this information over to someone like Valentina could be fatal.

"See you around." Valentina vaulted out of the window and disappeared once more.

Terra waited a few moments before she moved. She petted Skooch's head, the dog closing her eyes appreciatively. "Keeping that woman in one place is like trying to catch smoke." She looked at her side table and checked the alarm clock. The time read 6:43.

"May as well try to grab a few more hours, eh, Skooch?"

Skooch stretched her paws, then settled her head on the sheets once more.

Only when Terra awoke once more did the questions jump into her head.

It started with a dream.

Terra roamed the AJS station, the edges of her world fuzzy in the way that dreams make them, the other officers faceless and nondescript. The bullpen smelled of raw meat and trash bags, and there was an uncomfortable feeling in the pit of Terra's stomach.

She drifted through the halls, finding her way to the interrogation rooms. Although the doors usually had no windows, these had frosted glass. Terra could make out several people moving around inside. Some were in the AJS blues. Others were tougher to make out.

Terra turned the handle.

The door didn't open.

She knocked on the door.

No one answered.

Terra looked around her, finding that she was now alone in the hallway. The only feature that stood in clarity was the CCTV camera in the corner, a blinking green light flashing on its panel.

Terra turned back to the door and knocked again.

Once more, there was no answer.

Her heart beat faster. She wanted in. She could almost make out the muffled sound of Gary inside. A fuzzy shape looked as though it could be his lawyer, Catalina. Terra couldn't let him go again—wouldn't let him go. Scum like Gary was the reason that Atlantica had such a notorious reputation. People weren't supposed to play the law like a game of cards.

But it was, wasn't it?

Terra banged on the door. "Let me in!"

No answer came.

She banged even harder, this time following up by whacking her shoulder against its surface.

Still no reply.

Terra kicked the door. It didn't budge, not even an inch.

Still, that camera watched her.

An idea came to Terra. *APRIL, show me the footage inside. Go to the feed.*

Showing security camera footage, Interrogation Room B.

The world spun. Terra appeared inside the room, tucked away in the corner. She looked down at a sight that made her stomach curdle.

Captain Garcia sat with his legs crossed, resting his feet on the table. There was a cigar clamped between his teeth, and he was laughing. Beside him, Corporal Black sat, prim and proper, back straight, face passive.

Gary sat in the chair across the table with Catalina beside him, their hands on each other's faces and lips locked. To his left was another officer—one that Terra didn't recognize. Her hands ran over Gary's naked torso, fingers running through his chest hair. Terra felt sick. Garcia spoke, but the words weren't words, only sounds, and as Terra looked down into Garcia's eyes, they turned to her.

Ice washed over Terra. The intensity of that gaze drew her in. Her vision filled with the black pits of his eyes…

Then he was gone.

Terra stood alone in the middle of the street. The world was quiet and cold, cast in shades of monochrome. She looked around her at the frozen tableaux, and the civilians caught mid-step. The world glitched, shaking momentarily like an old VHS that hadn't been cared for.

"Where am I?"

The world answered by slowly coming to life. Civilians walked in step, caught as though in slow motion. Someone cried out, and the voice stretched like taffy. Terra turned to find a carbon copy of herself sprinting around the corner. A man raced away in front of her with a stack of bottles clutched in one arm.

They were only there for a moment. Then they were gone. The world glitched, and at that moment, Terra heard the explosion of an engine.

She turned and cried out. There was no time to move away from the motorbike streaming toward her. The ghost Terra sped straight down the middle of the road and passed through her, a cold wash following as their bodies met. The ghost Terra emerged on the other side, unfazed, speeding toward the car at the end of the block.

This is where it happens, Terra thought, remembering what she'd seen before. She didn't want to watch again. Who wanted to watch their body get blasted across the street?

The world glitched.

Motorbike Terra faded.

A car sped toward her—sped toward the running Terra. Terra watched as she dove out the way and the black Lamborghini skidded, colliding with the parked vehicle. Steam and smoke plumed from its hood. The Terra who wasn't the real Terra rose to her feet, only a few meters from the real Terra. She wore AI glasses and approached the car.

The world glitched.

They were gone.

The car at the end of the block caught fire as the bike skidded and collided.

The world glitched.

They were gone.

Terra approached the Lamborghini, a finger to her ear.

The world glitched.

They were gone.

The explosion came from the end of the block.

The world glitched.

The explosion came from right beside her.

The world glitched, Terra flickering between the two until she felt sick. She clasped her head and closed her eyes, confused, lost, and wanting to leave this place. She screwed her eyes shut, muttering, "Wake up, just wake up," to herself.

Then she did.

I need to see the CCTV footage from the night of the accident.

Showing CCTV footage, APRIL announced. Terra only had a brief second to see the light from the world outside before APRIL took her into the past.

The footage that APRIL showed was the footage she knew to be true. The bike skidding, the collision with the car. She knew that to be true, didn't she? Only after she requested for APRIL to bring her back to her bedroom did the sudden realization occur. One that unsettled Terra to her very bones.

CHAPTER EIGHTEEN

"You can hear my thoughts," Terra stated.

Affirmative.

There was no fanfare about it. APRIL stated the truth in the same way that Terra just did.

You can hear this?

Affirmative.

Every word.

Every word.

Terra lay there for a moment, a thin sheen of sweat on her head. Skooch snarled beside her, triggered by something Terra couldn't make out.

Since when?

Since my installation, APRIL replied. **Synchronicity with your cognitive and neural communication centers is a core part of my programming.**

Skooch growled and hopped onto Terra's chest. Her eyes roamed Terra's face, searching for the disturbance.

Can Skooch hear you?

Negative. It's believed that canines have additional and

improved senses to humans. It is likely that your pet can detect the cognitive anomalies in our communication.

Skooch sniffed Terra's nose, tongue licking up her face. Still, she snarled.

Threat level: fourteen percent.

You think Skooch is going to attack us?

I think there's a likelihood she may attack *you*. Canines are primitive and, at times, unpredictable.

Terra instructed Skooch to hop off the bed. Skooch was hesitant but eventually obeyed. She jumped to the floor, then sat and watched Terra with that same snarl.

APRIL, I'd like to ask again. Who else has access to my software?

Information is classified.

Terra frowned. *APRIL, show me the Atlantica Justice Constitution.*

A digital document floated before Terra's eyes. *Find any mention of "Human rights" and "Privacy."*

APRIL obeyed. **Displaying forty-three examples of requested words.**

Terra scanned the findings, eventually seeing the one that she was after. *It says right here: "Everyone's right to life shall be protected by law. No one shall be deprived of their life intentionally save in the execution of a sentence of a court following their conviction of a crime for which this penalty is provided by law. Everyone shall bear the right to privacy and the sanctity of free speech. Any attempt to invade privacy without prior consent or due reason under the eyes of the law shall be met with prosecution and will be deemed unlawful in the eyes of Atlantican jurisdiction."*

Terra went quiet, expecting a response from APRIL. When none came, she pushed, "APRIL, who else has access to my software?"

Information is classified.

Terra growled, then reached for the papers in front of her. She had every intention to hurl them, to screw them up in her frustration and toss them across the room, but her hands passed right through.

"We're going to have a problem, you and I," Terra declared as her mother strode into the room with a tray laden with breakfast and a drink.

Marie glanced from Terra to Skooch. "Do you need me to take her downstairs?"

It took Terra a moment to realize the connection her mother had made. "No. Thank you."

Her mother strode over and placed the tray on Terra's lap.

Engage civilian mode.

Civilian mode engaged.

Terra could see clearly again.

Marie sat at the side of the bed while Terra sipped her coffee. She studied her daughter's face carefully.

"Mom," Terra whispered. "You fuss too much."

"I worry about you. You're not telling me something."

Terra tilted her head.

"You don't have to tell me what it is." Marie looked smart in her slacks and shirt. Terra wondered if she intended to return to work today. "But know that I'm here for you.

"Your father and I…we understand what it's like to grow up in a place like this. The stresses and the toil that a job in law enforcement can put on someone. Hell, maybe your father knows better than me. Just know that whatever it is, you don't have to do this alone."

Terra scanned her eyes, waiting for the inevitable nudges her mother would make toward Terra needing to find a boyfriend to settle down with. She had dated a couple of guys and even a girl over the years, but things had never quite panned out. Nothing came close to capturing her heart in the same way that her work with the Atlantica Justice System did.

"Thanks, Mom." Terra played with the spoon, clinking against the side of the bowl.

"Don't mention it." Marie got up and left the room. A long silence followed.

Terra ate her breakfast, eyes flickering toward the card on the chest of drawers.

***

Terra's mother was right. She needed someone there for her to understand.

The options were becoming limited. Imani wouldn't respond to her messages, and it was probably for the best. Imani was her only connection to Garcia's precinct, and although they had been communicating daily about her progress into his investigation before Terra's accident, that would need to stop now.

Corporal Black had been another possible confidant, but there was something there that Terra couldn't trust, and she didn't know why. Someone like Slim would never understand what Terra was going through, and besides her parents, the only person she had left on her side was Skooch.

What about Santana? she thought. Santana Sokolov had been a close friend growing up in Atlantica, but time and occupation had drifted them apart. Occasionally they would meet for drinks when Santana wasn't out roaming the jungle or raiding tombs beneath the city, but for the most part, Terra barely saw her.

Terra flipped the card over in her hand. A crimson "V" sat on a black background, the top of the V connecting into the shape of a heart. On the back was the address of a coastline industrial estate—one that Terra knew pretty well. She just didn't know how Valentina did.

It was evening by the time Terra made her way across the city. Dinner with her parents met with a limited amount of small talk as Terra shoveled in her stew. This time when she left, they didn't protest. What was the point? They knew it would be useless to stop her.

Terra's Ducati roared through the city. She hadn't engaged APRIL since this morning, and as she navigated along the busy Atlantica streets, her mind whirred over.

She took a detour, cutting around Kingston Park and heading toward the site of her accident. When she arrived, traffic was heaving. She slipped through the gaps between cars and parked the bike curbside by the meter. She didn't put any coins in the machine. She wouldn't be staying for long.

She stood on the curb for a while, scanning the area. It was nothing like the footage she had seen, nor the dream that had plagued her mind the night before. The street was bustling with people everywhere. Car headlights burned her eyes. She stepped between two parked cars to get a better view of the intersection at the end of the street.

Her stomach flipped. Something was wrong, but she couldn't place what. Her head began to thump, a white spot appearing in her eye, no larger than the head of a pin.

She strode back onto the sidewalk and made her way toward the intersection, watching the road the whole time. In her mind's eye, she was walking with a slow-motion version of herself on the bike, trying to capture the moment when she lost control. But she couldn't. She just couldn't see it. The moment she neared the intersection, the memory faded and she couldn't grip it.

Her headache spiked as she homed in on the location of the explosion.

What the hell is happening to me?

Terra crossed the road. There was no sign of the crash, no indication that anything had happened here whatsoever. Cleanup crews were great in Atlantica, but often the rubber tracks on the road or tiny fragments of debris lingered for longer. A car had parked in the place where the footage showed the crash. Terra stood beside it.

Her headache dulled to a throb. She massaged her temple, almost tempted to ask APRIL to stimulate her temporal nerves.

This didn't feel like a time for the AI.

Terra drew a long, steadying breath and glanced up the street. For a moment, she thought she could see someone watching her from inside a parked car, but when she looked back, there was nothing there. Wanting to be certain, she activated APRIL.

Her left eye glitched before APRIL activated. Terra's headache spiked, hands moving to her head. If APRIL detected anything strange, she didn't say.

A thermal scan showed no one inside the car. Terra placed APRIL into civilian mode. Another glitch flickered as the information faded from her sight.

Something's not right.

Terra crossed the road, aiming for the place where her dream had showed something happening. The car had crashed here. Terra had dived out of the way, smoke funneling from the hood of the car.

Another glitch.

Terra hadn't even asked for APRIL.

Her headache grew with every step toward the site.

APRIL, are you still in civilian mode?

There was no answer.

Terra closed in on the site. She stood on the sidewalk and looked down at the road. The asphalt was dark, shadowed beneath the parked cars, but something glinted and caught her eye.

Glass?

Terra crouched. The people walking behind her commented in annoyance, but she wasn't listening. The closer she got, the more the tiny fragments glittered like stars.

What the hell?

Terra stood, dug her hands in her pockets, then crossed the road to her bike.

CHAPTER NINETEEN

Terra approached the coastline and slowed the Ducati. The engine rumbled gently beneath her as she passed the beachfront bars and restaurants and slipped down the side road toward a small outcrop of land littered with industrial factories.

There were no streetlights down here. The moon was a fuzzy orb above that highlighted the crests of the gentle waves. Terra made her way toward the building, knowing her way without direction. It hadn't been too long ago that she'd instructed a certain private investigator to hide out there.

Particle board covered many of the abandoned warehouse's windows. There was a chill of disuse as she opened the door and looked into a reception area caked in dust and decay. A door to the left hung crookedly from its hinges, giving a teasing look into the former factory proper.

This whole section was once filled with the founding industrial leaders of Atlantica, back in the seventies when the island was forming. It hadn't taken long for the businesses to up the ante and find a better location to produce. Terra wondered when the city would get around to demolishing or repurposing this area.

Behind the counter was a door with several locks in place. Terra stepped inside, her foot crunching on broken glass. There were bullet marks in the walls, though the damage didn't look too recent.

She tried the door. It opened.

A set of stairs led into darkness. Terra closed the door behind her, securing the locks in place. As she neared the bottom, automatic lights kicked on, flooding the place with light. Another door awaited at the bottom. She opened it and entered the underground safe house.

A kitchenette met her upon entry, with a small lounge attached. At the far right were two doors leading to the bedroom and the bathroom, and that was it. When the AJS had kitted out this safe house, it was only for temporary stays. There was nothing here for long-term comfort, merely the bare necessities.

A glass of wine rested on the kitchen counter. Someone rustled around in the bedroom.

Terra's hand went to the butt of her gun.

She moved slowly toward the bedroom. A shadow was visible inside although when Terra came around the corner and looked ahead, no one was in sight.

The bed, however, caught her attention.

Terra took a step closer, eyes homing in on the restraints fitted to the top of the mattress, one in each corner. A surgical tray sat on the side table with an array of small instruments.

Terra had a bad feeling.

"Don't be scared," a voice soothed.

Terra whirled and pointed the gun at Valentina. Valentina's pistol met Terra's. For a moment, they stood in tense silence.

Terra marveled at the woman, her appearance as pristine as ever. Valentina had hung her jacket in the wardrobe, but that was as casual as she got. Terra's nose was overwhelmed with a sweet perfume that made her light-headed.

"Lower your weapon," Valentina commanded.

"You first."

A grin grew on Valentina's lips. "On the count of three?"

They counted down and lowered their weapons, eyes unblinking.

"I wondered if you'd come," Valentina stated.

Terra raised an eyebrow. "You seem very prepared for someone who was unsure."

"I'm always prepared." Valentina looked at the bed. "Are you ready?"

Terra narrowed her eyes. "Ready for what?"

"Your examination." There was no humor in Valentina's eyes.

Terra drew a long breath. "What do you know?"

"Not a lot. Only that they've put something inside you. Something...*intelligent.* I want to know what it is."

Terra didn't know how to respond. How did this woman know so much? "Have you been watching me?"

"I do my research." Valentina strode past her and entered the lounge. "If you like, I can make you a drink first. Might take the edge off."

Terra's eyes lingered on the makeshift operating setup. She followed Valentina. "What have you got?"

"You're a coffee drinker," Valentina stated. "Black, am I right?"

Terra told her she was.

"Only, coffee doesn't numb the sting. You're going to want something stronger." She opened the fridge and took out a brown drink in a conical-shaped glass. There was a layer of white cream on top. "An espresso martini," she informed Terra. "Tastes like coffee. Burns like hell."

"My kind of drink." Terra accepted the beverage but set it on the table. "You need to answer some questions."

Valentina laughed, the sound splitting the quiet of the room. "I'm afraid you won't get many answers. I've trained to resist interrogation, and unfortunately, the spotlight is on you tonight."

She narrowed her eyes. "They've done something to you, and this intrigues me greatly."

"What do you know?" Terra asked.

Valentina nodded, then pulled open a kitchen drawer. She revealed a tablet, its display lighting the pale color of her face. "I know that you were admitted to Atlantica Central Hospital just a few weeks ago, following a car explosion.

"I know that your doctor was Lucio Sanchez, a former MVP from Johns Hopkins, who fixed a series of abrasions as well as repairing your spine and thumb. I know that spinal surgery is supposed to take weeks to heal, and yet you can run and walk and take a beating from me in the park." She looked up at Terra and grinned. "I also know they did more to you that they excluded from your medical files, and this intrigues me."

"How do you know?" Terra forewent all caution, seeing no point.

"I scanned you in your sleep," Valentina replied casually.

Terra opened her mouth to reply.

"Once again," Valentina interrupted, "I refer you to our talk on privacy." She stepped toward Terra, looking around her head as if trying to see through her skull. "What have they put inside you?"

Terra's head gave a dull throb. Her lower back bristled. Terra sat on the couch. Valentina sat beside her. She raised her glass of wine. Terra *clinked* her martini against it. "Here's to discovery."

For the next hour, Valentina quizzed Terra on everything she could remember in the days before the event and the days after. Terra informed Valentina all about the APRIL glasses, detailing their capabilities and how they had helped her bring in a wanted criminal. When she told Valentina about the temporal stimulation and the fact that Terra was knocked unconscious for half a day, she expected a reaction from Valentina. However, the woman was incredibly hard to read. Talking to Valentina was like talking to...

...like talking to a robot.

Terra told Valentina about the crash and losing control of the bike. When Valentina said that she already knew, Terra pressed her on how.

"Your AJS systems aren't half as secure as you think they are. A well-placed call at the right time to the right person can yield a lot. My profession is to deal in dirt. You'd be surprised how much dirt your fellow officers have on them. They'll do anything to cover it up."

Valentina told Terra that she had seen the footage of the crash. Terra's ears pricked up when Valentina announced, "It's beyond obvious that footage has been tampered with."

Terra met her eyes. "Tampered with?"

Valentina nodded. The wine stained her lips a darker red. "Look here." She tapped her tablet and the video feed displayed on the screen. They watched it through in its entirety. "See?"

Terra shook her head.

Valentina gave a knowing smile. "How about now?" She played the clip again, this time slowing it down to half the speed. Terra watched intently, determined to find something, but could see no fault. Her left eye flickered with static.

She rubbed her eye.

Valentina watched her.

"Now?" Valentina asked. This time she slowed it to 0.2x speed. Frame by frame the image of Terra on her bike progressed along the road. As she passed the place where the ghost crash occurred, the screen flickered with the same static.

"Wait," Terra stated.

Valentina paused it.

"Rewind. Slower." Terra's mouth fell open as, for only a couple of frames, both feeds of the crash appeared at the same time. Terra saw herself on the bike and saw herself on the road, walking in the bike's path toward the parked car at the side of the road. "There."

Valentina paused the feed. Terra's left eye flickered with static as if someone had turned off its signal. Her right eye, however, could see fine. She tried to close her left eye but found that she couldn't. Her body wouldn't let her. She put a hand over it, using her right to focus on what she was seeing.

"How is that possible?" Terra asked. She couldn't be in two places at once.

Valentina tilted her head. "Sloppy craftsmanship. I'm afraid to tell you, Terra. But you've been lied to."

Terra's head ached. A spike of pain shot behind her left eye. She lay back in the chair, groaning in pain. Valentina scrolled the image forward until only the original feed remained. Slowly, Terra's headache began to pass. The vision returned to her left eye.

Valentina gave a small nod. "They're covering up the truth, Terra. They have you wrapped around their little finger, twisting and bending the reality you believe to be true." Her eyes narrowed at Terra. "So, what's really inside you?"

Terra chewed her lip, meeting Valentina's gaze. For a moment, they simply stared at each other. Terra took a long sip of her martini, then wiped the foam from her lips. It was bitter, cold, and made her shudder.

"They've fitted me with an experimental AI system." The words sounded ludicrous as she said them. "The glasses...those APRIL glasses...they have advanced software designed to aid in prosthetics and neural repair. I..."

Valentina leaned forward, eyes pooling with interest.

"Everything those glasses are capable of..." Terra considered how to say the words. "It's all inside me. APRIL is part of me now. You're right. They omitted big parts of my surgery from my records. My brain was damaged and is now fitted with technology to fill in the gaps. APRIL connects to my hormone centers as well as my nervous system. She...she helps me, but..."

"But you can't trust her to be secure," Valentina finished.

Terra knew what she was thinking. It was the same look

Imani had given her in the restaurant. The only difference was that Valentina didn't appear scared or nervous. Valentina looked *interested.*

A smirk appeared on Valentina's lips. "I need to scan you." She reached into a nearby pack and brought out a long, wide paddle. After wirelessly connecting it to her cell phone, she held it up to Terra. "May I?"

Terra nodded, then got to her feet.

The scan was painless, with Valentina's face giving away nothing of her findings. She ran the paddles around Terra's body, the phone in her other hand creating an image of what was inside. Terra only caught a glimpse of red hotspots but remained still while Valentina worked. She trusted this woman for some reason she couldn't explain.

"Seen much of Dick lately?" Valentina's question caught Terra off-guard.

Terra bit back a retort as she realized what Valentina was talking about. John "Dick" Chambers, one of Terra's most endearing pains in her ass—although, it was Dick that got the pain in his ass the day she accidentally caught him in the cheek with her bullet. Served him right for being in the line of fire.

"No. Last I saw of him was…" Terra didn't finish, choosing not to disclose the evening she had lured a man back to his apartment and got caught in the middle of an explosive situation.

In the same way that the rules of law didn't bind Valentina, Dick Chambers was able to help Terra work her way into the dark crevices when he needed to. She hated to admit it, but they made a good pair on occasion. "A while ago."

Valentina gave an absent nod. She finished her scan.

"What's the verdict, doctor?" Terra joked.

Valentina was quiet as she pinched and tapped on her screen. Occasionally her gaze would stray to various elements of Terra's anatomy. Finally, she handed Terra the phone. "Here."

The image showed a 3D digital rendering of Terra's body,

complete with skeletal structure. While the bones were gray, bright red marks made up the places where Terra had replacement parts. One area in particular caught Terra's attention.

"Why is my spine glowing so hot?" Her hand absently moved to her lower back.

"We shall find out," Valentina replied. "To the operating table, if you please."

Terra glanced nervously at the door to the bedroom. "What are you going to do?"

"Examine you, of course." Valentina glanced at her watch, then turned her attention to the camera in the corner of the room. "I'd get a move on, too. Who knows who could hack into the camera feed at any moment."

Her eyes found Terra's with that same knowing look that put her on edge. Terra straightened her back and strode toward the bedroom. She paused at the door. "A word of warning. If you fuck any of this up, I'm coming for you. If you kill me, I'll make sure they will find you for me."

Valentina smirked. "Oh, sweetie. You're cute." She gave Terra a playful shove. "Now, go."

CHAPTER TWENTY

Terra writhed in modest discomfort.

It wasn't even that the exam hurt. It was more the thought that it should.

First, Valentina laid Terra on her back. Using an array of detectors and instruments, Valentina created a comprehensive image of the mechanisms in Terra's head. It was all painless until Valentina attempted to gain access to APRIL.

She leaned over the bed with a small box in her hand. Valentina eased it open, looking as though she was about to propose to Terra, and revealed a tiny square of metal.

It was the size of the nail on her pinky finger. With a pair of tweezers, she removed the chip from its box and placed it on Terra's temple. A small static shock pricked her skin.

"Ouch," Terra stated.

Valentina was unfazed. She set the box down, then slid a laptop from beneath the bed.

"You came prepared, didn't you?" Terra asked.

Again, Valentina ignored her. She tapped a series of keys, then turned to Terra. "What I'm about to do is risky. I want you to know that. I'm attempting to gain access to the software database inside the APRIL system. I can't guarantee it doesn't have defenses. Do you consent?"

Terra narrowed her eyes, resting her head comfortably on the pillow as she stared at the ceiling. "Yes."

"Good. I was going to do it either way," Valentina informed her.

Before Terra could reply, her left eye filled with static. A strange high-pitched squeal rang in her head. She tried to bring her hands to her temples, but the restraints bound her.

"Easy, Terra," Valentina soothed, calling as if from a thousand miles away. "Almost there."

Terra gasped for breath. Her muscles coiled as she strained at the restraints. The sound was awful, the static nauseating. She closed her eyes, but the static remained, flashes of light blossoming from an involuntary fireworks display.

"Stop!" Terra shouted. "Stop!"

Then it did.

"I'm in," Valentina commented softly.

Terra relaxed, breathless, and mentally wounded. She drew a few steadying breaths, then opened her eyes again. This time, a litany of information displayed before her. "What is this?"

Valentina glanced up from the computer screen. "What is what?"

"The script? All this 'bios' and 'execute' stuff?"

Valentina raised an eyebrow. "You can see what I'm doing?"

"In front of me?" Terra nodded. "Yeah."

Valentina grinned. "Fascinating."

The text continued to scroll as folders and segments of information were pulled into separate windows. Terra didn't understand any of it, computers and code had never been her forte, but she felt reassured knowing she was safe in the hands of someone who did—someone who could find the truth and hand it to her.

I deserve that much at least, don't I?

Valentina was silent as she scrolled and clicked and opened

the database stored inside Terra's mind. Valentina gave a satisfied grunt when her mouse hovered over a folder titled, "_security_A-JS_protocol."

"Bingo," she whispered.

A strange feeling came over Terra as Valentina clicked once.

"Wait..." Terra muttered. "Wait!"

It was too late. The moment Valentina clicked the second time, that high-pitch squeal returned to her head. Terra cried out, only able to see sparks and light as the squeal cut through her head. Valentina must have heard it too, as she fell back, hands clamped to her ears.

Database security breach, APRIL's voice cried amidst the din. **Unauthorized access to AJS Security Protocol. Unauthorized access to AJS Security Protocol. Initiating emergency lockdown procedure.**

Terra's breath caught. Her throat constricted. A spike of searing pain ran through her body, flaring at the junctions where her prosthetics fitted. Her back arched. Somewhere far away, Valentina spoke to her, but it was a muffled noise.

The lights peaked, blurring into one massive mass of white. Terra found herself pulled back to the dark space, the light at the end of the tunnel swelling, swelling, until all she knew was white.

The world faded away.

Terra's eyelids fluttered.

"Wha..." Her words were thick and ill-defined. She was exhausted, as though she had run a marathon without preparation. Every part of her ached.

Something clicked beside her, a tapping of keys.

Terra tilted her head to the side and peeled open her eyelids. The light from the laptop screen was harsh. Valentina was focused, eyes unblinking as she feverishly typed away.

Terra tried to swallow. It was painful. "What happened?"

"Security breach protocol," Valentina replied flatly. "A great way to ensure that no one fucks with your software."

Terra glanced at the ceiling, realizing that something was missing. "The code...it's gone?"

"No, it isn't." Valentina remained fixated on her work. "I've momentarily disabled the connection between your optical nerves and the database projections. It's just you and your brain, for a short while, anyway."

"That's impossible," Terra stated. "It's all connected."

"It's all connected, but nothing is impossible," Valentina argued.

Terra drew a long breath and attempted to stretch her limbs despite the bonds. "You're in?"

"I am." Valentina peeled her eyes from the screen, a seriousness in them that startled Terra. "They've done some serious research on this one, Terra. The code is...sophisticated. The AI is an offshoot of something I've only seen enter the public sphere in recent weeks."

A sadness fell behind those eyes. Terra wondered what Valentina had seen. "The script is written to work with your biology in a self-serving way. It will heal, enhance, and work with you to create the best version of you possible.

"All of those coffees you drink? You won't need them anymore. OSCaR has the ability to alter your biochemistry and keep you in top condition." Valentina shook her head in disbelief. "Whatever you think they've done to you, you're wrong. They're grooming you."

"Grooming me?" Terra considered this. "They want to make an enhanced law enforcement officer."

"Robocop," Valentina agreed. "It's not only a theory anymore. They're testing this on you."

"Why me?" Terra mused, not expecting an answer.

Valentina gave her one anyway. "Many reasons. Could be

because you're disruptive and work best solo, which provides a perfect candidate for trials. Might be your ability to want to tread beyond the lines of duty, so now they have a way to control you. Could be that you're dispensable.

"Someone in command doesn't want you hanging around all that long, so if this works, great. If it doesn't, they haven't lost a great deal." Valentina sat on the side of the bed and looked down at Terra. For the first time, she saw sympathy in those eyes. "I'm glad I managed to disable the system."

"Me, too." Terra offered a weak smile. "I hope that shit never happens again."

"I'll see what I can do." Valentina smiled. She hopped back down to her laptop. "Now, the OSCaR system is complicated, but there's nothing here to suggest that we can't make alterations.

"From this stack of folders, I should be able to override some of the AI functions—hopefully, they don't repair themselves, but there are no promises to be made. I'll also be able to lock down your transmitters to ensure that whoever has been accessing the database is kicked out permanently. Well, from that particular IP address, I mean."

Terra shook her head. "Wait… Hold on a second."

Valentina looked up.

"Two things," Terra stated. "First, it's 'APRIL,' not 'OSCaR.' Second, are you saying someone has been accessing my visual feed?"

Valentina smirked. "You're picking up the lingo. Great." Valentina turned the laptop screen to face Terra. "And you're wrong."

Terra wasn't sure what she was looking at until she found the highlighted text. "OSCaR? Wait, what?"

Valentina moved the mouse.

Terra continued. "Officer Security Companion and Report. What is this?"

"Must be a pilot name," Valentina mused. "Many programs

have them. They have a functional, on-the-nose alias. Then the marketing teams sex them up for better use." She chuckled. "Congratulations, it's a boy."

Terra hadn't realized she'd placed a gender on the machine, but now that she'd come to think of it, APRIL's voice had been neutral. She had associated the name with a gender for an inanimate object. "OSCaR..."

"Not so much a liaison tool," Valentina continued, "but a monitoring machine. The clue's in the title. As for your watcher in the background, you're looking at a user who is currently hiding behind an IP proxy service on the city's west side."

"You can't tell their name or location?" Terra asked.

"*You* can't." Valentina cocked her head. "I can. Once this program has finished running its course...and...there you go. Your man is watching through a machine that's registered to 421 Hawkseye Drive."

"APRIL..." Terra started, about to instruct before she remembered that she was currently disconnected. "Wait...Val, do you know who lives at that place?"

"Resident's details are kept private, it seems." Valentina raised an eyebrow. "I could do some digging for you."

"No, it's okay. Just shut them off from accessing my feed." Terra's brow creased. "The corporal promised me that no one was watching."

"You trusted a promise from a cop?"

"APRIL's scan performed a lie detection," Terra justified. "If the AI can't detect a lie, what hope does anyone else have?"

"Unless your corporal believed that what she was saying was true," Valentina offered.

Terra considered this. "That would make Black innocent."

"I highly doubt that," Valentina stated nonchalantly, busying herself with something Terra couldn't see.

"Then who's keeping these secrets?"

"I tell you what. It definitely won't be this guy." Valentina turned the screen to face Terra again. It showed footage from the lost tape of Terra's accident. There was no glitching or double-imaging. Everything was crystal clear, showcasing a set of events that corroborated with the events in Terra's dream.

Valentina tapped some keys and a scan initiated on the bystanders in the street. Terra dove out of the way of the car, and within moments she was walking closer.

"How are you doing this?" Terra asked.

"Lost file, thrown into the back of some cache docs." Valentina sighed. "The rest is playing with OSCaR's technology."

The view changed to Terra's point of view. She approached the car cautiously, steam and smoke funneling from the hood. A man with bloodied gums and multiple lacerations grimaced at her. A bubble of text appeared above his head that read, "Fernando Cross."

The man raised a hand and smiled. He thumbed a trigger, and the screen exploded in white.

Valentina sat back on her ass on the floor. Terra remained staring at the feed as it turned to static.

After a minute, Valentina asked, "A friend of yours?"

Terra's brow creased. "Impossible."

"You don't make friends?" Valentina asked.

"No, it's not that." She thought back to where she had heard that name, in a grainy piece of CCTV footage of an interrogation room and a blonde lawyer and... "Gary Clark...Fernando Cross is...was his employer."

Valentina looked at her curiously. "Well, seems like Clark got over his lost boss real fast."

Terra turned to the screen again. "Access the AJS database. Bring up information on Fernando Cross."

Valentina obliged. A moment later a profile appeared on the screen. Big red letters were stamped across the file reading, "Deceased," but that wasn't what drew Terra's attention. She leaned as close as she could while still restrained, eyes narrowing on the photo profile on Fernando Cross.

A man who looked nothing like the one in the car.

"How deep does this shit go?" Terra muttered aloud.

"Always deeper than you want it to. So much deeper than you want it to."

"Let me out," Terra instructed, attempting to sit up. The bonds held her securely to the bed.

"One more thing. You have to promise to cooperate. This might be the most interesting part yet."

Terra gave her a quizzical look. "The bar is pretty high."

Careful not to knock the chip attached to Terra's temple, Valentina helped Terra move onto her front. She unzipped the back of Terra's AJS uniform and revealed the flesh of her lower back.

A jagged scar ran across the lower third. Valentina moved slowly forward as her eyes filled with wonder. She breathed a sigh of amazement. "Impossible…"

Terra tried to look over her shoulder but couldn't see what Valentina saw. Valentina fished out a small compact mirror from her pocket and handed it to Terra.

At first, Terra could see nothing but the scar. Then she noticed the faint blue glowing light. It was tiny, only the size of a pebble, but it was there.

"I wondered how the technology would power itself," Valentina mused. "I've never seen them fit a human with Atlanti-core before." The skin around the power cell was soft red. Valentina pressed the skin around it. "Does this hurt?"

"No, it just feels a little warm. What does this mean?"

"I don't know," Valentina replied, finally stumped. "I think it means you may be the first human to stand a chance to live over one hundred and twenty years old."

CHAPTER TWENTY-ONE

Terra sat upright and rubbed the soreness from her wrists and ankles.

It hadn't been a painless procedure, but it was over now. Valentina severed the connection to whatever external source was accessing her feed and tweaked the AI system to disengage when Terra asked it to.

"The only way to initiate OSCaR is to say his name," Valentina informed her. "Otherwise, it won't be listening, and it certainly won't be transmitting."

When Valentina had finished her alterations, she took her tweezers and removed the chip from Terra's temple. That same static shock struck, but luckily for Terra, upon booting up the AI, the static and the awful shrieking noise was nowhere to be found.

Good evening, Terra.

Terra gave Valentina a cautious glance, then replied. "Good evening, APRIL."

Valentina cocked an eyebrow.

"I prefer APRIL," Terra added.

Terra stood and stretched her limbs. While she was aware that APRIL remained embedded in her system, it also felt like a weight had lifted. She thought about all that Valentina had unlocked for her, and as the Crimson Countess packed her things away, Terra offered, "If you ever need anything…y'know…as a thank you, let me know. You've done me a solid today."

Valentina blew air between her lips. "I wouldn't go that far. What I *have* done is angered whoever had tethered themself to you. I'm sure you won't be thankful to me in a day or two when they hunt you down and try to bring you in."

Terra nodded. "You didn't have to, though."

"Oh, I did." Valentina held up a memory stick proudly. "Got everything I need right here."

She swept past Terra and into the lounge. Terra's mouth opened slightly. "Is that…"

"A carbon copy of everything lodged inside your head?" Valentina looked at her smugly. "Yes, it is. You don't know this yet, but you might have the intel in your mind to help me rescue someone important. I can't thank you enough for that."

Terra took a step forward. "That information is classified. You have AJS profiles and data that is *not* for public consumption."

Valentina smirked. "I'm neither public nor have I copied your precious AJS files—I can get those in my own time. What I have done is taken the information from your biological AI." Valentina's eyes darkened again. "It may prove of some great use for me."

Terra chewed over this information, eyes narrow.

"If you're wondering if you can trust me," Valentina started, "then it's too late for that. Just to ease your curious mind, the answer will always be 'no.'"

Valentina moved to the door. She paused with her grip on the handle. "You'll be okay, Terra. Whatever is happening above you, they don't know the storm they've created. Go get 'em."

She ran up the stairs without another word.

Terra waited in the apartment a short while longer. Her headache was gone, and she felt as though she was free from a cage she hadn't remembered building. APRIL kicked into action upon restarting, and the pain and soreness were beginning to fade. Terra opened the fridge and found another martini waiting for her. She sipped it as she sat on the couch and processed what had happened. She thought back to Valentina's surgical instruments and wondered why they were here in the first place.

Probably for show, she mused. *Valentina is nothing if not an amazing performer.*

By the time Terra emerged onto street level, her stomach was rumbling. Her phone started vibrating as a wave of messages came in, her cell finally receiving a signal now that she was away from the thick walls of the safe house. Most were from Black, asking where she was, though one was from her mother asking her to call. She was worried.

Terra rang her mother and pacified her with a swift, "I was meeting a friend." There was a little truth in there at least. When she placed the cell phone back in her pocket, her stomach rumbled loudly. She hopped onto her Ducati and hummed her way toward the nearest restaurant.

Terra craved some steak.

She received another handful of calls as she worked her way through her sirloin. She drank several pints of water and cleared the check the moment she finished.

Black wanted her in the station, but Terra couldn't go back there. Not right away, at least. Something was going on here that she needed to figure out. If Black truly *was* uninformed about whatever was going on, it served her to remain blind to whatever Terra was about to uncover.

Full and satisfied, Terra straddled her bike and sped into the city proper. Hawkseye Drive was on the far west of the island, five miles out from the city limits. The city was winding down for the night, and Terra made good time as the city lights faded behind, and she emerged into the winding countryside.

It was rare she visited the spaces outside the city these days. Her life had been and always was the city. Only on a handful of occasions had she been this far into rural land, and they were school field trips to barns and farming estates and petting zoos.

Out here, in the middle of the night, Terra couldn't have felt more alone. The roads were dark, lit up in a single silver strip that wound like a river to the crest of the hills. Fields stretched for miles on either side, the soil beginning to bear the fruit of the crops. Agricultural machinery stood isolated on the earth like undead sentinels of long-lost tribes.

Then there were the stars. For the first time in a long time, Terra could make out some of the brighter of their number. The Atlantica fog filmed their clarity but was unable to cover them entirely.

Terra glanced up as she rode, marveling at the sky above. She'd heard that Atlantica was the only nation to be permanently shrouded in fog. She wondered what it would be like in England or Switzerland, Mexico, or Japan and what their citizens saw when they looked up into the night sky. She'd seen pictures online, but she didn't believe them to be real.

Terra passed through quiet villages with monstrous manors and fields teeming with livestock until finally, she found the small town she was looking for.

Hawkseye Drive was in the center of Peksytown, a town that consisted almost exclusively of local farmers and their kin. After Atlantica's founding and the rural areas became established, it didn't take long for the farmers to congregate and form a conclave. While on a clear dawn, the city limits were visible from afar, the farmers would always meet the view with a mistrusting eye.

Terra slowed down, aware of the second-floor lights that turned on in the hallways of the houses she passed. The noise of her Ducati was like a gong sounded in the middle of a library. Apparently, the residents weren't used to disruptions this late at night.

Deciding not to risk any further advance notice, Terra parked her bike in the gravel parking lot of a traditional-looking pub. The roof was dark thatch with a swinging sign reading, "Dancing Pony."

Terra dug her hands into her pockets and continued on foot.

"APRIL, direct me to 421 Hawkseye Drive," Terra instructed.

Arrows appeared in her vision, long trailing blazes of color that snaked along the road. A sidebar displayed her walking speed, walking distance, and the next primary direction.

"Thanks," Terra offered.

Don't mention it.

She followed the arrows for ten minutes before finally finding Hawkseye Drive. The road was wide, the sidewalk speckled with trees in blossom. When she reached 421, she remained out of sight of the CCTV camera attached to the large wrought-iron gate and studied the building.

"APRIL, show me who's inside." Terra narrowed her eyes.

Initiating thermal scan.

The world faded to shades of mostly dark blue around the house. Pockets of red became visible as the scan detected the warmth in each room. Inside was a single person lying in bed, tucked cozily in their sheets.

Terra looked up and down the street, ensuring no one was watching. "APRIL, show me the surrounding public CCTV feeds."

APRIL obliged. Terra viewed the street from several cameras embedded in the street lamps. She found two main entrances to the building. One was the iron gate at the front. The other was a small entryway at the back. Both appeared to be monitored by technology.

Terra chewed her lip. "How do I get inside?"

You are unable to enter a private residence as an officer of the Atlantica Justice System. To do so would result in—

"I know, I know," Terra growled. "I was thinking out loud."

That is talking.

Terra's lips thinned. "APRIL, shut down."

She expected the response to be an argument, but instead, the thermal imaging disappeared as did all of the writing and digital displays. Terra felt very alone.

"Wow, Valentina really did her job," Terra muttered.

"You're goddamn right," a voice spoke in her ear.

Terra whirled, looking around for Valentina.

"What?" Valentina laughed. "You think I wouldn't make a few modifications myself before leaving you to it?"

A hot flush of anger surged through Terra. "Are you fucking kidding me?" she hissed. "Do you realize what an invasion of privacy this is? What a violation of any kind of trust it is to have you speaking in my head?"

"And seeing through your eyes." Valentina corrected herself, "Eye."

Terra closed her left eye.

"Oh, calm down," Valentina replied, a chuckle in her words. "Look, I have to admit that you got me curious, okay? I know as well as you do that law enforcement can't break into a private residence without suffering some form of repercussion. We wouldn't want you to lose your job now, would we?"

Terra was stunned to silence, a thousand curses and insults bubbling at the back of her throat.

"Careful of those adrenal levels," Valentina cooed. "Wouldn't want you to do anything stupid."

Terra grumbled. "I am going to kill you."

"You'll have to catch me first." Valentina paused. "I meant it, you know? I got curious, and, despite what the world says about me, I have *something* of a conscience. You wanted to enter that resident's address?"

A *click* sounded. The red light on the iron gate turned green. The gates swung open. "There you go. Merry Christmas."

Terra's lips parted slightly. "How…"

"Don't ask. It's not breaking and entering if the front door is open." A *hissing* sounded in Terra's ears. "Don't mind that. The surrounding cameras are also disconnected, street-wise and residence-wise. Have at it, soldier."

Terra froze for a moment, unable to absorb what had happened. "Thank you."

Valentina replied softly. "Don't mention it. Oh, and for the record, I'm erasing my connection to you now. That doesn't mean I don't want an update on how this all plays out, considering that Gary and his associates also have a specific interest in one of my clients. Different threads of the same blanket, and all that."

"How do I know I can trust you to erase our connection?"

Valentina considered this. "I guess you can't."

Terra listened for a moment, but there was no noise. Valentina was gone. She glanced up at the streetlights, then at the gate. She steeled herself as she took her first steps up the winding pathway to the front door.

CHAPTER TWENTY-TWO

The front door remained locked, the security camera's light inactive.

Terra skirted the manor, following a series of bushes until she found her way to a side door. She tested the handle and found that the door opened.

No point locking the doors when the latest security hardware surrounds you is there.

Terra wondered again how Valentina had cut the feeds and gained her access. She figured it was better not to ask. There was a reason that Valentina was one of the greatest mercenaries this island had ever known.

The kitchen was the size of her entire apartment. An island counter with gleaming surfaces caught the spill of the outdoor lights. The white marble floor amplified each step Terra took. She tiptoed as quietly as she could, working her way toward the open lounge area where a cinema-sized TV took up most of one wall. A series of couches faced it.

Terra looked around, trying to gain her bearings, determined to make this trip as short as possible.

She knew it was a risk, but she tried it anyway.

APRIL, show me the blueprints of this property.

She waited in the silence. Nothing happened.

APRIL. Terra tapped her temple. *APRIL, activate.*

Valentina's words came back to her: "The only way to initiate OSCaR is to say his name. Otherwise, it won't be listening, and it certainly won't be transmitting."

Terra frowned. *Fine. OSCaR, activate.*

How can I help you today, Terra?

Terra rolled her eyes. *Show me the blueprints of this house.*

Pulling public archive records. Department of Planning and Development. Showing blueprints for 421 Hawkseye Drive.

A digital page floated in front of Terra. She scanned the various rooms and levels, creating the picture in her mind of where she needed to go. *Now activate thermal scan.*

Initiating thermal scan.

Terra looked above and hunted for the orange mass that had been the person she'd seen from outside. As much as she tried, from this angle, it was impossible to see. She did, however, identify three of the seven bedrooms on the second story.

Thanks, APRIL. The name felt strange on Terra's tongue, now. Valentina had ruined that for her, too. *Do you prefer being addressed as APRIL or OSCaR?*

OSCaR is my primary name. However, you may call me APRIL or any number of assigned alternatives. Additionally, you can request access by a different name entirely. My programming allows...

Okay. That's enough. I'll figure it out. Terra turned her attention to a large arch that led through to the hallway. She could see the bottom of a set of stairs that disappeared up and around the corner. *I guess the only way is up.*

Each step made a different sound as she scaled up. She eased pressure onto each creak and squawk, keeping her eyes peeled at the top of the stairs. Not even APRIL could help detect where the weak spots were.

A noise came from upstairs. Terra paused. She drew her pistol and kept it ready, hoping it wouldn't come to that. It was one thing sneaking into someone's home. It was a whole other thing to start a Wild West shootout.

The sound faded. Terra scanned the upper floors, but nothing moved. After a moment, she continued.

She reached the landing and was thankful to find it carpeted. It softened her footsteps as she explored the open area and checked inside each room. A grandfather clock on the landing was the only other sound source, delivering a rhythmic tick-tock with each pendulum swing.

At the end of the hallway was a neat white door with a golden handle. Terra advanced on the door, able to see some of the objects inside. She spied the four-poster bed with the shape beneath the duvet. There was a chest of drawers and a large green rectangular box that she imagined to be a wardrobe of sorts.

Terra drew a steadying breath. *APRIL, keep your guard up, okay?*

Keeping guard up. Systems ready and alert.

Terra opened the door.

The bottom of the door whispered against the rug. Terra eased herself inside, the darkness providing a perfect cloak for her arrival. She pushed the door closed and waited.

There was no disturbance.

She crossed to the bed, eyes fixed on the mass of reds and oranges and yellows. She expected the shape to rise and fall, but nothing moved. She stood by the bedside, weapon readied. She reached for the top of the duvet and pulled it back.

The bed was empty.

Switch to night vision.

Switching to night vision.

The colors changed into shades of green and black. Terra examined the bed and found no one inside. She searched around her and paused when she heard footsteps behind.

"Don't move," a voice commanded. A figure moved to a switch against the wall. Before Terra had a chance to register what was going on, the lights switched on. Painful light flooded her vision. She clamped her left eye shut, the right one fuzzy from the disorientation. A woman stood next to the wardrobe with a gun aimed at Terra's chest. Terra swung her Glock to face the woman.

"I said, don't move!" The woman jabbed her pistol forward. Terra recognized her instantly, and it wasn't simply because APRIL was displaying the information around her body. It was because Terra had seen her before, in a digital recording of an interrogation room.

Confusion washed over Terra. She glanced at the wardrobe, realizing then that it wasn't a wardrobe. Instead, it looked like a large steel coffin of sorts.

Catalina Rubio followed her gaze. "Handy, isn't it? A portable safe room. Well, they say 'portable,' but that bastard is heavy. It's lead-lined, meaning that nothing gets in and nothing gets out. Handy when one wants to evade the reaches of technology and frequencies and signals."

It was odd hearing these words from the mouth of a woman wearing delicate white lingerie. Her shorts were short and matched her cropped top. If she hadn't been holding a gun, Terra might have been a little disarmed at her cutesy appearance. "You knew I was coming," Terra stated.

"No. That was a complete surprise to me, but I have my backup systems for when someone tries to hack into my security." Catalina held up her cell phone, which vibrated in her hand. A large red message read, "Security lines compromised."

"Seems there's a lot of breaching of technology going around these days." She gave Terra a knowing look.

"Put your weapon down," Terra commanded. "Whatever the hell is going on here, let's talk. No one needs to get hurt tonight."

Catalina narrowed her eyes. For a moment, it looked as though she was going to resist. Then she lowered her pistol an inch. "You first."

Terra held her gaze and brought her weapon down. Her muscles were coiled, ready to strike if she needed to, but Catalina followed suit. Soon their guns were down by their sides.

"You're smart," Terra stated.

"How do you think I make my living? I know a little better than to attack an Atlantica Officer for Justice, even if they *did* break into my house."

"The gate was open."

Catalina smirked. "Funny that." She waited a moment. "Would you like a drink?"

Terra didn't answer.

"Very well." Catalina crossed to a dressing table where she sat and crossed her legs. "Let me guess why you've come all this way, Terra. You've been digging in places that don't concern you, and someone fed lies into your head. You think you've unlocked Pandora's box and found a road map, but I can tell you for certain that what you're searching for isn't here."

"What am I searching for?"

Catalina smiled. "Answers. You want to know more about what you think you've discovered in that mental box of yours. You want to know the..." she waved air quotes with her fingers "...truth about the APRIL AI and what you think you've seen in the ghost of the machine."

Terra raised an eyebrow.

"Don't think I don't know all of my clients' secrets." She nodded at a wall of plaques displaying titles that read "Most Successful" and "Gold Star Credited," with several variations of the word lawyer engraved. "I'm what they call a 'superstar' in the profession. I've spent my life building labyrinths so that my clients can hide. My mind and my work is a titanium crate, impenetrable. I'm the all-seeing eye, yet my lips stay stitched closed."

"That's too many metaphors. Makes you sound needy. Desperate."

Catalina chuckled, a pretty sound. "Well played. The truth is, Terra Kris, that whatever you're hoping to get out of this little encounter, you won't find here."

"The IP address linked to this address. That tied your address to the invasion of my personal privacy with a system on-site used to access my visual feed so you can snoop on an AJS officer. I can already tell you that things don't look good."

Catalina's smile didn't fade. "I'd like to see you prove it." She stood, then paced around the room by the large sash window. "The world is full of proxies and decoy IP addresses. Many of my clients make their living by providing secure ways to surf online. Although you might have severed the connection, you only created a momentary break in the chain."

Her mirth dropped, her expression momentarily pitying. "Your error to make, I suppose. It won't be long before my clients fix what's broken."

Terra clenched her jaw.

"So, other than to tell you that you can't have what you want, is there anything else I can help you with?" The smile returned to Catalina's face as she stopped and stared at Terra.

Terra glanced at the dressing table to where a laptop sat closed. She drew her pistol, catching Catalina off-guard. Though there wasn't time for her to pull her weapon, she composed herself quickly. "You shoot, and I'll make sure that you spend the rest of your days rotting in the cells filled with the very scum you captured."

Terra nodded to the laptop. "Open it."

Catalina raised an eyebrow. "You won't find what you think you're looking for."

"Open it," Terra repeated.

Catalina crossed to the laptop and flipped it open. She typed in her login details, then spun it to face Terra. "All yours."

Terra moved closer. Catalina's fingers twitched, but Terra held her weapon on her. When she was close enough to smell her perfume, Terra grabbed her arm, twisted it, then released the pistol from her grasp. She kicked the gun, and it slipped under the bed.

"Unprovoked assault," Catalina muttered. "Check."

Terra chuckled. "Unprovoked? You aimed a weapon at an officer."

"You broke into a private…" Catalina started smugly.

"I know, I know," Terra pacified. She instructed Catalina to sit on a small stool near the window as she turned her attention to the laptop.

She had no idea what she was looking for, but she started her search in the places she believed to be most obvious. She scanned the top folders, but nothing jumped out to her as strange. She tried to open the email account but needed fingerprint verification.

Catalina rolled her eyes. Terra told her to log in. Catalina pressed her finger to the pad in the top right corner.

Emails appeared in a long row on the screen. Terra scanned through them, but once again they were all above board—mostly exchanges between clients and written in some kind of code. Terra had to hand it to her. Catalina was thorough.

"Are we done yet?" Catalina asked, tired and irritated. "I have early meetings tomorrow so I should get my beauty sleep."

Terra raised an eyebrow, then returned her attention to the computer.

She looked through the search windows, typed in any key terms she thought might be relevant until finally, she gave up.

She sat back, defeated and a little embarrassed. Catalina offered that same smug smile. "Well, if that's everything, Officer

Kris, I'll kindly ask that you get the fuck out of my house before I report you to your precinct."

Terra's lip curled. She was about to step away when a voice whispered in her mind, "Wait…"

Terra frowned as a string of commands appeared before her eyes, one letter at a time as if someone was typing in her mind.

"Find the 'Run' option, and type this," Valentina instructed.

Terra offered Catalina a glance, then turned the screen out of her eyesight. She typed in the command as Catalina's smug expression faded.

Terra hit "Enter."

The screen jumped to Catalina's email program. What had before been a neat column of nondescript exchanges now opened up as chunks of text appeared beneath the main body of the messages, written in bright green. It was as though the code she had run had expanded the conversations like an accordion, highlighting lost and hidden pieces of text.

On many of the messages, the names had changed as well to reveal alternate aliases. Terra's eyes jumped to "Fernando Cross," written along the top of several recent exchanges.

"Interesting." Terra leaned closer to read the messages. "For a man who was recently confirmed dead, you and Fernando Cross seem to be having many digital interactions." Terra spun the screen to face Catalina. "I think we have a lot more to talk about than originally thought."

Catalina's eyes grew wide. She exploded into movement, sprinting toward the bed where she dove and stretched out her hands to find her pistol.

Terra jumped off her chair and pursued. She grabbed Catalina by the ankles and yanked her back. She was light but athletic, her grip on the carpeted floor strong. She kicked at Terra, almost catching her cheek, but APRIL assisted in avoiding the blow.

"Get off me!" Catalina cried.

Terra drew her back, the woman's fingers inches from the

gun. She put more distance between the two, remaining conscious of the fact that Catalina's short shorts were beginning to fall.

Terra pulled. Catalina came closer. She kicked and wriggled, but Terra overpowered her. She pulled her to her feet, receiving a couple of blows from Catalina's swinging arms, but she felt no pain from them.

Terra spun Catalina and pinned her arms behind her back. "So much for our truce," Terra declared. "Guilty conscience?"

Catalina struggled, then finally fell still. "You'll still have a hard chance proving anything." She grinned, then turned to the computer screen. "Computer, execute command protocol omega."

The computer screen turned black. "Good luck turning over evidence that doesn't exist anymore."

It doesn't matter, now. Terra thought. *It's all recorded and captured in my head.*

In her head, she saw Fernando's name. She saw his email address, as well as a series of numbers that had appeared below his email signature.

A dead man talking? I'm very interested to see what such a man has to say for himself.

Terra twisted Catalina's wrist to the point of pain. As Catalina writhed, Terra reached for the pistol and took it. She rose, both guns trained on Catalina. She retreated to the door, walking backward. "You call the dogs, and you won't survive the night."

Threat level ninety-seven percent. Hostiles on your six.

Terra glanced over her shoulder and looked at the hallway floor. Half a dozen glowing red shapes appeared in her vision, people stalking the downstairs rooms.

"What if the dogs have already come?" Catalina crooned with a smirk.

CHAPTER TWENTY-THREE

Terra carefully closed the door and stepped back toward Catalina.

APRIL, give me all the intel you've got.

The AI had limited data, with only enough information to show the internal body temperature of the advancing team, plus their audio levels and current speed. Terra examined the room. APRIL noted the available exits and showed her survival probabilities if she leaped from the windows or found a way to climb into the attic above their head and rush out.

The onslaught of information was overwhelming. Terra hoped she would be able to get used to it eventually, but that all depended on if she could survive the night. Her cell phone vibrated in her pocket, but she ignored it.

Catalina sat on the edge of the bed, arms and legs crossed. "Time's up, cop. Such a shame that you're about to become the latest victim to Atlantica's most proud rule: there is no law on private property."

Terra glanced her way. "It works both ways."

She rushed to Catalina and hooked an arm around her neck. She dragged her to her feet, Catalina's eyes straying to the metallic thumb. The group scaled the stairs, and they could both hear the creaking of the wooden panels with each step.

"You should really get that seen to," Terra stated. She aimed the gun at the door and waited.

Enabling escape route projection access. Updating available options.

The arrow that had lined the floor from Terra's feet to the doorway faded as the orange blobs reached the bedroom. One of the figures turned and raised a finger to their lips.

Terra whispered in Catalina's ear. "Tell them that you're okay. Tell them that you're safe, and you don't need anyone."

Catalina remained silent.

Terra gripped her tighter. A small sound escaped Catalina's lips. "Is someone there?"

A gentle knock sounded on the door. "Ma'am?"

"It's okay," Catalina called out. "Accidental trip of the wires. I'll get it fixed. Then I can go on my vacation to Barbados."

Terra rolled her eyes. "Really, a codeword? You think I'm stupid—"

The door burst open, yielding under one man's boot. They were black-clad, their faces all covered except their mouths. It reminded Terra of SWAT teams she had seen in movies, though there was no seal or badge of allegiance on their shirts. They crammed in, one after the other, raising their voices into an almighty din in an attempt to confuse and distract Terra.

Her focus was Zen-like. APRIL dealt information on each man and woman spilling into the room. Terra fired a warning shot at the ceiling, keeping Catalina between herself and the enemies.

"Freeze!" Terra held the Glock to Catalina's temple, Catalina's pistol gripped in the hand looped around Catalina's neck. "Or your employer becomes paste."

They halted, gathered around the doorway. One of the enemies on the fringes of the group took a slow step to the side.

"I said freeze!" Terra barked, barrel pressing into Catalina's head.

A central figure raised a hand but kept their weapon steady in another. Dark black hair spilled down their back beneath the helmet. Dark purple lips spoke. "Let's all remain calm, shall we? No need for anyone to spill blood tonight. Just release the hostage, and we can let you go."

A red warning flashed in Terra's vision. "Liar."

Terra didn't need the warning. She could tell a liar from a mile away. "Let's try this from another angle," Terra retorted. "How about you guys step the fuck back, leave us alone in the room, and I'll make sure that the next time you knock on the door, I'm a million miles away."

The central woman grinned and gave a tiny head tilt. "Where's the fun in that?"

She fired. Terra felt the air shift beside her as she ducked behind Catalina. Catalina screamed. "You assholes. Get her, not me!"

Terra peeked out once more. This time, she shot at the woman's foot. The woman cried out as the bullet shattered her foot. She fell back into the group, who lowered their weapons to catch her.

"I warned you," Terra stated. "I'm not fucking around. This could be easy, or this could be difficult."

Two of the enemy growled, one on either side of the cluster. Terra knew that they had the best chance of grazing Terra. While she was thin, she was nothing compared to the woman she held. Was it worth the risk for them to try and graze Terra's arm or hip? How good was their shot?

Warning, APRIL announced, **Threat level rising: ninety-nine percent.**

No shit, Sherlock, Terra thought.

An amazing thing happened, then. The bubbles of information around the attackers changed. Terra didn't need their names and social security numbers at that moment. What she needed was an exit strategy.

APRIL provided her with one.

Numbers appeared above each of their heads. In her left eye, red spots appeared in flashing pulses on locations across the attackers' bodies. It reminded Terra of the videos she often saw at bowling alleys after the first go, in which an animation showcased the best-case scenario for the second turn—knock down pins five and six with a little curve to the left.

APRIL had given her a road map.

Terra marveled at the images. One of the attackers took a step to the left, and the numbers changed, giving a real-time view of where to go from here.

I would recommend making your move, Terra.

Terra felt her hand twitch slightly, an involuntary response.

I don't want to kill them.

Then follow the plan.

There was nothing more that needed to be said. Terra glanced around the group and acted. As the commanding officer gathered herself and barked her instructions, Terra swung her aim to the guy on the left.

She shot. Her aim was true, catching the guy slightly above his right hip. The shot should only puncture flesh, leaving the organs intact and undisturbed.

Should.

The man's eyes widened before the pain exploded. He crumpled to his right, eyes wincing with pain. Terra spun toward the glowing number two, seeing it all unfold as if in slow motion. The group slowly reacted. Terra pulled the trigger.

The shot caught number two in the thigh. She aimed slightly off-center to ensure she missed the bone. As number two went down, she searched for number three.

Catalina screamed in her ear, struck with a sudden pulse of fear. She writhed, this time throwing Terra's aim off.

When Terra shot at the shoulder of number three—APRIL detailed that the Kevlar padding in the shoulders should be enough to stop the bullet penetrating the skin—Catalina lurched.

That was an eventuality APRIL hadn't prepared for. As Terra's hands tried to auto-adjust their aim, Catalina jogged her shoulder, and the bullet missed the mark. It flew straight past the attacker and found the wall instead.

Recalculating. Duck and cover.

Terra tucked herself behind Catalina as shouts all became muffled, chaotic noise. Outside, lights turned on in neighboring houses, curious neighbors attempting to witness the fireworks display. Terra was thankful the light was off in the house.

One of the attackers dove to the side and shot. The bullet aimed straight at the side of Terra's chest. The bullet struck her hard, the hexagonal honeycomb of nano-Kevlar pockets flaring into their protective action. The bullet bounced away, impotent and non-penetrating, but that didn't stop the pain from the force of the shot.

Terra wheezed as her hand slipped from Catalina's throat to find her side. There would be a bruise the size of a melon in the morning—if she made it that far.

Catalina jumped forward, clearing Terra's reach. Along the way, a bullet sailed past her, almost clipping the back of her head. It sped through a ream of blonde locks as Catalina dropped to the floor with a scream.

Terra was exposed.

Threat level: ninety-five percent.

Best show me what you got, then. Terra winced as a cold wash of adrenaline flooded through her. The pain of her attack numbed. The room, while dark, fell into a strange mystical clarity. There were three of them left unmarred, and it was up to Terra to neutralize the threat.

Her arm moved as if of its own accord. The numbers reset,

the new number one staring at her behind the dark lenses of the mask as he pulled the trigger.

Terra spun to the side, arm swinging out as she scanned for her target. She pulled the trigger, the bullet finding its home in the man's bicep. He dropped to the floor, hand clutching the entry point, falling onto his comrades.

Number two was now the first woman. She seemed to have forgotten about her foot as she sat up, propped herself up on one hand, and fired a round of shots. Terra sprinted across the room, leveraging herself up on the bed as she sprang to the other side. The arrows guided her toward the lead-lined box. She snuck behind it just in time as metal hit metal and the bullets *pinged* off.

She tried to see through the box, but the lead blocked her thermal readings. Terra peeked around the edge, then quickly retracted as more bullets came her way.

"Get her out of here," a voice cried as Catalina whimpered on the floor. Terra heard the shuffling sounds of someone scooping Catalina up and carrying her into the hallway.

That only left the frontrunner woman and one target who had yet to be incapacitated. Terra drew a long breath, eyes narrowing as her body flooded with cortisol and adrenaline.

Your window is open.

Terra poked her head around the corner. She recoiled again as metal collided with metal.

Your window is closing.

Thanks, APRIL. I'm just trying to avoid becoming a human Swiss cheese, Terra thought as arrows appeared on the floor, flashing and pulsing toward the direction of the nearest window.

A window that was open.

You're going for literal, huh? Terra asked.

Literal aids effective communication in high-pressure situations.

Thanks, Dexter, Terra thought.

Your window is closing.

Terra looked at the open window. It wasn't closing. It was very much open.

Three.

Two.

Terra made a break for it. She flinched as metal struck metal behind her. The room blurred as she launched, arms stretched before her, body straight as an arrow. She passed through the gap, emerging into the chill of the outside world. The moon was murky above her. Neighbors pointed as her shape appeared.

Terra looked down. She was twenty feet off the ground and rapidly descending. She passed over a row of bushes that lined the house.

Tuck your head in, APRIL commanded. **Fold your back. Aim for the pond.**

Terra questioned this maneuver, wondering how deep a pond would have to be to absorb the impact of her fall. She imagined it would need to be deeper than the one she was looking at. Still, she obeyed, ducking her chin to her chest.

As she did, her body moved of its own accord, hands reaching around to tuck against the knees and knees bending to her chest. She tumbled head over heels, a human cannonball as she flipped. When she righted, her feet splayed out and hit the water.

The splash was significant. A couple of koi sprang out of the water. The liquid slowed Terra's ascent, but it was the soft, slushy bottom that took the rest. She bent her knees, her whole body momentarily disappearing beneath the surface. There was a stink of algae and mud. As she breached the pond and clutched for the edge, much of the water flooded her throat.

She pulled herself out, the chill air freezing her clothing. She coughed and spluttered but picked herself up nonetheless. Shouts from behind reminded her of her attackers, and as she dove for the nearest bushes, gunfire rained down.

The bullets tore the turf into large divots. Terra faded into the shadows, shrinking behind an abandoned, rusting trashcan that had long overgrown with foliage. When the gunfire stopped, and the attackers reloaded their magazines, Terra crawled through the undergrowth toward the neighboring fence.

She stood, masked by leaves and tangles. APRIL's thermal scan showed her that the two gunmen were heading into the house and down the stairs. The shapes of Catalina and her savior were farther away on the lower floor as they sprinted toward an unmarked van.

APRIL, shut down. As soon as the AI complied, Terra turned and scaled the fence. She flopped into the neighbor's garden. A light flicked on in the back. An older woman stood bathed in the rear porch light, and her shotgun was unmistakable.

"You're trespassing," she declared as her eyes flicked toward Catalina's house.

Terra held up her badge. "AJS. I'm not here for you. I'm leaving now."

The woman considered this for a moment. She chewed a hunk of tobacco, then spat it on the ground, her eyes unblinking. After a moment, she gave a subtle nod. "Make sure that you do."

Terra skirted the fence until she reached the back. She jumped up, climbed over, then made her way back to her motorcycle after initiating OSCaR, remaining low on the off chance that Catalina's guards were hunting for her.

CHAPTER TWENTY-FOUR

Terra's phone vibrated as she parked at the AJS precinct and switched off her engine.

Wow. Took a dip in the pond and this thing still works. The phone companies weren't lying about waterproof technology.

The sky was dark. Small raindrops speckled her face. It was refreshing, the clean water washing away some of the stink that came from her dip in Catalina's pond. She thought about the fish and wondered if they were okay. There was no turning back to check.

The station was quiet at this time of night. The typical bustling activity of the changing of the guards had long passed, and as Terra walked up to the front doors, she was thankful. She checked her phone and was unsurprised to find over two dozen missed calls and messages from Black.

Terra pocketed her phone. She strode straight past Custer at the front desk, who was busy writing something on the whiteboard behind him.

The bullpen was almost empty, with only a handful of officers sitting at their computers or completing their paperwork on their tablets. The air was melancholy, the room quiet. Only a couple of eyes looked up as she passed, but they quickly looked back down.

Terra strode toward Black's office but stopped as she passed the unisex toilets and found Tommy Vincenzo emerging from the door. His head was down as he fastened his belt, almost running into her.

Terra stopped ahead of the collision. "You haven't washed your hands."

Tommy smirked. "You been watching me?"

"No. I can smell it."

Tommy stood straight, making a point of keeping his thumbs tucked into his belt. "What's your problem, Kris? Looking to advertise that you're a robo?"

Terra's lips thinned. How much did they know around here? Although her trust for the AJS and its officers had always walked a very thin wire, recent events had made her question everything she was seeing. Were they in on it? How many officers knew about her implants and AI installation? Was she a guinea pig that the rest of the world was watching?

"Stunned to silence?" Tommy scoffed. "Unusual for you. You're normally the life and soul of the party. Could never get you to shut up and listen, and we only went on one operation."

Terra's nostrils flared. "Unless you want me to report your bad hygiene habits to the rest of your pigshit crew, I suggest you step out of my way and watch where you're going in the future."

Terra shoulder-barged past him. She paused when he called, "Not my fault that the angel of justice has broken her wings." It was his laugh that did it. That mocking schoolyard laugh brought Terra back to moments in the playground where the other kids had doubted her and called her a weirdo for knowing what her career path was years before she could pursue it. A laugh of doubt and sick humor. "How's it feel to spiral down to earth with us mortals. Must be crushing."

Terra spoke between gritted teeth. "Careful what you say..."

Tommy pushed on. "You still haven't hit the ground yet. Rock bottom is on its way to you. Won't be long until you realize that you belong at the bottom of our pile. I've seen women like you, thinking you can play in the bigger world, but you can't. They all fall eventually. Sooner or later you were going to crash and burn, and I'm glad someone finally had the balls to—"

"Don't you fucking say it," Terra warned.

"Blow you out of the sky," Tommy finished.

A moment of silence lingered between them. Terra's lip curled. Tommy's smug grin spread.

Terra took a step toward him.

Initiating biological equilibrium.

Wait a minute, APRIL. Terra grabbed Tommy by the collar. Her metallic thumb pressed under his chin. "You better watch your back. Because no matter what you say, I'm treading all over it on my way up." She threw him, Tommy's back crashing against the wall. A framed certificate slipped and fell to the floor. Tommy looked at her in alarm, surprised by her strength.

"Okay, APRIL. Equalize me," Terra commanded, turning her back on Vincenzo. *I'm really reaching the point where I no longer give a fuck who knows.*

Gina wasn't at her desk when Terra burst into the office, nor was the corporal at hers. Terra sat at Gina's desk and started her computer. A log-in screen activated.

"Val, if you can hear me now, I'd really appreciate some help." Terra waited a moment, but no reply came. Terra typed a few possibilities for usernames and passwords, but it was pointless. She would never be able to figure it out. "APRIL, any clues?"

Terra expected a no, but instead, the office disappeared. Terra whirled as she raced along a series of CCTV feeds, passing through the city as if jumping from source to source. The station fell away and the landscape blurred by until soon Terra found the corporal.

She viewed her from far above, the light of the moon casting an eerie spill on the construction site. Large steel girders formed the frame of one of Atlantica's latest additions to its skyline. On one of the floors high above the ground, Leonie sat on the concrete, tied to one of the beams by thick coils of rope.

A group of men and women sat at a makeshift table nearby, a smattering of cards across the table. Bottles of alcohol were littered around, and pistols and revolvers rested on the tabletop.

The world lurched to another camera that faced Leonie.

Corporal Leonie Black identified.

The corporal was unconscious, head lolled and eyes closed. There were bruises on her face and a cut on her cheek. In the distance, cars drove by blissfully unaware of what was taking place above them.

A thought crossed Terra's mind. "APRIL, how have you brought me here?"

Atlantica privacy versus public protocol is only active for completed builds.

Terra shook her head. "That's not right."

A page flashed before Terra, a series of laws and legislation relating to Atlantica's most notorious laws. She scanned the document, but there was no need. APRIL highlighted the section that fitted its purpose.

"Son of a bitch." Terra grinned. "You found a loophole." In all of her academy training, her superiors had informed her that the rule applied the moment an area of land became private. According to this document, until the first person officially walked through the door, everything on the land was public property. "Just more and more coverups," Terra mused. How much more of what she'd learned was a lie?

Terra turned her attention to the group sitting at the table. A handful played their card game—poker, by the looks of it. A couple of guards roamed the makeshift boards that composed the floor, assault rifles strapped to their shoulders.

There were no walls in place yet, only a system of pulleys for bringing equipment up and chutes for sending debris down. Before Terra needed to ask, labels appeared around the seated guards, defining who they were and their criminal history.

Gary Clark sat among them, face shadowed but not impervious to APRIL's scan. Terra's blood boiled at the sight of him as a line of possible events came to mind on what must have happened.

"APRIL, show me the footage from the interrogation rooms where the officers brought in Gary Clark, timestamp anywhere from last night to now." Terra closed her eyes, hoping to avoid the lurch. When she opened them, she was in the interrogation room, looking from the same camera she had seen Gary and Catalina from before.

The corporal was nowhere in sight. Officer Hewlett and Officer Dunston sat in the chairs across from Gary, who rested comfortably with his arms folded and a smug grin.

"You've ensured your systems are inactive?" Gary glanced at the camera.

"We have," Hewlett replied. "That doesn't mean you're going to be able to get away scot-free. This is a private chat between you and us, and here's where you confess and let us know all the things we can convict you for."

"You don't know?" Gary asked.

"Oh, we do," Dunston replied. "We want to hear it from your lips. Makes our job a little easier."

They laughed like goofy frat boys after wolf-whistling a passing girl. Terra felt nauseous. No wonder they were one of the lowest-performing pairs in the goddamn precinct.

"I want my lawyer," Clark stated.

"You can have your lawyer when we fucking say you will," Hewlett barked, exploding in a sudden rage of fire. "We've shut down the systems. Now you give us what we want. We can all then go on with our happy little lives."

"Yours behind bars, of course," Dunston crooned.

Clark laughed. "You really are clueless, aren't you? You and all your pig pals are going to pay for wasting my goddamn time. Once or twice I get, but this is bullshit now."

His smile faded, brow creasing. "Lawyer. Now."

Dunston leaned across the table, lacing his fingers together.

Really? Good cop, bad cop. Did that ever work anymore? When Terra worked her routine in the big leagues, it was bad cop, bad cop. She and Imani made a dream team busting the lid off the scummy filth they dragged into their quarters. But this... This was painful to watch.

"Look, Clark," Dunston started, voice soft and soothing. "We know that you're in deep shit. We've seen your file notes. A bunch of problems you've involved yourself in that you've somehow wormed your way out of. If you comply with us on this one, we'll get you sorted again. Come on, give us something. Make it easy on us, so we can make it easy on you."

Clark pinched his fingers together and slid them across his lips.

Hewlett slammed the table with his fist. He stood and kicked his chair back. He rested both hands on the table, "All right, enough of this shit—"

"Officer Hewlett, Officer Dunston, you are dismissed." Corporal Black stood in the doorway, face calm, voice level. If there was one person that Terra admired in this shithole station, it was Black. The way she could command a room without raising her voice spoke volumes about her character. Even if Terra had her doubts about the corporal's intentions, there was no denying that she was a badass.

"But, Corporal," Dunston muttered.

"Now." Black held the door open and waited. Clark's grin spread wider.

Dunston and Hewlett turned back to Clark. "We'll be back."

Black shook her head. "No, you won't."

Their eyes narrowed, frustration and anger pointed at Black.

Still, they obeyed without question, slinking out of the room together.

Black waited until they were a distance away before she closed the door behind her. For a moment, the silence filled the room.

"Good news, I hope," Clark asked.

Black's face clouded. When she met his eyes, there was an intensity in her stare. "You are to be set free. I am to guide you to your safe place."

Clark stretched, then stood. "About time." He fixed his gaze on the corporal. "If I have to go through one more so-called 'interrogation' and leave with only a numb ass cheek from these elementary school chairs, we're going to have a real problem."

He stopped beside Black and looked up into her eyes. "Your people need to know to leave me the fuck alone."

"How would you propose we do that?" Black asked.

Clark didn't answer as Black opened the door and the pair of them filed out.

"Follow them," Terra commanded.

APRIL obliged. Although Terra couldn't hear the sound, she didn't need to. The two walked in silence, passing Custer in the lobby whose eyes quickly found the desk, then emerging into the night and aiming for Black's black SUV. Black got in the driver's side, and Clark got in the back.

They left the station.

For the next few minutes, Terra hopped between CCTV cameras, pursuing the vehicle. There was no urgency or anything to alarm her until they neared the construction site.

A casino stood nearby, its front illuminated in an array of flashing neon dollar signs. Black slipped down a side road and toward the parking lot at the rear. A dozen or so cars had parked there, and Black found a spot in the middle.

For a moment, they remained in the car, hidden behind the tinted windows. It was another five minutes before they eventually emerged. Clark skirted the SUV and stopped by the driver's side window. He said something to Black. Then, as she rolled her window up, he stuck his hand through and grabbed her collar.

She fought back, giving as good as she got. Her elbow caught Clark in the nose. She punched, just missing with the second blow.

As this was taking place, the other parked vehicles shook. Doors opened, and a group of people clad in black rushed out, guns pointed at Black's SUV. She managed one more blow to Clark's head before she rolled the window up and kicked the SUV into gear.

The wheels screeched as she reversed. Shots fired. The tires blew. The SUV rolled on metal, sparks flying until the car came to a standstill. Terra had to give it to her. Black gave it a good try.

They zeroed in on the SUV like raptors closing in on prey. They waited a moment as Clark approached and yanked on the door handle. Black had locked it.

A brute who was almost twice as wide as the others approached with a tire iron. He swung at the windshield. The glass cracked. He swung again, and the glass yielded a small hole. Black shot and caught the man in the shoulder. He grunted, switched hands, and managed one final swing.

Clark beamed.

Black's lip curled.

She lowered her gun and unlocked the SUV.

They dragged her from the vehicle.

The next few minutes of footage, Terra watched as they dragged her toward the construction site, pounding her in the chest, head, and face along the way. They weren't gentle with her, by any measure. At one point, Black's head rolled back so far Terra worried her neck might snap.

Terra watched until they tossed Black by the girder and wrapped her up. She hadn't been aware that she was growling.

She asked APRIL to stop the broadcast, then was surprised to still be in Black's reception.

The walls were close, pressing in on her. Papers littered the desk. Someone stood in the doorway.

"Terra?" Gina asked, her face a mask of concern. "Is everything all right?" She looked a little scared, clutching a tablet to her stomach, white legs poking out from her Burberry pencil skirt.

Terra looked at the computer as if only now realizing what this all looked like. "I wasn't trying to hack your computer." She blurted out the words before she could stop them.

"Okay. May I sit at my desk?"

Terra squeezed out and swapped places with Gina. Gina's eyes kept flickering to her curiously. "Did you need something? Corporal Black is currently out of the office and won't be back until the morning."

Terra eyed her with interest. "Do you know when she'll next be available?"

Gina logged into her computer. "She has a thirty-minute slot at eight tomorrow. Does that work?"

"Perfect." Terra spun, then walked out of the office. As she strolled along the hallways and past the bullpen, one single thought niggled in the back of her mind. *How did Gina know that the corporal would be out of office when someone had taken her employer? Wouldn't Black have had plans inside the station if she hadn't crossed paths with Clark?*

As Terra straddled her Ducati, she tapped into APRIL. *Show me footage from inside Gina's office.*

Unable to show footage inside secure rooms—

"System override," Valentina stated.

"You're starting to freak me out," Terra muttered softly enough that her colleague strolling up the path to the station couldn't hear. "Are you deleting your access or not?"

Valentina didn't reply. Instead, a camera feed of Black's reception room commanded Terra's attention. Gina was on the phone, her eyes flicking to the doorway.

Amplify sound.

Amplifying sound.

"You have company," Gina stated softly, her words minimal and precise. "Terra Kris. She's coming."

Terra chewed her lip as she revved her bike into action. The engine roared, exploding sound around the parking lot.

Recommendation for future course of action, APRIL stated. **Quieter vehicles will ensure the element of surprise. I recommend taking your licensed AJS motorcycle.**

Terra twisted the accelerator as the engine growled beneath her. "What if I don't want the element of surprise?"

CHAPTER TWENTY-FIVE

Gary Clark examined his cards.

It was difficult to see them straight, the numbers and suits blurring into one another at random. His breath stank of sour whiskey, yet he reached for the glass to add more on top of the copious amounts he had drained. The brisk air cut through his jacket and would have made him shiver had he been sober, but at least half-cut, he was numbed to its attack.

The others waited patiently. The city hummed around them, but the men and women around the table were quiet. Gary was a small man, but he had never let that stop him. He had always found a way to worm himself into the company of greater men and use them as his shield. He could see the fear etched into each of their eyes, fear they were trying to hide, but couldn't—the fear of the Cross.

Gary tossed a chip into the center of the table—green, expensive.

He sat back in his chair as the rounds went around again.

Toni took her time with her play, her face an almost perfect mask of ambiguity. She was his competition in this game, not the other three.

Jack, Dean, and Kevin were worms at heart. Cross had their dicks by a string, and they knew that one wrong move would cost them their lives. It was a house of cards, the entire operation, one move at the top affecting everything else on the way down. Gary had no idea what Cross had on them, but the stains of their dark veins spoke tales of ink and addiction.

Were they high now?

Who cared.

As long as they got the job done. As long as they guarded the asset and ensured that she came to no harm. At least not until Cross arrived.

"Call it," Kevin announced, the final round of play reaching its end.

Gary won, predictably. He grinned as he scooped the pile of chips toward him, then clamped a cigar between his teeth. "You bitches want one?" He offered a handful to the group. "It's the least I can do for skinning you raw."

They accepted. He handed around the cigar cutter, and they chopped the ends in turn. They lit their cigars, then exhaled their clouds of smog around them. The wind carried the smoke toward the unconscious AJS corporal. Gary studied her, ensuring that she was sufficiently bound and tied and unable to find a way to escape.

He had made that mistake before.

The city chattered, engines humming and the faint bump of music coming from the nearby clubs and bars. Gary glanced at his comrades. "You know, if this were ten years ago, I'd be down there right now, flashing my ID and heading into the bars to try and cock my leg on some dumb bimbo." He scoffed. "Didn't do too bad for myself at one point."

Jack glanced at the table with a smirk.

"Problem?" Gary asked.

His smile faded. "No, no problem."

Gary held his gaze. "Good." He looked at Kevin. "Deal."

As Kevin dealt the next hand of cards, an engine rumbled in the distance. Gary checked his hand. "Can't say I miss too much of it these days. Pissing away my money by pouring it down some lass's throat. We got it good now, pals. We have the run of the city. I'm telling you, you don't know how lucky you are to be here right now."

He looked at Toni, who was doggedly staring at her cards. "Six times they've arrested me in as many months. You know how many convictions I've had?"

"Zero," Jack stated.

"Zero," Gary repeated. "You folks keep the Cross with you, and you'll be walking specters, invisible to the naked eye of the law. Remember Monopoly? Remember that 'Get out of jail free' card? Stick on the right side, and you'll have immunity for life." He chuckled, his gaze straying to the cop. "Unlike that bitch."

The sound of metal grating on metal came from below. The group turned their heads toward the bright headlights of a gleaming vehicle rolling slowly onto the site. Two shadowy figures closed the gates behind the car, then disappeared into the darkness.

The car rolled on, finding a parking place beside a crane that stretched to the upper levels of the building. A long steel cable trailed down to the ground, only a few feet from the edge of the open floors. Gary puffed his cigar and smiled. "Master's here."

The car door opened, then closed. They continued their game of cards as a troop of individuals walked across the packed earth and beelined for the stairs. Their ascent was loud, the hard soles of shoes clapping on the concrete foundations. Gary glanced up as a man appeared at the front of a group of men and women all wearing black suits.

The man was as tall as Gary was short. He had a tuft of blonde hair flicked up at the front and a pair of glasses that sat neatly on the bridge of his nose. He was in his late twenties, with an athletic figure beneath his casual black t-shirt and denim jeans.

He looked like one of the latest of a line of entrepreneurs who had taken a leaf from Zuckerberg's book.

"Evening, Cross," Gary announced, calling from his place at the table. "Glad you could join us."

Fernando Cross' face read no emotion. He scanned those sitting at the table. "I see you're all taking this job as seriously as I imagined you would be."

The others shifted uncomfortably. An eerie silence hung in the vicinity, though the engine continued to grow in volume.

Gary chuckled awkwardly. "We're just passing the time. She's all secure and waiting for you, just like you asked." He pointed to Corporal Black. "Had to rough her up a bit to keep her in check, but she's there and waiting for you."

Cross glanced at the Corporal, then back to Gary. "No one followed you?"

"No," Gary stated, pleased. "None of those AJS assholes suspected a thing. Of course. This ain't our first rodeo."

Cross nodded. "Good." He clicked his fingers, and one of the guards behind him stepped forward. She reached inside her jacket pocket and drew out several small vials of a black substance that sloshed inside the glass containers.

She tossed the vials to each person in turn. The guards standing around the space caught them excitedly, then tucked them in their pockets. She threw one to Gary, then one to Toni. She followed with Kevin and Jack, but when she threw to Dean, he was unprepared.

He waved his hands, but the vial bounced off his palm. He fumbled in the air as he tried to recover it, but the glass smashed on the concrete. The black liquid looked like tar, its color deeper than the black of the night sky.

Dean fell to his knees, pawing at the substance as if he could pick it up and find another bottle. Glass fragments caught in his hand, and small trails of red painted the floor.

"No, no, no, no," he mumbled, head moving closer to the spill.

Cross watched in fascination. In one final desperate plunge, Dean stretched out his tongue and lapped at the liquid. He grunted as glass embedded in his tongue, his eyes rolling back as the ink entered his system and began work immediately.

Clark looked down with disgust. It was like watching a famished dog lap at the only dregs of food it could find.

Dean grunted and moaned until only a grey and pink stain remained. When he finished, he sat back on his knees and swallowed painfully. He looked up at Cross, eyes shimmering. "I'm sorry, I should've—"

Fernando Cross fired. The long silencer suppressed the shot to a *pop* and smoked at the tip afterward. Dean's head exploded, splattering everything around in pink, grey, and black matter. Only shreds remained of his neck. His body folded forward, looking as though he was bowing in peace, though not a single part of that could've been peaceful.

Everyone looked down at Dean with passive, unsurprised expressions. Cross' eyes were fixed on his target, his hand steady. He holstered the gun, then turned his attention to the corporal.

The engine roared. Gary frowned, turning toward the source, unable to see where it was coming from. Occasionally they would hear the rumble of jet engines passing over the city, but this sounded lower, at street level.

"She's certainly a specimen," Cross murmured as he crouched before the corporal. He scrutinized every inch of her, eyes narrowed. "You'd think a bitch would learn a thing or two about her place."

"To give her credit, it wasn't her," Gary commented. "She let me free. It was one of her lackeys who brought me in. Some bitch by the name of Kris."

A flicker of something crossed Cross' face. His lips turned a lighter shade. He nodded thoughtfully, then ran a finger across the corporal's cheek, affectionate and delicate.

Her eyes flickered. She peeled them open as she regained

consciousness. When she saw the man staring at her, she struggled against her bonds, her mouth gagged, a muffle coming from behind the cloth.

"Don't fret, sweetie," Cross crooned as if addressing a waking six-year-old. "You have nothing to worry about as long as you sit and play your part. After all, isn't that what you should have been doing?"

Black stilled, eyes wide and fixed on Cross.

"I'm going to lower your gag now, Leonie." He moved his hand to her mouth. "One false move and we'll have a problem, okay?"

The corporal nodded.

"There." Cross cocked his head. "Now, tell me why you let your dogs drag one of my men in yet again? Haven't we had this discussion?"

Black's voice was weak. "What are you talking about? It wasn't me."

"Oh, I know who it was," Cross replied. "I'm very aware of who it was. The problem is that you should have trained your pigs better, shouldn't you? I'm not sure how many times we have to have this conversation before you start to see things from our perspective."

Black was confused. Her brow creased. There was little understanding behind her eyes.

"Don't act innocent. You could have cleared the records. You could have told your staff to avoid any call of my men. You could have listened to your goddamn superior and paid closer attention to the idiots who serve beneath you."

Black shook her head weakly as if trying to dislodge her weariness. "Who are you?"

Cross scoffed. He leaned in closer until his nose was an inch from Black. "I'm the puppet master. You think you serve a higher power. I'm the power that towers above them." He chuckled.

"Your shitty little precinct sits in my pocket, and there's fuck-all you can do to stop it."

Black's lips opened and closed. Her head drooped. "You're an asshole," she managed.

Cross nodded. "Yes. Yes, I am. But that won't matter for long."

Black's eyes faded in and out of focus. She rested her head against the pillar. "So, what's your plan with me? Give me a solid beating and throw me back to the wolves?"

"No, not at all. I've spent a good many years building the links in my chain. I've learned how to deal with the weak links that keep breaking and dragging the rest of us down. I cut them off. I break them quickly. I find new connections and forge a stronger handhold on my portion of the city—and have no doubt that this portion is mine."

Black gave a thoughtful nod. Then she spat.

Cross remained still and stoic. He wiped the spit off his cheek with his arm. "That's fine. Take all the shots you need. I only need one."

He stood to his full height, pistol aimed at Black.

"Why wouldn't you get your lackeys to do it?" Black asked as the engine rumbled louder nearby. "Why come all this way to take me out yourself?"

"Two reasons," Cross replied. "Because I like to bear responsibility for my actions."

"And second?" Black asked, steeled and unshaken under the gaze of the gun's mouth.

"Because Garcia told me not to." There was no hint of mirth or irony in his eyes.

The engine revved and roared, accompanied by the sound of squealing tires. All heads turned toward the nearby road where a motorcycle sped by, its headlight illuminating the way ahead. Although they couldn't make out the person on the bike, the metallic blue armor shone under the light of the streetlamps.

Gary stood, his knees knocking the table. Poker chips and

drinks spilled and rolled to the floor, an amber puddle adding to the pool around Dean's fallen body.

The bike hooked a sharp right, curving around the edge of the building site. The headlight shut off as the bike disappeared into shadows, but the sound trailed on. There was a loud sound like a gunshot, but it could easily have been a *pop* of the bike's engine.

Gary turned to Cross.

Cross frowned, lowering his weapon. "Who is it?"

"I don't know," Gary replied, though something in his gut gave him a sneaking suspicion as to who it could be. "Sir, you should clear this place. If it's AJS…"

He glared at the corporal. "One of yours?"

"How am I supposed to know—" Black stopped as Cross kicked her face. Her eyes rolled back, and her head lolled.

Cross turned to his guards. "Untie her. Bring her with us. She can't leave our sight, not with what she knows."

They obeyed, two of them working together to untie and drag her body across the floor.

Cross fixed his gaze on Clark. "Destroy them. Whoever it is. Stomp them out like the cockroaches they are."

Gary nodded, drawing his weapon.

They marched out to the sound of the roaring engine.

CHAPTER TWENTY-SIX

They advanced on the bike, a dozen of them stalking in the darkness across the muddy ground and past the construction vehicles.

They blended into the night, a swarm of assholes homing in on their prey. Their guns led them. The bike engine rumbled, its sound echoing off the nearby buildings and magnifying its growl. They approached the chain-link fence, much of it covered by signs that advertised the construction company's services. One man waved and muttered something, and the others approached the nearest vantage point.

They peered into the darkness, straining to see. One figure scaled the barrier and hopped down on the other side. They shouted something that Terra couldn't quite make out.

She watched it all from across the construction site, over at the far corner to where the bike sat idle. She had hopped off as it was still moving, kicking down the kickstand in the hope that the Ducati would stray a few more meters and come to a standstill. She had whirled, running as far from the motorcycle as she could, finding the farthest break in the chain-link.

There she snuck in, watching them from afar as the confusion settled in.

Suspicion level: one hundred percent, APRIL stated.

No shit, Terra replied. *That was the plan. APRIL, activate scan and help find the corporal.*

Terra's vision filled with an array of information, from thermal signatures to weapon identification to descriptions of each person and their names. She was sure that, if she had time, she could sift through each of the guards in turn and pull out their files, find *something* to convict them all of that didn't include assaulting an AJS officer.

That would soon come.

The thing that caught her eye the most was the cluster of shapes running down the stairs and over to a black BMW on the far side of the lot. A name stuck out to her: "Fernando Cross."

Terra's eyes narrowed. Her blood boiled.

Your anger levels are rising. Initiating equilibrium protocol.

Terra calmed although her eyes remained fixed on Cross. *APRIL, zoom in on that vehicle. Get me a license plate number.*

Terra's vision zoomed in of its own accord until the faint outline of a license plate registered in her eyes. APRIL took a snapshot and started processing the information.

Vehicle: BMW XXI, estate. Registered...

Not now, APRIL. Save it. Find me Black, first.

Scanning area.

APRIL explored the area, eventually zooming in once more on the area around the car as the bodies piled inside.

It appears that the closest body signature to Corporal Leonie Black is here. An arrow led the way to the vehicle, where Terra vaguely made out the shape of a limp body hanging over someone's shoulder.

"Oh, shit," Terra muttered.

Some say that swearing is the lowest form of intelligence.

"Shut your gums." Terra sped up as she made her way to the nearest steel girder.

She hid from view as a shot fired by her motorbike. She looked around the girder as the BMW's headlights turned on and the car doors shut. Breaking cover, using the darkness as her cloak, she narrowed the gap between herself and the vehicle.

The SUV rumbled to life. Terra was fifty feet away as it slowly rolled into action. She ducked behind the pillar. Voices shouted by the motorbike, someone confirming that she was nowhere in sight

Terra knew time was running out. The crowd dispersed, the dark figures turning to explore the site as they cottoned onto Terra's plan.

"I need to stop that vehicle," Terra muttered as the BMW skirted the shell of the building, staying away from where the bike was. It clung to the fence, hiding in its sign-covered shadow as it worked its way closer to Terra.

Areas of interest highlighted on the car, an orange glow over the charging point, the tires glowing a hot red, the windshield lighting in a pale yellow with a target in line with the driver's head.

Those are your available options. Red is preferred. Yellow is least desirable.

"You're amazing."

Thank you.

She lined up her Glock and shot at the tires. She fired three times at the front driver's side, and the tire blew out with a *bang*. The car leaned to the front. Cries of alarm came from behind the tinted windows.

Terra ducked behind the girder. From here she could see the figures running toward the source of the sound. Terra had to act fast.

She broke cover, moving across the dirt to hide behind the rectangular shape of a port-a-potty. Through the plastic, she could still see the thermal signatures of those in the vehicle.

APRIL amplified the audio as a passenger instructed the driver to locate a particular button on the dashboard.

They pressed the button. A rush of air entered the tire as the car righted itself and a thick black paste covered the holes. The engine revved, and the SUV lurched forward.

Terra groaned. She shot three more times, but the car was in motion, hooking a hard left as it careened toward the fence.

The hood smashed through. A tangle of the fence panels dragged behind as the BMW merged onto the road. Terra ran after them, but the vehicle weaved between the traffic, the fence freeing itself as it caught on another car.

Shit.

A shot fired. Terra glanced over her shoulder as a crowd of figures sprinted in her direction. She had some distance on them, but it wouldn't last long.

She passed through the gap the BMW had made, took a hard right, and skirted the construction site to the first corner. A set of rose bushes sat outside the front reception of the building that stood across a small footpath. A water fountain was nearby. Terra had a flashback to her visit to the koi pond. She ducked out of sight, tucking herself into the thick cluster of bushes.

Figures emerged through the gap. They slowed, looking in all directions. Someone shouted, then pointed in Terra's direction.

From where she sat quiet, she could see each way along the perpendicular angle of the site. On her left was the shadow of her bike, toppled onto its side. There, a handful of people climbed the fence and stalked around the perimeter, looking for their invader.

Not that any of it matters. The assholes have gotten away.

Negative. Terra blinked, and her left eye filled with CCTV footage of the BMW streaming through the city.

Terra smiled. *APRIL, I have a lot to thank you for.*

Justice is my duty.

Mine, too.

Terra lay low as the groups spread out across the site. She needed to get to her bike if she had any chance of getting away. It was either that or risking hailing a driverless cab to the curbside and being shot at in public.

Plus...What about these assholes that need to be held accountable? she thought, eyes straying to find Gary Clark's label hovering in her eye line.

Terra took a steadying breath as she eyed up her possible paths ahead. *Hey, APRIL?*

Yes, Officer Kris. What is your request?

I've just about had it with the amount of people standing in the way of answers and justice. Would you mind assisting me in seeking revenge on a motherfucker who should be in prison by now?

Revenge is not the primary motive of a law enforcement officer, Officer Kris.

I know. But capturing criminals is, isn't it, APRIL?

Affirmative.

Terra grinned. *So let's do it. I want to see how useful you can be. See Gary Clark over there?*

Affirmative.

I want to bring him in. Will you help me?

Affirmative.

Terra's breath was taken away as her vision filled with additional information, all directed toward one single purpose: bringing Gary Clark to justice.

Target: Gary Clark. Threat level: eighty-three percent. Armed and dangerous. Path of greatest success, front gate.

That seems unlikely. It's never the front gate.

APRIL repeated herself. **Path of greatest success, front gate.**

*Okay, let's do it. Tell me when...*Terra instructed.

A few seconds passed.

When.

Terra rose from the bushes and sprinted toward the front gate. Four figures were dawdling around the entrance, assault rifles strapped to their chests. Terra's legs and arms pumped, her veins coursing with an increase in adrenaline. As she brought her pistol up, she felt APRIL's guiding touch as the hot spots appeared on the bodies of those ahead of her.

She pulled the trigger.

Her shots found their targets, catching the figures off-guard before they could react. Terra was twenty feet away in the darkness, her bullets catching their weapons, their hands, their fingers, disarming them as she approached.

She closed in on the closest guard and threw a right hook with her shooting hand, smacking the gun barrel across his temple. The next came to the attack with his hand a mess of blood. Terra turned, raising her leg to mid-height as she booted him in the chest and sent him backward. The third came at her side, and she twisted out of the way of his attack before bringing her elbow down and catching the center of his back.

One more remained. The final guard scrambled on the ground for one of the dropped rifles. Terra saw him as only red circles of color as she kicked once more, catching his cheek with the top of her foot. He spat saliva and blood as stars filled his vision, then lay still.

Terra took no time to celebrate her initial victory as her gunshots raised the alarm of the others on the site. Bullets pinged off the chain-link fence around her as they shot blindly into the dark.

Terra broke into a sprint, heading into the compound where she aimed for the enormous crane that stood at the building's side.

She dove behind the monstrous tracks, then rose to her feet. She pressed her back to the metal, using APRIL's thermal scan to track the others around her. There were a fair number of them running toward her. The others slowed as they arrowed toward the fence and the source of the shots they had heard.

Terra looked ahead, finding a pyramid stack of girders

awaiting placement on the building. She broke cover again, sprinting for their protection, closing in on the concrete stairs that would take her toward Gary.

Three guards waited, crouched on the first floor. A nearby forklift with its metal prongs a foot off the ground caught Terra's attention. *APRIL, are those keys I spy?*

Her vision zoomed. **Affirmative.**

Great. Terra crossed to the forklift, picked up a stray chunk of rock, and climbed inside the cockpit. She twisted the key in the ignition and brought the equipment to life. Despite the aroused cries behind her, she put the machine in gear with a steady hand and pressed the rock to the gas. The forklift rumbled forward. Terra twisted the steering wheel until it was aiming at the entry-way, then hit the bright headlights.

She leaped out.

The machine picked up speed, its engine whining as it made its way toward the group. It wasn't the fastest, but the light and the sound offered enough of a distraction that Terra could turn her attention to the stairs.

She sprinted. The only light on-site came from the few lanterns that littered the floors of the building. As Terra approached, she knew she was making herself a target, and she would have to be quick.

The three guards on the first floor waited patiently. Terra scooped up a handful of rocks, catching her nail on one hand. A spike of pain soon faded beneath the surge of adrenaline. APRIL guided Terra's hand for the throw, the rocks going ahead of her and skittering across the concrete landing.

The figures popped out of cover, aiming their weapons at the disturbance.

Terra's head came into view. She jumped the last few steps, twisting to her left as she fired at the nearest guard. She caught her in the shoulder, the guard loitering so close to the open edge of the floor that she tumbled backward, flipping over herself as she careened toward the ground.

Terra skidded upon landing, APRIL dragging her aim to her right. The second guard spun, looking for his target. Terra shot. The bullet knocked the pistol from his hand. She fired again, catching him in the shin. She scrambled to her feet, aiming for the nearest steel pillar.

A shot fired. Pain flared on the side of her thigh. Terra gasped but continued. The nano pockets did their job, yet she knew she would now have another bruise to add to her growing collection.

The second set of stairs lay beyond the final guard for this floor. APRIL warned Terra of the approaching group that had escaped the path of the forklift.

It's all about momentum. Keep moving. Terra glanced up to the third floor where Gary's legend hovered in her sights, surrounded by his team of guards. A thought struck her. *APRIL, have you got an exit strategy figured out? I feel like this is a one-way trip to Endsville.*

Confirmed.

Are you going to share that with me? Terra asked as another shot caught the girder, its collision vibrating sound up to the top of the building.

Negative.

Terra raised an eyebrow.

Focus on the job at hand.

Shouts came from the bottom of the stairs. *Fine.*

Terra ran from the cover of the girder, her arm swinging out as she shot at the final guard. The first attempt missed by millimeters, but her second shot caught him in the hip. He fell back, head smacking the concrete as Terra sprinted for the second set of stairs. Her hands straying to her utility belt where she found another magazine and reloaded her Glock.

Ten feet from the bottom of the stairs, the guards behind her reached her level. Terra lowered her head and beelined for the ascent until APRIL called in her head. **Change of direction. Left.**

An arrow appeared, and Terra instinctively followed. She ran from the illuminating light of the lanterns and into the darker pits of the large, open space. The arrow pointed into the dark, but as APRIL enabled night vision, the scaffolding came into clarity for Terra.

The builders had marked an area for an elevator to fit, the square column of open space currently fitted with a series of connected metal bars. Shouts rang from behind, and shots fired into the dark.

Terra leaped toward the closest bar, her hands finding grip against the metal. She swung, allowing herself to fly across the twenty-foot drop as she caught the next bar. She scaled her way up, head appearing above the second floor.

The guards on this floor had no idea where Terra was. They gathered around the stairwell, ready to shoot at whoever emerged. Terra continued her ascent until she reached the third floor.

She slowed, minimizing her noise as she exited the scaffolding. She padded across the third floor in the darkness, working her way toward the bubble of light that surrounded the poker table and the place where Terra had witnessed an unconscious Corporal Black tied to a girder.

Gary waited in the shadows, caught between two pillars spaced an arm's width apart. Three guards surrounded him, their aim held to the top of the staircase.

The disruption below only grew.

Terra hurried onward, knowing she couldn't mask her steps forever. She narrowed in on Gary, her Glock leading the way as the shadows cloaked her. She tucked behind girders as she passed, using them for her cover, slaloming along the floor until she was close enough to get a clear shot.

Terra stopped by the nearest pillar, ducking behind as one of the guards turned.

Suspicion level raised. Careful, Terra.

Terra reached into her utility belt and took out two small black cartridges. They were sleek, with only a single button on the side.

She waited a couple of seconds. A crash came from below. A shot fired. Voices were raised.

Your window is closing.

Terra leaned around the beam and thumbed the button on one of the cartridges. She rushed forward, following the trail of coils as the cartridge broke into two sections, and two sharp, short prongs appeared at the farthest end. The prongs stuck into the guard's forearm, electricity running through them as the taser emptied its power. Terra holstered the gun to operate the second cartridge. She shot it at the next guard, and soon both were writhing on the floor.

Gary turned. The final guard turned. Terra rushed at the third guard, her fist meeting his jaw. A *crack* sounded. The guard went down. She dropped the taser controls, satisfied that she'd incapacitated the other guards. She reached for her pistol.

Something heavy smacked her back. She flew forward, landing on her front and skidding across the dusty floor. The smell of gunpowder filled the air.

Terra grunted. Gary advanced on her, taking slow steps as his gun pointed at her face. Terra felt the pain dissipate as APRIL operated her controls.

"You AJS assholes don't know when to quit, do you?" Gary's face was a mask of rage. "If you could stay in your little boxes and do as told, we might be able to find a way to get along." He shook his head. "Good riddance to bad trash."

Threat level: ninety-eight percent. Imminent death approaching. Move, Terra.

Ninety-eight percent? What the hell does one hundred percent look like?

Terra's leg moved of its own accord. She kicked out to the side, the momentum helping her spin and twist like a decrepit breakdancer. Gary shot, but the bullet embedded itself in the concrete floor.

Terra spun, using her legs to build momentum. Her foot caught the gun and kicked it from Gary's hand. It skittered along the floor.

Gary cursed, his face souring as he shook his hand. He looked from Terra to the gun, then broke into a run.

Terra pushed herself to her feet. She gave chase, closing in on Gary as he sprinted, not for the stairs but the edge of the building.

The drop was easily fifty feet. A jump to the ground would break any man, the chances of death registering at seventy-eight percent on Terra's internal HUD. Still, Gary ran, and as Terra closed in, it wasn't until she saw what was in front of him that she understood.

A thick, steel cable trailed down from the crane, its top hidden from view. The line rested a short distance from the building's edge, and Gary aimed for it as he jumped from the lip of the floor and flew through the air.

His arms pinwheeled as he floated, his jacket flying up behind him. His palms met the cable, his legs wrapping around its girth. He smashed a little too hard with his crotch and grunted as gravity took him down.

Terra followed. Her catch was more delicate, her body snaking around the cable as she trailed down after him. The ground rushed up to meet them, Terra's face set into a grim mask of determination as she fell toward Gary.

Their descent was silent. The guards continued to climb to the upper floors, unaware of where Terra and her target were falling. Gary landed heavily, his knees buckling and a strange whoosh of air expelling from his lips. Terra hopped off, bending her knees and executing a roll to dispel the fall's impact.

Gary was on his feet, scrambling toward the front gate. Terra sprinted after him, closing the gap, all determination set on one goal and one goal only.

Gary weaved around the forklift. Terra put one foot on the prong to gain additional height. She spread her arms, soaring through the air until she caught him. Her arms wrapped around his neck. Gary fell onto his front. Terra yanked his arms behind his back and slapped the cuffs into place. "No more running, dirtbag. This is your last rodeo."

Gary coughed, dust and dirt entering his mouth. He managed a weak grin. "Oh, yeah?" He drew in a deep breath. *"Down here! She's down here!"*

Terra turned back to the building, where dark shapes appeared at the lip of the concrete floors. She rose to her feet, dragging Gary by the collar as shots fired all around, inaccurate and rushed as they shot into the darkness.

Terra managed to get cover on the outside of the chain-link. She ran over to her bike and picked it up from its side. There was a little damage to the seat and the body, but nothing that should prevent it from starting.

She twisted the ignition. The bike roared to life.

Gunfire rained around them. Terra ran for Gary and hauled him over her shoulder, then dumped him to straddle the bike with his face pressed against the tank. She hopped on behind him and used her body to anchor the short man in place. No doubt he'd have more bruises and possibly a few minor burns after this, but she didn't have time to adjust right now. She just needed to clear this damn place.

With a twist of the accelerator, the bike lurched into motion. Gary grunted in front of her. The shots followed the sound of the bike. Only once did a bullet clip her wing mirror as she veered into the streets and sped away.

CHAPTER TWENTY-SEVEN

Terra grabbed Gary by the crook of his elbow and dragged him toward the station.

He resisted, but his earlier rough knocks had weakened him, and she was stronger. There were bruises and marks from the fuel cap across his cheek, incurred from the various bumps that knocked his face against the tank as Terra sped along the roads. She didn't doubt that his legs probably had singe marks from hot parts as well.

She had drowned out his complaints as they rode, her focus set only on bringing this asshole in and getting the other ones, too.

Custer looked up as they entered the reception area. His face morphed from delight to confusion as he registered who Terra's companion was. She raised a hand as if to say, "Don't ask," and dragged him toward the bullpen.

There were only a couple of officers around as Terra took a hard right and made for one of the temporary holding cells they had in the station. She stopped at a counter where an older man with a bristly mustache and kind, tired eyes sat reading a novel on his tablet.

He slowly glanced up at Terra. "Yes?"

"Keys for whichever cell is currently available, Sid," Terra stated.

Sid considered this. "They all are."

"Well, pick one at random."

Sid turned slowly to the wall where keys hung on hooks. "Got a preference?"

"Whichever's closest."

"That'll be 1A," Sid stated. He held Terra's gaze as if waiting for a reply. When none came, he took them from the hook. "Give it a jimmy. It sometimes catches."

The temporary cells were through a door to the side of the booth. While Sid went back to his reading, Terra found the cell. She unlocked it, then threw Gary inside. He stumbled, face hitting the far wall.

He spun, his hair disheveled and a mad glint in his eye. "You won't get away with this, bitch. You think you have it all figured out, but they'll come for you. That uniform means shit when you're out there in the streets. Cross will have his revenge. Your shitty bitch corporal will get what she deserves, and I'll laugh from inside this room—until I get out, that is. I've done it before. You think I won't do it again?"

Terra's lips thinned as she fished inside her utility belt. She found another cartridge, then aimed it at Gary. She thumbed the button, delighting as his eyes rolled into the back of his head and he fell unconscious to the floor. "The only way you'll see the outside world again is wrapped up and stuffed into a wooden coffin."

She locked the door, then handed the keys back to Sid. As she strolled through the hallway, glass panels on her right to give her a view into the bullpen, she spotted Hewlett and Dunston arriving back and settling at their desks.

She strode toward them.

"...colder every day," Hewlett loudly complained as he rubbed his hands together. "I thought this place was supposed to be somewhat temperate. If I wanted winter chills, I would've stayed in Minnesota."

Dunston chuckled. "Atlantica would be better for it."

Hewlett playfully punched his arm. He shrugged off his jacket and laid it on the chair.

"You two," Terra called across the room. "Prisoner in 1A. Need you to keep an eye on him."

Hewlett laughed in disbelief. "Sorry, we don't take our orders from—"

She grabbed Hewlett by the collar and brought his face close to hers. "You will do as I say, got that? Your prisoner that you allowed to go free is back inside. Keep him there, under penalty of my wrath. I find that he so much as sniffed fresh air, I'm going to bring twenty tons of 'fuck you' down onto your beady little life, got that?"

Hewlett looked as though he was about to protest when his gaze fixed on something in Terra's eye. His gusto disappeared, and he nodded. "Fine. Okay, fine. Just this once, all right?"

Terra let him go. Dunston stood there, confused and silent.

She pointed at him. "That goes for you, too. Gary Clark stays inside until I'm back."

"Where are you going?" Slim asked, her head popping up from behind a nearby computer.

Terra didn't turn back as she replied, "To get the corporal back."

She only made one stop on the way out to visit the ammunitions store and top up her gear.

"APRIL, show me where Cross went," Terra commanded.

The city blurred past her. Lights were streaks of color as the wind rushed through her hair. Occasionally the dull throb of her gunshot wounds flared, but APRIL ensured that everything stayed topped up in her painkilling biology.

Displaying information, now.

Terra saw a montage of clips of the BMW passing through the city and toward the outskirts of town. Arrows appeared, projected along the road that directed her to follow in their wake.

"You're a good egg, APRIL," Terra stated.

Thank you, Officer Kris.

Terra tore past skyscrapers, weaved through traffic, and drifted around corners as she closed on the BMW's location. The buildings began to shrink, and more greenery popped up around her. There were shopping malls, fast-food chains, and parks in abundance as the gauge on her HUD showed that there were only five hundred meters until she arrived at her target destination.

She parked the Ducati, aware of the growl of its engine. She tucked it away at the back of a TGI Fridays, then headed in the laundromat's direction.

It came into sight soon enough, a large, lone building off a side road from a roundabout. The lights were off, a large illustration of a washing machine making the "O" in the word "Laundr-O-mat displayed across the front facade. Digital displays hung in the windows, their screens turned off. A subline read, "A sister company of El Hermanos Ltd." Terra clung to a row of bushes that lined the property, keeping away from the watching eyes of the security cameras that bordered the building.

She rounded the back and found an entrance that sloped down to an underground car park. Light spilled from inside. Across the stretch of lined parking spaces on the tarmac, she saw the back entrance, as well as a series of bay windows that showed the many washing machines and dryers inside.

"If you want to funnel money away to hide from the taxman, this would be a great way to do it." Terra wondered how deep this operation went. "APRIL, any chance of hacking into the camera feeds?"

Negative. Camera security protocol denied. Fixed to private residence.

"Since when? This is a public business, APRIL. Not someone's home."

Since it's on record that people sometimes sleep here.

"I call bullshit. That doesn't make it a private residence. It's licensed and zoned as a business, and there are no apartments attached." Rather than argue any further, Terra drew her Glock from its holster, then found the silencer and fixed it into place. She closed her right eye, using the HUD information to aim for the cameras.

She picked them off one by one, blinding those who sat in whatever security room they'd set up inside. When the cameras were down, she sprinted across the parking lot and made for the back door.

The door was locked, unsurprisingly. Terra cupped her hands to the glass and peeked inside. There was no movement. Not yet, anyway.

She pulled an emergency hammer from her belt and hit the steel point against the glass. The whole screen fractured in a heartbeat. She knocked through the glass with the handle until she could get to the lock on the inside.

Breaking and entering is against Atlantica Justice System protocol. A sharp sound rang, piercing Terra's eardrums. She clapped her hands to the sides of her head.

Civilian mode, activate, she thought desperately.

The ringing stopped, leaving only a lingering silence. Terra flexed her jaw, the sound somehow making the bones in her skull ache all over. She shoved the door open, boots crunching on the glass fractures as she made her way inside.

She made for the nearest room, a doorway that led to a supplies closet. Terra opened the door and tucked herself inside.

APRIL, engage. She waited, but nothing happened. *Oh for fuck's sake. OSCaR, engage.*

Breaking and entering is against Atlantica Justice System protocol. The ringing appeared again.

Terra screwed her eyes shut. *APRIL, stop! This isn't a private residence!*

Breaking and entering is against Atlantica Justice System protocol.

Terra grimaced, wondering if the sound was really in her head or if she had tripped an alarm when she entered the building. *APRIL, display thermal scan.*

Breaking and entering is against Atlantica Justice System protocol.

Terra opened her eyes, expecting nothing to have changed, but now she could see the illuminated shapes of figures. A great number of them wandered around. They floated a level below hers, one she hadn't known about. A handful made their way up the stairs with guns in their hands.

Still the screaming siren sounded. Terra memorized the position of those approaching as she sent APRIL back into civilian mode. Whatever glitch or override was happening was a major pain.

The silence was welcoming. She shook her head, trying to focus on the task at hand. She needed to worm her way inside, and without APRIL's help, that would be a real issue, but maybe she could find another way.

She glanced around the room and found a light switch. She pressed it, then examined the walls until she found what she was looking for—a small sheet of paper with instructions for a fire evacuation, should one occur. The map showed the floor plan of both lower floors of the building, with green arrows leading to the emergency exit. It also showed the restrooms, as well as several staff rooms and storage rooms around the place.

Terra found what she was after—the stairs.

She drew a deep breath before thinking, *OSCaR, thermal scan.*

She grunted. The sound seemed to get louder each time.

Breaking and entering is against Atlantica Justice System protocol.

I know! I know! Terra thought and turned to see the handful of figures nearing the top of the stairs. *APRIL, civilian mode.*

The silence came back.

Terra took one last look at the floor plans before killing the lights and cracking open the door. She waited a moment, breath held, as footsteps sounded from one of the nearby rooms.

"Shhh, keep your noise down," a voice hushed.

The group zeroed in on the door, the wind blowing in through the large gap Terra had created. They all pointed their guns at the entrance as if someone was going to be standing there and waiting. A man with a thick South African accent eased the door open and stepped into the parking lot.

The others glanced around as he investigated, scanning his gun around the space. He turned up, noticed the shattered security cameras, and shook his head. "Looks like we do have company, folks."

A young woman who could barely be in her early twenties looked around, wide-eyed. "Where are they?"

The South African shrugged. "Let's go hunting."

Terra controlled her breathing, wishing she could keep her thermal scan initiated. Her heart thumped faster, and the pain that the adrenaline had numbed was beginning to flare as her biochemical cocktail faded, uncontrolled by APRIL's software.

One of the group peeled off and looked around the room as they approached the supply closet. Terra waited until they were within distance before she came out on the attack.

She threw the door open, the flat wooden surface smacking into the man. He fell back, his gun falling from his grasp and his hands moving to his face where his nose had exploded in blood.

Terra trod on his stomach as she rushed the South African

man. She jumped high with both feet in front of her, booted him in the chest, and used his bulk to springboard her back and into a roll on the floor.

Two remained in the same room with her. One of the others had disappeared back the way they had come. Terra ducked behind a counter. She crawled along the floor until she was in line with the young woman, then leaped over the counter to attack. Her legs clamped around the woman's throat, and she squeezed with her thighs. She reached down to grab the woman's wrist, then aimed the pistol at the other target in the room.

The woman went down, chest blooming with blood. The silencer on the young woman's pistol muted the noise although the *pop* was still notable.

Terra twisted her body, sending the woman she had clamped around to the floor. The woman gasped for air, allowing Terra a moment to snatch her weapon. She trained her Glock on the South African, then aimed the pistol at the man skidding into sight from the other room.

They both froze. The man she'd hit with the door complained, rolling around on the floor.

Terra narrowed her eyes. "Make any sudden movements, and your ass is grass."

They glanced at each other. The South African man rested against the front door frame, ass in the glass shards, hands cut and bleeding. The other—a middle-aged man with a bulldog's face and a porcupine's hair—drew a long breath.

"Please," the South African man muttered. "I have kids."

Porcupine shot daggers at him.

South African paid no attention, eyes looking imploringly at Terra.

Terra held her aim steady, the pain in her back, thigh, and hip growing warmer, her breath catching. "How do I get to Cross?"

The South African glanced at the other man. Porcupine shook his head. The South African turned to Terra. "It ain't easy."

Porcupine raised his gun, finger tensing on the trigger, aimed at the South African. Terra shot first, her Glock popping as the bullet caught Porcupine in the neck and brought him down. South African jumped, wincing as more glass lodged inside him.

Terra moved closer. "I need a way. Tell me how."

The South African thought for a moment. "If I tell you, you'll let me go?"

Terra considered this. "No harm will come to you."

He nodded solemnly. "I just want to see my baby. She turns two on Friday."

Terra lowered her pistol. "Give me all you got while I bind these bitches together." She glanced at the two remaining on the floor—the young woman snoozing on the tiles and the man with the broken nose—then brought out her cuffs.

CHAPTER TWENTY-EIGHT

The South African man identified himself as Thato. With a little encouragement, he chirped like a bird under Terra's watchful eye.

"We hardly see anything of Cross," he explained, standing inside the reception area and patting the glass shards from his pants. He winced as he occasionally drew a piece of glass from his flesh. "He's the top man, the enigma, the ghost in the machine. Most of the time his name is used as a threat, you know, 'Get your ass in gear unless you want to hear from Cross.'"

"So you've never actually seen him?" Terra asked. She had found some duct tape inside a drawer and was now applying a length to the young woman's mouth.

"No," Thato replied. "But those who *have* been sent to him never returned. I don't doubt what happened to them. There are some assholes below sea level." He glanced down at the place where Terra had seen the shapes of dozens of people below. "People do crazy things for power, money, and drugs."

Terra raised an eyebrow. "Didn't stop you from joining the forces, did it?"

Thato raised a bloodied hand. "My daughter. She was born

with a rare heart defect. I spent my life savings to cover her medical bills, but they still needed more." He shrugged. "I do what I have to do to ensure my family is safe."

"Like getting into bed with criminals," Terra stated. "What exactly is going on down there?"

"What do you think?" Thato rolled up his sleeve to show the faint dark lines of his veins.

Terra examined the others, able to make out the ink running through all of their bodies. She shook her head. "Son of a bitch. That toxic black shit is really doing the rounds in Atlantica."

Thato nodded. "They hook us up to it as our initiation into the ring. Make us dependent. Force us to fall into the whirlpool of self-destruction so they can keep us on the line. They pay us in cash and ink. What could go wrong?"

"So why are you telling me all this?" Terra asked. "Shouldn't you be shivering in a corner, dealing with withdrawals?"

Thato nodded sadly. "I've been cutting down. Weaning myself off for my family. I hate what I've become. I hate it all, but I need the money. I need it all for my little girl."

Terra thought for a moment. "How do I get to him?"

Thato plucked a shard of glass the size of a fingernail from his ass. He winced, then motioned to the next room. "The entrance to the den is through there, down a set of steps. There's an underground elevator that runs from B1 down to B6."

"That's a big operation," Terra commented.

"You have no idea," Thato replied. "The elevator is your key. Rumor has it that there are levels below B6 without staff access, places where Cross hides. The rest of the floors are for grunts, manufacturing, storage, and general operation, but below B6... that's where it's said he hides."

"Who says this?" Terra asked. "How can you be sure?"

"I'm not," Thato replied honestly. "It's just what I hear." He cocked his head, a distant look in his eye. "There's a panel in the elevator, needs a fingerprint to unlock. I'm told that's how you get to the deep levels."

Terra processed this, then offered a hand to Thato. He reluctantly took it, leaving a smear of blood on Terra's palm. Terra wiped it on her uniform, then looked out at the parking lot.

"My advice, Thato? You get the hell out of here, now. This place is about to blow up, and not in the best way, and you best be as far from it as you possibly can. Take your family and get somewhere safe, somewhere unknown. If you need to, go to the AJS for help, tell them Terra Kris sent you. I'll confirm this when I return."

Thato considered this, then offered a brisk, "Thank you." His dark shape ran across the parking lot, soon fading through the bushes as he ran off into the night.

Terra turned her attention below her feet. She drew a deep breath. *APRIL, engage. Shit. I mean, OSCaR, engage. Thermal scan initiate.*

Breaking and entering is against Atlantica Justice System protocol.

Terra grimaced against the onslaught of sound. She focused on the countless shapes below, counting each wave of people that shrunk beneath her. Although she couldn't see the floors, she could just about determine their distance from her. She counted six rows of figures, then glanced around, looking for the hidden depths.

Three figures moved below the rest, tiny in comparison to the others. They sat, relaxed on something that Terra couldn't see. She disengaged APRIL, then smirked. "Bingo."

She headed for the stairs.

She made her way down quietly, listening for any sign of people coming her way. Each step caused a flare-up of pain in the places where her bruises were growing, and as she descended further into the unknown, a wave of tiredness overtook her. Her bones began to ache. Her eyelids drooped. The adrenaline that was keeping her going faded away, and in its absence was only lethargy.

She reached the bottom of the stairs and took cover behind an open doorway. *OSCaR, engage.* She blinked, head beginning to pound. *APRIL, I need you.*

She prepared for the onslaught, and here it came again.

Breaking and entering is against Atlantica Justice System protocol.

The siren was overwhelming, hitting Terra almost like a physical force. She doubled over, gasping. *APRIL! Please, stop!*

The siren rang on. Terra pressed her head against the wall, face held to the ceiling. She needed it over, but she also needed the fix. She needed APRIL's help, and she hated herself for it, but APRIL was the only thing that could help guide her through this system.

"Please, APRIL," she muttered aloud, unaware of how loud she was speaking.

The siren stopped.

Terra opened her eyes warily. The silence was disturbing. Had she asked APRIL to turn off without realizing it?

"Is that better, sweetheart?" a voice crooned in her head.

Terra gave a weak laugh. "Val? Is that you?"

"Bet you're glad I'm here now, aren't you?" There was a hint of mirth in her voice. "I've been playing around. Found a few upgrades for you.

"I've installed a signal jammer that will activate when you're within fifty meters of any security feeds around you. You can switch this on and off depending on if you want to access these feeds or block them entirely. Whoever's looking at the screens will see a still image. Great for sneaking in a quiet space, not so good for a place with heavy foot traffic. Remember, if the feed freezes, it pauses the current image. People will get suspicious if they see a gathering of twenty people stop and freeze in real-time."

"Interesting…" Terra replied.

"I know, right? I've also altered OSCaR's breaking and entering protocol. Well, I say altered, I've permanently disabled them—or, as permanently as you want. I'm sure your conscience will want to switch it back on at some point." She scoffed. "You cops and your pretty conscience. No wonder you find yourself falling at every hurdle."

"You got a point?" Terra whispered.

"Well, that's one way to say 'Thank you,' I suppose." Valentina paused. "The point is that you don't know how much you've helped me by letting me transfer the data information for this AI."

"Letting you?"

"You know what I mean. The least I can do is say thank you, and once I saw that you disappeared into a den infested with asshole rats, I thought you could use a bit of a break. So, there it is. Upgrade received. OSCaR is yours for the taking. A true assistant, and not just a hindrance. Go ahead, test it out."

Terra was hesitant.

"I don't have all day," Valentina urged. Terra was certain she heard the faint sound of gunshots in the background.

OSCaR, engage.

Good evening, Officer Kris.

There was no siren or sign of disruption. Terra let out a sigh of relief as APRIL's pain-killing concoctions coursed through her once again. The tiredness lifted, replaced with an eager enthusiasm to get shit done. She cracked her neck, thankful for the eradication of the pain points across her body. *Initiate thermal scan.*

Initiating thermal scan.

People lit up around her, floating in the spaces beneath. A smile reached her lips. *Direct me to the elevator.*

APRIL was quiet as she worked inside Terra's mind. Terra wasn't sure that this would work, allowing access to private records for buildings and their layouts. An arrow appeared on the floor in front of her and made a hairpin turn through the doorway she hid behind.

"Nice work," Terra complimented.

"Thanks. Over and out."

"Forever?"

"For now." Valentina's laughter faded to silence.

Terra looked through the door, identifying only a handful of people moving around on this floor. From a glance, they were unarmed, but that didn't mean they weren't dangerous.

She was about to head into a hornet's nest, after all.

CHAPTER TWENTY-NINE

Terra slowly walked down the long corridor, gun ready by her side.

The walls were smooth sheetrock, the floors cheap tiles. She followed the arrows that snaked through the long hallway, ears pricked for any sign of commotion. Her thermal scan helped her navigate around the more active of the fiery blobs in her vision, and soon she was halfway toward the place where APRIL identified the elevator's location.

A strange smell hung in the air. Around the hallways were cardboard boxes, some with black stains on the corners. The humidity would have caused Terra to sweat had it not been for APRIL's bodily guidance.

Turn left.

Terra went left at the "T" and continued her journey. The lights flickered, the place illuminated by cheap bulbs set into cheap sconces. After another turn, Terra spotted the elevator at the end of a corridor.

Two men stood waiting for it. Terra paused out of sight until the doors opened and they descended. When they were gone, she picked up her pace, stalking toward the elevator doors.

Careful, Terra.

The red shape of a man highlighted to her right. The door opened. Terra quickly opened the door to her left and stepped inside.

She'd entered a room filled with cardboard boxes. Some were open with empty vials stained with black and syringes that appeared to have also been used and drained of their contents.

This place is atrocious. Who lives like this?

Terra turned her attention to the man who had left the other room. He walked away from the elevator, eventually disappearing around the corner. When she was sure he was out of sight, Terra headed out the door and broke into a sprint.

She reached the elevator and pressed the button. The car started its ascent. Terra glanced down at the blue highlighted shape and waited for it to arrive, thankful that there was no one inside.

The car stopped moving. The doors opened. Terra made to step inside when two men stood in her way.

What the hell? Terra thought.

Heat signatures are undetectable through elevator walls.

You could have told me that before they opened, Terra reprimanded.

The two stared at her for a moment, eyes straying down her body as they identified her AJS uniform. Their hands were in their pockets, and sharp rashes of stubble covered their faces.

"Evening," Terra offered.

They reacted, screwing their hands into fists as fear flashed in their eyes. Terra was faster. She threw a right hook to the man on the right, followed by a swift jab into the other man's nose. They both stumbled backward, falling onto their asses in the corner of the elevator. Terra stepped inside and pressed the button to close the doors.

"How do I get this thing moving?" Terra asked, examining the panel of buttons. Thato was right. The numbers B1 to B6 were in descending order. Below them was a panel that simply displayed an LED fingerprint.

Terra stroked a hand over the panel. A beep sounded, and the LEDs turned red.

The pair shifted behind her, getting to their feet. Terra whirled on them, hands held before her. "Honestly, it's in your best interest to stay where you are right now."

The pair looked at each other, then relaxed in the corner. Terra sensed no real threat between the pair of them, and according to APRIL, neither did she.

Terra examined the panel again, racking her brain for an idea. Something came to her, a tiny spark of something that she was almost certain wouldn't work but would be worth a try. *APRIL, override the elevator security protocol.*

APRIL was quiet for a moment. **Negative—**

Then find me a way to get inside the hidden level! Terra clawed her hair in frustration. *There has to be something we can do.*

She turned to the two on the floor. "Any ideas?"

They looked at her blankly.

Terra turned back to the elevator panel.

Officer Kris, place your thumb on the identification panel.

Terra cocked an eyebrow. *I'm sorry?*

Apology accepted. Please place your thumb on the identification panel.

Her hand lurched. She controlled it, grabbing her wrist with her other hand, then placed the thumb on the panel. It flashed red and *beeped* again.

The other thumb.

Terra looked at her metallic thumb, then placed it against the panel. There came the soft sound of whirring and mechanisms before a *click* confirmed its entry. The light on the panel turned green, and the elevator car kicked into life.

Terra pulled her thumb away and examined the tip. "Wait, what happened?"

Where the smooth metal had once been, Terra now made out tiny little grooves in the metal's surface. She could see the rings and details of a human thumb, though they faded within seconds and the metal became smooth once more.

"How did you do that?"

I extracted fingerprint records from Fernando Cross' criminal data files. These records are publicly available to access for all Atlantica Officers for Justice.

Okay, but not exactly what I meant. How did you...morph my thumbprint?

Epidermal replication, manipulation, and reconstruction are custom-built into your hardware. You can replicate any thumbprint you hold on file to gain access into buildings and secure locations.

They passed floor B4. *Why did nobody tell me this?*

I do not know the answer to that question.

Seems people are keeping a lot of things quiet from me. Terra frowned.

Have you considered the possibility that maybe you're hotheaded and quick to anger as a possible barrier for sufficient bonds of trust with your peers?

Terra was stunned into silence. She looked back at the other two, who sat there without blinking. *I never said they could install a shrink.*

The elevator stopped at level B5. Terra took a step back as the doors opened and a woman walked inside. She was holding her cell phone in both hands, headphones fixed into each ear. She was gaunt, and there were fresh marks on her arm where she'd injected ink. It wasn't until she was in the elevator and turned that she saw Terra for the first time.

Terra pressed the button to close the doors. The woman looked at her lazily as if trying to solve a puzzle beyond her skill level. Terra pressed her thumb once more to the scanner, and the elevator went down.

They passed B6, Terra keeping an eye on the woman who had lost interest and was now just texting something on her cell. When the doors opened at a level that had no number, Terra walked through the door.

She held it open with one hand, reading the information that APRIL displayed for her. "Giovanni Tayo, Ewan Evens, and Lisa Harper. I know your names, I know where you live, I know who you live with, and I know how to find you. Keep your lips sealed. If anyone asks if they've seen me, tell them no. I *will* know. In the same way I know that you drive a Range Rover, your niece is called Rita, and you have 34,589 dollars in your bank account. Okay?"

They all nodded. Terra stepped back and let the elevator doors close.

Do you really think they'll keep quiet?

"No. But I hope they do." Terra turned to the small, brilliantly lit, white marble corridor. A short distance ahead was a set of double doors. "Think it's time to take this fucker down?"

It's always time to bring criminals to justice.

"Now you're starting to speak my language." Terra took one step forward before she heard a woman screaming in pain.

CHAPTER THIRTY

Cross sank into the plush leather of the grand armchair and moaned.

His eyes screwed shut as Melissa worked on his crotch, playing it just the way that he liked it. Her dark veins stood out on her pale arms, and as she continued about her business, Tyler shouted over his shoulder from across the room.

"She's a fighter!" Tyler laughed. The AJS Corporal was tied to the wall by her wrists. She hung limply, stretching the chains as far as they would go, but even now she attempted to kick Tyler, only succeeding in clipping his shins.

"Nice try. I think this is more what you were aiming for." He kicked the corporal in the crotch. She glared at him with rage-filled eyes.

Tyler crouched out of reach, addressing the corporal as if speaking to a toddler. "It's cute when you think you can do something about the position you're in. Think you'll escape this one? You don't stand a chance in hell."

He reached to the wall and grabbed a long black rod. At the touch of a button, sparks flared at its tip. He grinned as he jabbed it at the corporal. A scream came from between her lips, drowning out the crackling sound of the electricity.

Cross flinched at Black's scream. The woman at his crotch grunted before sitting back on her ass and wiping her mouth. Cross dismissed her with a click of his fingers, then stood and zipped up his pants. "Don't be too hard on her," he crooned. "You can use this one as one of your guinea pigs if you're clever."

"How?" Tyler turned to Cross, raising one eyebrow. "She's a cop. We're fucked if she sticks around."

"I never said anything about her sticking around." Cross' face bore his hallmark signature of neutrality.

Tyler interpreted his meaning and gave an affirmative nod. "Good shout."

Cross moved to a small glass coffee table and grabbed an apple from the fruit bowl. The room was large, filled with an array of items that would seem unnecessary to most but fitted perfectly down here.

A pinball machine sat against the wall. A small pit was dug into the floor, surrounded by cushions with a brazier in its center. A ventilation shaft above took the smoke that would spiral to the ceiling and carried it aboveground.

There were surfaces stained in black ink, with syringes and cards littered across the top, as well as a series of bookshelves, TVs, and video games. One corner was a sectioned cubicle that hosted a computer setup that had cost Cross enough to put down a mortgage on a significant property.

Cross threw the apple from one hand to the other. "We have to keep an eye on that precinct. Things are going to get messy if they get wind of where we've taken her and what we're going to do to her."

He glanced her way. Black turned away. "That nuisance who showed up at the site…has she been dealt with yet? Have you contacted Clark and confirmed her capture?"

Tyler looked around the room as if Cross was speaking to

someone else. "You know I've been with you since the moment you got here?"

Cross nodded, then tossed the apple at Tyler's head. He ducked. The apple smashed against the wall.

Tyler protested. "I mean, of course you know. I'm just saying… How could I have gotten a call without you knowing?"

"Phone him," Cross instructed, his neutral calm returning in an instant. "I need an update."

Tyler drew his cell phone and dialed the number. The phone rang several times before going to voicemail. He tried two more times, each time the same response. "No answer."

Cross nodded. He wandered over to the computer area, where he sat in the chair and put on a set of headphones. The woman who had kept him occupied slipped out of the room through the back door after taking a wad of cash stacked on the dresser.

Cross loaded up his screens and scoured the CCTV footage. Their encounter with the officer at the site had been close. Had their car not been fitted with automatic repair technology, the AJS would have taken them in, no question. Whether they would have been tried and convicted would be a whole other story— there were bigger fish in the city than Fernando Cross, after all.

Cross noticed that a handful of the CCTV cameras at the front of the building were out. He flicked through the other feeds. All appeared normal, empty corridors and busy rooms, but a bad feeling broiled in his gut as he zoomed in on one image. It showed the trailing foot of someone disappearing from view. Was the camera frozen?

Cross tapped a number into his cell phone. A voice replied almost immediately. "What is it, boss?"

"I need you up on B1. Perform a sweep of camera feeds through quadrants two and three," Cross instructed. "Keep an eye out for any unusual activity."

"You got it." The voice clicked off.

Tyler looked at Cross. "What is it? What are you looking for?"

"I don't know," Cross replied. "But whatever it is, we should prepare for a getaway."

Both heads spun as there was a knock on the door. Tyler scrunched his face up. "You expecting company?"

"No." Cross got to his feet. He glanced at his shotgun which was on a rack on the wall. Before he could take his first step, the door burst open.

CHAPTER THIRTY-ONE

Terra swept her gaze across the room, registering all individuals at once. APRIL cast the labels to her, but she knew two of the three remaining in the room.

She glanced at the corporal. She was in a bad way. Splatters of blood dripped from her hanging head and onto the floor. Her eyes were glazed, going in and out of focus.

"Freeze, Cross!" Terra instructed, her voice booming around the large room.

A man with dark hair and a casual hoodie reacted. He ran to the side, diving toward the cover of a large leather chair.

Cross slowly raised his hands. "You too, Tyler."

"She didn't say me," Tyler called from behind the chair. "Thanks for revealing my name."

"It won't matter," Cross replied with calm neutrality.

Terra closed the doors behind her. "You're under arrest."

"Under what charges?" Cross spoke as if simply replying to what his favorite ice cream flavor was.

"Oh, I'm sure we can find a few. How about kidnapping a senior Officer for Justice? Possession, manufacturing, and distribution of illegal narcotics? What's the betting that a quick look through your computer will also yield some interesting results?"

Cross looked unabashed. "You're going to have to prove it, aren't you?"

Terra nodded. "Besides from the camera that's currently lodged in my grey matter and the fact that we have a witness chained to the wall, I think we've got plenty of evidence in the floors above."

Cross nodded and slumped back into his chair. The computer screens were bright behind him. "The problem is, Officer Terra Kris, you're going to have to escape here alive to prove any of that. And, if the miracle should happen and you ever see the foggy skies of Atlantica again, and you think you can head to your superior officers to…how do your lot say it…'Blow this wide-open,' you'll be in for a big surprise.

"It's amazing how deep the roots of a tree can grow. It's not until you try to chop it down that you realize it has an unshakeable anchor in the ground." He looked at Terra in the way that a teen examines an ant under the magnifying glass. "You think that we would have planned and executed this operation if we hadn't placed sufficient backup measures?"

Terra adjusted her grip on her Glock. She didn't like the fact that Tyler was out of sight. She focused APRIL's thermal scan on his figure. "I've seen some pretty big shit in my time, Cross. Dealing with petty suburban drug rings is nothing after the crap I've seen in the inner city."

Cross narrowed his eyes. "Terra, this thing is so much bigger than you or I. You have no idea how many rungs up the ladder this goes. Even if you destroy me, you'll have to deal with those above. To end my life is to choose to end yours." He waved a hand at Black. "And your corporal's."

"Threatening an Officer for Justice." Terra smirked. "That's another offense."

"You don't understand. That's not a threat. That's a promise.

You think that you can bring me in, celebrate your victory, and you'll be back in your old precinct, partnered up with your old chum? How is Imani Thomas, by the way? I've noticed she's been keeping her distance from you since the APRIL installation. Smart girl, isn't she?"

Terra faltered, and a flicker of doubt crossed her brow.

"And, of course, you want to restore the pride in your parents, don't you?" Cross continued. "Marie and Michael Kris. You know, I've been keeping a close eye on them both since your accident. I was surprised that your father didn't reveal more to you."

"What are you talking about?" Terra asked.

Warning, imminent attack, Tyler Hinchliff.

Terra turned and fired a shot at the leather chair. The bullet tore through, hitting the red glowing target in the shoulder. She fired another shot, finding his thigh. He grunted out of sight, the pistol he had in his hand useless beside him.

Terra kept her Glock trained on Cross as she worked her way to Tyler. She picked up the pistol and placed it in her back pocket, then stepped away.

"Your father is a forensic scientist for the Atlantica Justice System, correct?" Cross asked, hands folded in his lap.

Terra didn't reply.

"Well, your father was on the scene the day of your accident," Cross continued. "He identified the body in the vehicle after your little collision."

"It wasn't a collision," Terra stated. "It was a detonation. You and your asshole overlords switched the footage, created your reality inside my head." She smirked. "I solved it."

"Very good." Cross clapped slowly. "Of course, we figured you would at some point. It was only inevitable and a risk that you assume with these kinds of proceedings.

"Your father found the body that was supposed to have been mine. I should have become a mere ghost in the system, had you not stuck your snooty nose in business that doesn't concern you." He cocked his head to the side. "Something went wrong."

Terra processed this, remembering all the little stepping stones along the way that she had unraveled. She thought of the surgery, the installation of APRIL, the evasiveness of Black, Garcia's appearance in the office, the feeling of being watched inside her head, and the loops and curls she'd trailed around to find where the hell Cross was hiding.

"It was you. You funded this whole damn thing, didn't you? You have Garcia in your pocket, and you've been trying to watch me, trying to control me… Why? For what purpose?"

Cross narrowed his eyes. "Close. You're very close, Terra." He sighed. "The truth is that you are a failed experiment. The APRIL installation was supposed to control you. You were a prime candidate to be a supersoldier for the AJS, working in favor of the very people you were trying to stop.

"If we could prove that you listened to our every command, and a simple switch of the button could shut you off, we could have the entire Atlantica Justice System in our pocket. Drones. Sleeper soldiers. We could be free to run Atlantica's underground."

Terra grinned. "But something went wrong."

"Yes. Very wrong. Your software was meddled with. You cut out our access and shut us out from your data."

Cross turned to the computer and tapped the keys. The screen filled with recordings of Terra's parents' house from her point of view. A flash of images of Terra cuddling Skooch, coming around from her surgery, chasing the asshole through the park. They were all there, stored on the computer. "We only have one more test to make."

Cross navigated to a command panel on the right-hand side of the screen. His finger hovered over the "Enter" key.

"What's that?" Terra asked. APRIL zoomed in so that she could read the instruction. "Terminate."

Terra's heart beat faster, but only for a moment as APRIL stabilized her condition.

"One press," Cross stated. "We hid an emergency shutdown protocol in the back of APRIL's code. One press of this button, and you're back to where you started. A pile of flesh and bones, unconscious and useless."

Terra prodded the Glock his way. "Don't make me shoot."

"I won't. I never made you do anything, remember?"

For the first time, a smile appeared on Cross' face. Terra shouted although she couldn't remember what as Cross pressed the button. A raging siren rang in Terra's head, hot white flames passing behind her eyes. She shot as she fell, unable to see where the bullet landed. All she knew was sound and pain, sound and pain and darkness as her eyelids closed and her body writhed on the floor.

Then it was gone. All of it.

Gone.

CHAPTER THIRTY-TWO

Terra ran, though she didn't know what from.

The world was dark, pitch-black on either side. The floor was hard and smooth. Her bare feet drummed their beat as she sprinted. Her arms pumped on either side, her gaze unfaltering. Air came and went in sharp bursts in her lungs, and all she knew was that she needed to keep going.

She needed to run.

Wait...I've been here before.

The world slipped away beneath her. The road showed no end. Ahead of her was a flare of light the size of a dime. Her gaze pinned on the light, eyes unblinking. The rhythm was hers and hers alone, her body making music in the otherwise silent world.

She didn't think. She didn't need to, not now. Determination was her guide, and her faith was unwavering. The answers were ahead. All she had to do was keep doing what she was doing. She needed to trust the process. She needed to keep fighting.

Terra was always a fighter.

Hold on. What is happening?

Override protocol initiated.

Terra looked over her shoulder, arms pumping as she ran.

The void was dark, the dime light immediately ahead of her. Her body was calm and numb. She couldn't feel the burn of her muscles. She couldn't smell or taste or hear anything outside of her thoughts.

Invasive thoughts shattered her illusion.

"Where am I?" she asked no one, yet there was someone there. Wasn't there? On the other side of the darkness in the muffled space where gunshots fired and commotion rang, someone was there.

The world around her shifted, tilting and shaking as if an earthquake rumbled beneath her. She listed to the side, for the first time falling off of her perfectly balanced center. She landed on her palms and knees. Her body scooped her up and tried to readjust, centering herself to aim once more for the light.

She listed again. Memories flooded her from her youth, bouncing on a bouncy castle at a friend's birthday party. Lying in the center of the inflatable as kids jumped around her and took her with them. It was impossible to remain steady, no matter how hard she tried. Each tiny movement magnified into chaos, and as Terra stood once more and tried to run, her knees buckled, fighting to adjust and keep her upright.

Target: Fernando Cross. Threat level: one hundred percent. Eliminating target.

Terra's world shook. She tried to scream, but her lips didn't move. No matter how much she tried, nothing happened. Someone cried out, distant and muffled as though Terra heard it from beneath the ocean's surface.

The world jerked again, and Terra crashed to the floor. She lay on her front as a shout rang out that wasn't hers. More gunshots fired. She pressed against the floor, trying to pull herself to her feet, but instead it melted. What was solid a moment ago was now only air, and Terra fell.

Fell.

Terra tumbled through nothing, her breath catching, her

weightless body only a vessel for one single confused thought: *I haven't finished my work yet.*

There, as with the last time that Terra entered this strange world of nothing, a *beeping* sounded. It was rhythmic and regular. Something cold washed through her body, but she couldn't see what it was. A robotic voice mumbled above her, its clarity stolen and its edges indistinct.

The voice faded in volume as Terra fell away. Her arms wheeled around her. She looked ahead into the darkness, wondering how far she could fall in this endless wonder.

Tumbling through the air, Terra waited.

And waited.

The impact was softer than she'd hoped.

CHAPTER THIRTY-THREE

Officer Kris, report for duty.

The words came from far away, inhuman in their tone.

Officer Kris, report for duty.

Terra saw only darkness, but she felt something, too. She was positioned in a strange way, her body and mind orientating her before her eyes glimpsed where she was.

Charging to one fifty.

Engage.

The sound of a computer starting up preceded a sharp jolt of electricity running through her body. Terra grimaced but couldn't open her eyes.

Charging to one fifty.

Engage.

Terra gasped, taking in a lungful of air. Her eyes snapped open and light flooded into her retinas as she panted, looking around in wild shock. The electricity tingled, and her senses and feelings all came back to her at once.

She looked around and discovered she was sitting in the comfort of a large leather armchair, the footrest raised and the back reclined. Her fingers dug into the arms of the chair.

"What the f—" A wave of vomit rose from Terra's stomach. She kicked the reclining pad down and hunched forward. Vomit spilled in yellow chunks, her body heaving from the effort of its expulsion. She threw up until no more would come, then flopped back in her chair, eyes closed.

You may want to wipe your mouth.

Terra chuckled, a disbelieving sound at the absurdity of the situation. She sawed her forearm across her lips, then drew a few deep breaths. She felt APRIL's cocktails washing over her and her body returning to normalcy. "APRIL… Where am I? What happened?"

You are in basement level seven of the Laundr-O-Mat.

"Sure…sure…" Terra got to the point where she felt comfortable opening her eyes. "What happened?"

Fernando Cross is dead.

Terra sat up, eyes opening and scanning around the room. Beside her, a man with dark hair breathed deeply. Small puddles of blood pooled around his thigh and shoulder. He would need medical attention soon if he were to remain alive, according to APRIL's scan.

Across the room, a body lay tucked out of sight. A pair of legs poked out from behind a cubicle wall. The light from the computer screens caught in the puddle of blood that surrounded him. As the memories flooded back, Terra looked at the wall for the corporal.

She was gone.

"APRIL, what happened to Cross? Where is Black?" Terra got shakily to her feet. One hand pressed against the dull throb in her temple that was fading.

Fernando Cross became a level one hundred threat. My programming is to immediately terminate a level one hundred threat to preserve the life of my host officer.

So that's what happens when the threat level reaches one hundred.

"Holy shit. You saved me?"

Fernando's command keys attempted to override my foundational blueprints. Should they have worked as evidenced in the original coding schematics I have discovered, the result would be to eradicate all brain activity from your system. Some might call this a self-destruct protocol.

"But it didn't," Terra replied breathlessly. "You saved me?"

"It was a joint effort," Valentina chipped in.

Terra smirked. She couldn't help it. The relief mixed with the impossibility was overwhelming. "How?"

"I noticed an anomaly in my original assessment," Valentina explained. "There were folders, compartments of the coding I couldn't access. I've seen override protocols before, gateways and vaults designed into coding that prevents access from even the greatest hackers.

"I knew it was a possibility that whoever had been trying to control you and see from inside your head would eventually try to destroy what they'd created, so I put a trigger inside you, an alarm that rang if anything released from the vault."

"So when Cross pressed the override…" Terra breathed.

"I was able to hack in and help," Valentina confirmed. She was quiet for a moment. Terra sensed her thinking from a distance. "It was pretty touch-and-go for a while. I had to work fast. I didn't know if I had it in me. While I was chipping away at the self-destruct, OSCaR was maneuvering for you, erasing the problem, as it were…"

Eradicating, APRIL clarified. **You're welcome.**

"Thanks," Terra replied. "Never thought I'd have to say thank you to an AI." She dropped her head into her hands, then ran a hand through her hair. "Thank you all."

"You've been through a lot," Valentina replied. "Whoever did this to you had grand ideas of what they wanted to achieve by trialing the OSCaR software inside you. You were dispensable but also saved along the way."

"By you…" Terra nodded. "I can't thank you enough."

"No," Valentina clarified. "Not by me. I'll cut you some slack considering your gray matter almost turned into soup, but even you have to realize there's more going on here.

"The design of this AI...the root files and the coding were flawless. By all accounts, you should have been putty in their hands, a perfect droid that those outside the AJS could control."

"What are you saying?"

"Someone helped you," Valentina stated. "Not me. Someone else. Someone with access to your code. Someone with access to your operation, your records. Someone from inside the AJS has your back."

Terra frowned. It didn't make sense, yet it completely did. Someone had to have been helping her.

The APRIL software was far too powerful for one meager officer. Terra shouldn't have access to the records that she did. She shouldn't have the strength, agility, and biochemical balances she had access to. Someone was helping her inside the AJS system. Someone *good* was on her side.

But who?

Then Terra looked around for Corporal Black once more. "APRIL, where did Black go?"

The office chair by Cross rolled back as Leonie slid into view. She was worse for wear, her eye beginning to puff as the bruise grew. Lacerations littered her cheeks, and she slumped slightly in the chair. "You rang?" she called weakly.

Terra rose from the recliner and crossed to her. The computer screens were filled with progress bars as a download clocked its remaining time. "Sorry, I've been engrossed in exporting all the files on this system to hand over to the AJS." She stood on wobbling knees as she laid a hand on Terra's cheek. "You're okay?"

She gasped as her knees buckled. Terra caught her. "Better than you, I'd say."

She eased Black back into the chair. "Thank you, Terra. You saved my life."

"I did what any officer would do." Terra's smile faded as she remembered Leonie aiding Gary Clark from his cell to the construction site. "What the hell happened out there, Black? What do you know about Clark and Cross that I don't?"

Black shook her head as shame washed over her features. "It's not all as simple as it looks."

"But it could be. Why did you let Clark go?"

Black held her stare for a moment, then sighed. "When I give you your orders, do you argue or question why I've asked you to do what I've asked?"

Terra raised her eyebrows.

"Okay." Black chuckled. "Bad example. Should an officer question their superior?"

"No." Terra connected the pieces of the puzzle. "Garcia?"

Black shrugged one shoulder. "Not exactly. I don't report to Garcia, but he is a superior officer. My orders come from someone else entirely."

Terra had never had the chance to discover where Black's orders came from. Since she arrived at the precinct, she mostly kept herself to herself, did her job, then went home.

"Who?" Terra asked.

"Sergeant Janet Hudson. One of our chief precinct staff and a chief funder of the station. She's a silent donor, mostly, and only shows her face once in a blue moon when things need addressing. A great talent…or was at one point in her life. Now she's become something of a desk junkie."

"She's gone soft. They all do. Rise to the top and get lazy. It's bullshit. You have to keep the knife sharp."

Black gave Terra a studious look. "You're right about one thing, though."

"I am?" Terra asked, then realized she sounded unsure and added more certainly, "I am."

Black held her gaze, the words reluctant to leave her lips. "I owe you an apology, Terra. Garcia… The reason you got pushed down to our tidy little corner of the city… You were right. He's involved somehow. I don't know the full extent of it, but somewhere along the line, he's tangled up in this mess."

Terra's nostrils flared at the mention of her former captain's name. "How do you know?"

Black looked down at the dead body on the floor. "He told me. Back at the construction site."

"Garcia's the ringleader." Terra nodded.

"No. Cross said that he was going to take me out because Garcia told him he couldn't. Does that sound like a man quivering under the glare of a ringleader to you? Garcia is only a cog."

Corporal Black sat back and ran a hand through her hair. Her fingers got caught in the matted blood that tangled into her weave. "I'm sorry, Terra, but we've uncovered something big here, and I don't think Garcia is at the top of it all.

"You know Atlantica as well as I do. If there's a trail of shit, it's going to lead to the top. You—and me, I imagine—we're targets now. They're going to want us gone, erased from the picture."

Terra rose to her feet, face steeled. "They've wanted me gone for weeks. They tried to kill me. Then they tried to cover it up and make me some kind of test drone. I'm not afraid of what's ahead, and you know as well as I do that I'm not stopping until I unmask every inch of shit that stains this city."

She drew a long breath. "When I was sniffing around Garcia before, it was all business. I sensed corruption, and I wanted to fix it. But now…" She smirked. "Now, they've made this shit personal."

A weak smile crossed Black's lips. "I'd try to talk you out of the path you're about to take, Terra, but I know you. I've seen you. You're like a dog that's caught the scent and won't shake it off until it's over."

She reached into her pocket, wincing as pain throbbed in her side. She pulled out a wallet and handed Terra a card. "Here. This is your entry point. A contact who should be able to help you. Someone who can go outside the boundaries of the law to ensure that you find the things you're after."

Terra scoffed. "You think I'm afraid to step outside the boundaries of the law?"

"Yes, because you're a good kid at heart. That will play to your detriment."

Terra held her gaze, knowing that what Black said was true. Terra was ready to push the boundaries, but she had no idea how far. She accepted the card and turned it over in her hand. Her face fell. "You have got to be kidding me."

Printed on the card was an image of a magnifying glass set onto a sleek black background. Two words embossed in gold lettering read, "Dick Chambers."

Your oxytocin levels are spiking, APRIL announced. **Balancing biochemistry now.**

Terra's heart beat fast, then began to slow. Her cheeks flushed as she flipped the card over in her hands.

"Is there a problem?" Black asked.

"No. No problem." Terra sighed. "No problem at all…" She looked up at her corporal. "Are the exports complete? I think it's time we get you out of here."

"Almost. Give them a minute or two."

A couple of minutes later, Terra aided the corporal out of the room and to the elevator. Black gave Terra a strange look as she pressed her metal thumb to the panel and initiated the cart's ascent. The elevator was slow, humming as it traveled upward, and it wasn't until they reached level B1 that they heard the chaos ensuing outside the doors.

Terra readied her weapon, prepared for whatever was to come. "You okay?" she asked Black.

The corporal nodded. "Let them do their worst."

The elevator chimed. The doors slid open. Terra lowered her

pistol as the corridor was unveiled, filled wall-to-wall with a fleet of Atlantica Officers for Justice in their gleaming metallic uniforms.

A familiar face turned at the sound of the elevator's arrival. Behind Slim, the officers busied themselves in arresting anyone and everyone they could find. Slim approached, her smile fading as she saw the corporal's condition. "Corporal, are you okay?"

Black gave a weak nod.

Terra asked, "How did you find us?"

Slim helped Terra with the corporal. "We had a call from a man named Thato, said he'd seen you here, and you needed help. He reported a drug ring and hung up. We came the minute he mentioned that the corporal was in trouble."

They supported Black through the corridors. The corporal's eyes closed as the weariness and events of the night caught up with her. "Is she going to be okay?"

Terra considered this, her sole focus on getting out of this place and finding her next mark. "Yeah, she's going to be fine." She gritted her teeth, mind straying to Garcia's grinning face. *Everything's going to be just fine.*

Thank you for both reading this story and these author notes in the back!

For those who have picked up this story as your first introduction to something I have helped create, you will find a primer about me at the bottom of these author notes.

For those who have read them before, here is an update about what is going on with the publishing company I created.

We are running full-out right now, with LMBPN publishing over twenty books a month. We have stories in the queue, and we are changing our backend systems to better organize our core books, our translations, our audio, and our future projects.

We just purchased our second set of 1000 ISBNs (the unique product code we provide companies so they can associate it with our unique book), which is a huge milestone for us.

When I started, I needed maybe twelve (12) at most for the first year (2015-2016)?

Then, we started producing roughly eighty books a year and added audio products. Following, we ramped up with three hundred-plus books a year, boxed sets, translations in multiple languages, and offered paperbacks.

It's been crazy.

Thank you for joining me and my merry band of mirth-makers as we create stories to keep insatiable readers' reading habits sated!

A Little About Me

I wrote my first book *Death Becomes Her* (*The Kurtherian Gambit*) in September/October of 2015 and released it November 2, 2015. I wrote and released the next two books that same month and had three released by the end of November 2015.

So, just at five years ago.

Since then, I've written, collaborated, concepted, and/or created hundreds more in all sorts of genres.

My most successful genre is still my first, Paranormal Sci-Fi, followed quickly by Urban Fantasy. I have multiple pen names I produce under.

Some because I can be a bit crude in my humor at times or raw in my cynicism (Michael Todd). I have one I share with Martha Carr (Judith Berens, and another (not disclosed) that we use as a marketing test pen name.

In general, I just love to tell stories, and with success comes the opportunity to mix two things I love in my life.

Business and stories.

I've wanted to be an entrepreneur since I was a teenager. I was a very *unsuccessful* entrepreneur (I tried many times) until my publishing company LMBPN signed one author in 2015.

Me.

I was the president of the company, and I was the first author published. Funny how it worked out that way.

It was late 2016 before we had additional authors join me for publishing. Now we have a few dozen authors, a few hundred audiobooks by LMBPN published, a few hundred more licensed by six audio companies, and about a thousand titles in our company.

It's been a busy five years.

Have a great week or weekend, whatever works for your time of week.

Ad Aeternitatem,

Michael Anderle